shanda

LOUIS ROMANO

ISBN 978-1-66780-586-3

FOR MARY LYNN BOLOGNA-ROMANO

Acknowledgements

I wrote a lot of this book in Rockland County, New York at the Nanuet Social Club of which I am a founding member. I was able to spend time in the nearby Hasidic communities gathering essential information and learning about these interesting and wonderful people.

In my early days in business, I had quite a few Orthodox and Hasidic clients who made an extremely positive influence on me. I have the utmost respect for them. I have used some of their names in this book, substituting first and last names for my characters.

My list of people who helped me with this project is long.

I have the honor to call Trislam Cruz my friend. He helped me enormously with information on ballistics, guns, target shooting and information on the physics of shooting. Tris made several trips into the community to verify distances and report back if some of the action is this book is freezable. Thanks also to my dear friend Brian Schuley for his guidance on guns and ballistics.

Barry Werk, helped me with many of the Jewish customs and has great insight on the Jewish religion. He helped make this book fun for me to write.

Thanks to EMS retired Captain Kevin Haugh for his professional information on procedures and his friend Abraham Glatzer for information on the Orthodox community.

Thanks goes out to Jason Feliz for his help with Spanish words and translation.

Ben Roth's help was critical in many ways. Firstly, he obtained most of the Yiddish translation I needed to make this book authentic. His knowledge of Rockland County was also an enormous help. I asked him many questions along the way and he was always happy to help.

Alan "Freddy" Urps was my go to guy for streets in Monsey, and a whole list of other information on logistics.

Professor Clark Hill gave me an incredible amount of help with all police matters in Rockland County. This is the fifth book he has helped me with on law enforcement procedures and history.

Thanks to Mike Baer and Steve Pandolfelli for cop information. Vic's driver Pando is modeled after Steve.

Laura Green did a fabulous and creative cover.

Thanks to Thomas Dellatore once again for pre-reading and editing the chapters and giving me great information to make the story better. Leticia Protami also did a masterful job of editing this book and smoothing out some rough spots.

Thanks to Alison Lorenz for my updated jacket photo. She's a genius, not a magician

Thanks to my entire family for letting me do my thing and never losing faith in me.

Farewell to my 17-year-old Jack Russell Rocco who was with me on every book I've written. He passed away during the writing of this work. Truly a Shanda.

Chapter One

Broomall, Pennsylvania • September 16, 2020

It was the third night that his temperature had reached 103.F.

Everything Gary Olsen read or heard about on television and on the radio while he was making deliveries indicated he had the Covid 19 virus.

He could barely lift his head off the pillow in the Queen-sized bed which he shared with his wife until she died eleven years ago. His head was pounding like it never had before in his fifty-four years.

Chills racked his body despite several blankets and a comforter he was buried under. Beads of sweat ran down Gary's forehead into is blurry eyes.

His son would ferry bottles of cold Poland Spring water from the refrigerator to his father's bedroom, but after a while the water bottles were unopened and untouched. Every movement seemed to bring another chest pain or add to his dizziness.

Gary Olsen was an old school Norwegian stoic who wouldn't complain about his condition or reach for the telephone to call a doctor or the emergency room at the Crozer-Ketstone Medical Clinic, three miles away from his home. He hadn't been to see a doctor since his son was diagnosed as being on the Autism spectrum, specifically with Asperger's syndrome when the boy was six years old.

Even though he and his wife knew their son "wasn't right," the news of his medical condition hit Gary so hard he wound up at the clinic with what his wife feared was a heart attack. Instead he was given Xanax and told he had had a panic attack. He never took one pill. Instead he dealt with the reality of having a child who would be different.

Now, with his boy just turning twenty-seven Gary worried what would happen to his son if the Covid would take him like it had with so many others the media was claiming. Gary had heard the horror stories on the news and from the few friends he had. If you got Covid and went to a hospital, they put you on a ventilator and you died. End of story. He figured he was strong and still young enough to beat this with Tylenol and lots of water as he did with any flu.

All the while his confused and frightened young son Edward would stand in the doorway of his father's bedroom, looking lost and occasionally asking if his dad was going to be okay. It was he who found his mother dead on the kitchen floor when he was eleven. The boy had come home from school, while his father was working, and there Ruth Olsen was splayed out with her eyes open, her oxygen tank lying on her chest. Years of excessive cigarette smoking took her not long after she was diagnosed with COPD.

The young man hated smoking of any kind so much he would tell anyone he saw smoking how stupid they were in those words. He didn't have any filter due to the Asperger's and would sometimes go into a fit of rage if a smoker spoke back to him.

Father and son became almost inseparable after Ruth passed. Gary became the boy's hero. He had the patience to deal with his son's difficulty socializing. The boy, brilliant in mathematics, physics and chemistry had no desire to make friends or play sports. The young man didn't speak much, but loved to hug his dad sometimes whispering how much he loved him.

They went hunting together, worked in their home machine shop, watched game shows where the boy had an uncanny ability to answer questions and figure out puzzles before any contestant. Gary would praise his son after any achievement whether it be shooting a ten-point buck in the thick woods near their home or answering twelve consecutive questions correctly on Jeopardy in their small dimly lit living room.

It took the boy three years to go back into the kitchen after he found his mother dead on the floor. Gary had unbound patience with his son, making him secure enough to eventually be able to cook supper for them. They would wash and dry the dishes together while listening to music from a brown box radio that Ruth had always played literally all-day long.

Father and son often read hunting, fishing and gun magazines together talking about what kind of fish were running in the local streams. They made detailed plans for overnight hunting trips and the type of guns and ammo they would be using. Gary and his son made several scrap books from photos taken of their hunting and fishing outings. They were father and son, and great pals.

The young man often quoted from his collection of college level math and physics texts with Gary feigning understanding anything his son was saying. Gary loved his son unconditionally. The boy adored his father.

In his sweat soaked bed, Gary could now barely breath. Every short breath of air brought a tremendous pain to his chest and back. When he coughed, which was increasing each night, the pain was excruciating.

Gary asked his son to go to the local CVS drug store and get more Tylenol and a Primatine Mist inhaler. He thought that might clear up the phlegm that seemed to be increasing by the minute. Gary Olsen was fighting off the worst global pandemic in the history of the modern world with nearly useless over-the-counter medication. Too stubborn or too afraid to call for help, Gary was beginning to hallucinate. He saw his wife standing in the bedroom doorway next to his son.

Edward took his father's van and did as he was asked. It never dawned on him to call for help. His father knew best in every aspect of their lives and he would be fine. That's exactly what Gary would say when his son asked how he was, "I'll be fine." Gary thought to himself, *"What will Edward do if this thing takes me? I thought I would have had more time to prepare for this. Please God, let me live for my son."*

When he returned with the useless meds, between coughs, Edward could hear his father talking to someone. He brought yet another bottle of water and what he picked up at the CVS, placing the items on the nightstand where his mom and dad's wedding picture stood in a silver frame. Father and son designed and made the frame together from silver ingots in their workshop.

Gary was now sucking in air between every third word. No one was in the room other than his father shivering under the covers.

"I never should have made that damn delivery to Monsey, but we needed the money. Had to get those hinges delivered. Those Jews up there gave me this damn Covid. What do they know? They all have Covid. They don't listen for shit. I should have known better. They're good people, they're good to me but they gave me this…this virus."

Gary said a few other things about the long black coats and the hats the Jews wore in his babbling fever induced rants. His breathing became more labored. The young man stood in the doorway watching his father as he suffered from something he couldn't understand. In a seeming catatonic trance, he watched as his father's chest heaved as he sucked for air.

An hour later Gary Olsen was dead.

Chapter Two

Gary Olsen had worked for twenty-eight years at Lamonia and Company molding various metals into a variety of specialty products. Burt Lamonia began his company twenty-eight years ago with a single government contact for tank parts and grew it into one of the largest machine shops in the state of Pennsylvania. Garry was a big part of the firm's success but always wanted his own shop and the ability to be his own man. He left two years ago, on good terms with Lamonia's blessing. So much so that Gary was able to convince the owner to hire his son on a part-time basis to work the computerized lathe machines.

"Burt, the boy is brilliant mechanically. He may act a lot differently from everyone else but if you show him something once he will be perfect at it. He may even come up with ways to do some things more efficiently," Gary Olsen said.

Lamonia, with tears in his eyes replied. "Gary, I owe you big time. I know Asperger's people are highly functional and generally hard workers I'd be happy to give the kid his first job under one condition.

The day your company grows to the point where you need your boy, just come in and get him. Until that time, he will have a spot with us."

Gary struggled to keep his small company afloat and used Edward from time to time at night and on his days off. Edward was a working machine. He knew nothing about life except working and reading his text books. He showed no emotion except when his supervisor had to tell him the plant was closing and he had to go home. He would get scarlet red in the face and stomp out of the building.

Edward Olsen could not process his father's death. Intellectually he knew his dad was dead. Emotionally he was vacant.

At 6:30 in the morning, the day after his father passed, before going to work at Lamonia, Edward looked into his father's room. His dad's corpse stared up at the ceiling, his mouth wide open, with his tongue dried into a shriveled, dried out dark brown mass from sucking in air.

Edward worked the entire day without saying a word to anyone.

On Friday, two days after Gary died, Burt Lamonia was walking through the plant. He spotted Edward melting some silver, preparing to pour it into a mold.

"Hello Edward. Everything okay?"

The young man nodded without a verbal reply.

"How's you dad?"

"He's fine," Edward mumbled.

"Well, give him my best okay?"

Edward shook his head in the affirmative, never taking his eyes from his task.

On Saturday morning, Edward's immediate supervisor noticed the young man had worn the same clothing for the past three days. As he approached Edward, an acrid aroma of decay set off the man's gag reflex.

Holding a handkerchief over his mouth and nose, the older man who had worked with Gary Olsen for twenty-six years blurted, "What is that smell son?"

"My dad is dead. The Jews killed him."

• • •

Months went by with many of the good country folks at Lamonia and Company doing their best to support Edward with his daily activities. Some of the wives of the young man's co-workers would prepare hearty stews and casseroles so he could eat a home cooked meal most nights. They would leave the food on a small wrought iron table on the front porch as Edward would not open the door to interact with anyone. Neighbors and their teenagers would maintain the small lawn during the fall and shovel the heavy snow during the winter. Edward would often be seen peaking from one of the front windows.

Edward would not accept help with housekeeping even though Burt Lamonia offered to hire a weekly cleaning and laundry service for him. He wouldn't let anyone enter the house where he lived his entire life.

Several weeks after Gary was buried next to his wife, Edward was seen sitting next to his parents grave rocking back and forth for hours. One early Sunday morning, Kate Lamonia, Burt's wife went to the Olsen home to drop off some breakfast muffins and homemade pie on the porch table. Kate at first thought she heard an injured animal howling from inside the house. After a few moments, she realized it was Edward, crying hysterically. Kate left sobbing at the desperate situation Edward Olsen was forced to be living in. "Something has to be done for that poor boy," Kate said to her husband when she returned home, trembling from what she had heard.

Chapter Three

Mendel Glick had to wear his round sunglasses for the first time in weeks, to shade his eyes from the bright sunlight. A cloudless blue sky on this cold, early March Friday was a welcome canopy over the Ultra-Orthodox and Hassidic Jewish Community of Monsey, New York.

Monsey is a town in suburban Rockland County, New York, a forty-five-minute drive north of New York City. Of the three hundred thousand persons living in Rockland, one hundred thousand are Jewish.

The winter had been dreary and cold and global pandemic Covid-19 threatened severe illness and death throughout the entire region, but especially among the Jewish Communities in Williamsburg, Brooklyn, Monsey and Kyrias Joel in Orange County, the next northern county from Rockland. The Orthodox community was rattled with a high incidence of the pandemic, well above other towns and communities, largely because social of distancing and the practice of wearing masks was largely ignored. There was a statewide ban of all weddings and funerals and other large group gatherings which was totally ignored by the Hasid's. Perhaps the Rebbe didn't give strict enough orders for the faithful to adhere to secular directives and laws. Perhaps their faith that Hashem would look over His people was most probably the reasons to ignore what elected officials were demanding.

Mendel was full of excitement for the remainder of his day and for the weeks ahead. He left his workplace at noon today to give himself plenty of time to get things done as he did every Friday afternoon. He planned to take the small list of groceries his wife wanted and shop for his family at the massive Evergreen Super Market at the Towne Square Mall on Route 59, the main one lane thoroughfare that dissected Rockland County east-west through Monsey, from the towns of Suffern to Nyack on the Hudson River.

After shopping, the twenty-seven-year old follower of the insulated Satmar Hassidic group would walk to the Congregation Yetev Lev Synagogue to join a minion of at least ten men for prayer. After his devoted davening, intently praying while slowly rocking back and forth in his prayer shawl, Mendel would take time at the Shul, the temple, to study Torah. This was not only his obligation as a Jew to enhance his religion, but he truly loved learning.

This week's *parshat,* or reading from the holy book, was one of Mendel's favorites. The story of Moses leading and exiting the chosen people out of Egypt had many sage lessons to convey and contemplate. After study, the young father of three girls and two boys and a baby soon coming, would use the *mitvah* inside the shul to bathe and prepare for Shabbas, the Jewish Sabbath. The *mitvah* is a spa-like pool of warm water used for ritual bathing. It is used especially by women after their monthly menses.

The excitement of being in the month of March Madness was giving Mendel something to look forward to in the weeks to come. Although he was not permitted to have a television or a computer in his home by rabbinical rule, (news would only be conveyed through the Rebbe), Mendel loved basketball. During the College March Madness tournaments, he would sneak off with his not so religious friend Barry Werkman, a Reform Jew, and watch the games at Barry's home. Mendel would especially liked Virginia to repeat winning the trophy this year. His excitement watching the games was building as it did every year since Mendel was sixteen. Talking basketball and watching the television with Barry was the highlight of his year.

Mendel was on the short side, at five feet six inches tall. His color was pale, almost anemic but his piercing blue eyes and blond hair and fluffy beard, accentuated a warm, welcoming smile which seemed to brighten his still youthful face. He wore the traditional white shirt, four corned *tallit gadol*, a prayer shawl under his shirt with *tsitis,* woven stings on each corner, a black suit, a woven yarmulke under his black hat. His *payot*, his long blond side locks, were wrapped around his ears and flopped in ringlets, lazily along both cheeks to just beneath his jawline. This tradition was found in scripture that commanded a man not to "round the corner of his head."

Mendel walked everywhere and extremely fast, almost like he was in a race to get to where he was going. His black laced shoes always seemed to need polishing and new heals. Mendel was more interested in making his wholesale photographic equipment business flourish, to provide well for his growing family, than he was with his shoes and personal grooming.

His long, open black coat was swirling on either side of him in the wind on this cold early afternoon and Mendel raced into the crowded Evergreen Supermarket.

In no time, he gathered the items on his wife's grocery list. Two dozen eggs, a large container of fresh, plain yogurt, six yellow apples, and a container of sweet butter. Not on this list were the five dill pickles that he took from the open barrel. He and his wife Hanna loved to have them with a brisket sandwich or with Hanna's homemade Chulent, a hearty beef, potato and bean stew that they would enjoy on *Shabbas,* the Sabbath day of rest, for lunch. Mendel also picked up a small bouquet of fresh flowers for his wife as was his habit on every Friday afternoon

The thought of watching his wife and two of his eldest daughter lighting the *Shabbas* candles at sundown tonight, following the Jewish tradition of thousands of years, and the wonderful meal Hanna was preparing, seemingly quickened his already speedy gait.

With three plastic bags in his left hand, Mendel left the market, his right hand at the ready in case Hanna or someone would call. He wore a Bluetooth earpiece to listen and speak into, allowing him to leave his phone in his coat pocket.

Mendel made his way to Route 59 and walked east toward the Shul to fulfill his plan for the afternoon, all the time excited about being home with his family for the festive meal.

There is an old Yiddish proverb. *"Mann tracht. Un Gott lacht"* Man plans and God laughs. Mendel noticed that traffic on the road was building in anticipation of the events everyone would be sharing with their families in a few hours. Busses and trucks zoomed by as did many sedans and other vehicles seemingly all in a rush to get somewhere. He also noticed the remnants of the last snowstorm from a few weeks ago, as some of the snow along Route 59 had not yet melted. He thought all of the ugly black dirt on the snow was mostly from car, truck and bus exhaust and how everyone was breathing in this terrible pollution.

After about a quarter of a mile up the road, Mendel's cell phone rang. For some reason, his Bluetooth earpiece wasn't working so he reached into his coat pocket. It was difficult to take the phone from his coat with the bags he was carrying. A tractor trailer truck, moving at a rapid speed barreled close to the curb on Route 59.

The last thing Mendel experienced in this life was a bright flash of light.

This *Shabbas* was not to be.

Chapter Four

Vic Gonnella and his sweetheart slash partner Raquel Ruiz, were planning a quiet evening alone in their Manhattan townhouse on tony East End Avenue. The same townhouse where two foreign terrorists met their maker, on the street, while attempting to kill Vic and Raquel during one of their acclaimed cases.

After school, their daughter Gabriella, would be doing a sleepover with her girlfriend Shoshana Rosen and a few other girls, chaperoned by her attorney parents at their nearby Park Avenue apartment. The Rosen's were taking in Chinese food for the girls and had a bunch of board games in mind. The girls would likely be sneaking a peek at the Tic-Tok app on their cell phones instead.

Raquel's mother, Olga, was spending the weekend up in the Bronx with her old neighborhood lady friends. She missed the local people, gossip and Spanish food in spite of Raquel's dislike of the ghetto-like neighborhood.

It was a rare occasion that the famous couple would have time alone together at home.

Vic left the office at two o'clock that afternoon to get an early start on an intimate evening. A bottle or two of their favorite California Pinot Noir, a pizza and a veal cutlet parmiggiano sandwich from Patsy's on 117th Street in East Harlem and hopefully a bit of loud, uninhibited sex was in the plan.

Raquel hadn't been in the office since the Covid pandemic invaded New York, just about a year ago.

"Pando is bringing our dinner at about five. How about let's start early with a couple of drinks?" Vic asked.

"Sounds good," Raquel mumbled.

"Something wrong?" Vic inquired.

"No."

"C'mon baby. I can tell. What's up?" Vic put his arms around a pouting Raquel.

"Honestly, I'm just sick and tired of this whole damn Covid thing. We haven't been away in a year, we can't even go out to a nice restaurant without those friggen masks. I worry about getting sick and business has really sucked this year. And my arm is killing me from the vaccine I got yesterday. Other than that, I'm just peachy," Raquel blurted, her rapid Bronx, Puerto Rican accent came out, she not taking a pause to breathe.

She buried her head into Vic's chest, her lips quivering, holding back tears.

Vic hugged Raquel closer.

"I know, it's been a rough time. Look, let me draw you a nice bubble bath, make you a drink, put some Sinatra on the stereo and…

"Only if you take the bath with me." Raquel interrupted. The fading scent of Vic's cologne was turning her on.

"I think that can be arranged."

"When is this shit going to be over? It's really dragging me down, honey."

"Raquel, I need to say something. I've asked a number of times for you to get away with me. Maybe Florida? Maybe the Islands? You always had the same answer. Covid! I get it. You won't even go out for dinner. I think you've taken this thing a bit too far. And of course, you're not happy to fly. Jesus, sometimes I hope that we catch this fucking Covid virus to put it behind us. I've had enough of this too!"

"What are you trying to say? I know I'm very neurotic about catching this virus. I stay awake at night worrying about my Gabby, you, my mom and me. You see how I stay away from everyone at the office, double mask, no meetings except on Zoom. Vic, I'm scared shitless."

"I'm not saying anything except I want to help you. I think maybe you should see someone about this fear you have. I just think you are a bit over the top," Vic said softly.

"A shrink? A damn shrink? Yea, maybe I need my head examined for staying with you. You have no empathy and I'm done with this horseshit."

Vic saw the venom in Raquel's eyes and knew the night was over. He took a deep breath as Raquel stomped out of the room.

"Well, that came out of left field," Vic announced.

"Drop dead!"

"Enjoy the pizza!" Vic shouted after her.

"Fuck you, asshole!" Raquel screamed.

Vic called his driver, Pando.

"Yes sir?"

"Pando, can you get the pizza early? Drop it off here and drive me up to Patsy's please. I have pizza on my mouth today and I'm having it come hell or high water."

"Sure boss. No problem. Sounds like a Ten-Fifty-Two to me." Pando answered with the NYPD signal code for a domestic dispute.

"You nailed it, pally."

"I feel like pizza too. Want company?"

"Ten-Four...my treat."

Chapter Five

"911 what is your emergency?" the male dispatcher asked.

"There is a man, lying on the ground on Route 59 in Monsey. He may have been hit by a car or something," a heavily accented voice replied.

"Where exactly on Route 59, sir?"

"Near the TD Bank. Not far from the Evergreen."

"We will dispatch an officer. What is your name please?"

The line went dead.

The Rockland County Sheriff's office logged in the 911 call at exactly one-eighteen p.m. The caller's phone number was captured by the Emergency Services System, even though there is no crime in hanging up and not wishing to be identified.

The dispatcher notified the Ramapo Police Department, which handles Monsey and a code 108 went out for an auto accident with injury with the location of the incident. A Hatzola ambulance, a volunteer emergency service organization that works in Jewish communities was immediately dispatched.

Officer Jessie Banks, was so close that he could see a crowd gathering at the scene from his patrol car. Much of the crowd was already standing on the roadway. He noticed traffic was backing up in both directions and radioed for assistance. With lights and sirens, Banks maneuvered his cruiser, coming upon the scene within two minutes of the 911 call.

Banks exited his vehicle and the crowd parted to allow the tall, strapping African American officer access to the injured man.

Banks knew immediately this was no 108.

The front of the victim's head was splattered along the sidewalk. Blood, brain tissue and bone were sprayed from under the victims face down position for about four-feet. At first glance, it looked to the veteran officer like a shotgun wound. He had seen several suicides and murders where the persons head was totally or nearly gone. Banks knew the man was dead but checked the corroded pulse to confirm the obvious. Banks stood up from the body and addressed the crowd, putting his hands up and waving for everyone to move away from the horrific scene.

"Please, everyone, move back. Back away from the scene. Now!" Banks bellowed.

There was a murmuring from the twenty or so Hassidic men who gathered around the body, all wearing long black coats and a variety of black hats. No one moved as ordered. It seemed none of the men were willing to give up their vantage point of the grizzly scene, or perhaps they were too shocked to move away, or simply did not like to be told what to do.

From his two-way microphone, attached to his shirt epilate, Banks called into the Ramapo PD Desk.

"No 108 here. We have a DOA. Looks like a homicide. We need crowd control, officers to redirect vehicular traffic, an EMS unit, detective squad and a supervisor."

A Ramapo PD SUV immediately pulled up to the scene. Another patrolman, this one seemed a good deal younger than the forty-year old Banks pulled up and went directly to his colleague. He looked down at the body and nearly gasped. His face went ashen and he quickly turned away.

"Do me a favor, would you? Get these people far away from here. Across 59 is best. Get some barricade tape for me." Banks knew the young officer was about to lose his lunch and rightfully thought it best to kept him busy and away from the body.

Within a few minutes the troops arrived, tape was set all around the crime scene, and traffic was rerouted around Route 59 in both directions. The supervisor arrived, took Banks' verbal report, then called the Rockland County Medical Examiner's Office to officially report the murder even though some how they knew and were already in route. He then called the Rockland County Sheriff's Office who commands the BCI unit. The Bureau of Criminal Investigation would assist in putting up a ten-by-ten tent to keep the crime scene intact and to protect it from the elements as they gathered forensic information, took photos and worked with the Medical Examiner. As protocol demands, the EMS team had arrived to make the first pronouncement of death.

Dr. Angela Rush, the County Medical Examiner for the past five-years arrived thirty-five-minutes after the Ramapo Detective squad began doing some preliminary investigation.

The lead detective, Mike Sassano had thirty-nine years on the job making him one of the senior men in the county. He knew enough to wait for the M.E. to prevent hard feelings and not to disturb the body.

For a guy who was maybe five foot eight, he still had a full head of salt-and-pepper hair. Deep, dark Sicilian eyes and an aquiline nose that had a good-sized bump on it from having been broken at least once gave Sassano a don't screw with me look. His plastic gloves looked a bit small on his large hands. Sassano had massive hands. The guys on the job called him "Mitts."

"Dr. Rush. This one is a bit ugly." Sassano said as he reached into her vehicle to shake the Medical Examiner's hand.

"Come on Mike, you coached me in girl's-softball with your daughter Rosa. So suddenly I'm Doctor Rush?" Angela chuckled.

"Respect for the office is all. I'm old school."

"Fine, I'll call you Detective Sassano and make you feel official. I heard Rosa is in North Carolina."

"I hate it. Only see the grandkids a few times a year and weekly on Facetime. Stinks."

"What do we have detective?"

"Young Hassidic guy. Looks like a high caliber bullet from behind. By the looks of the spray, and I'm only guessing, it may have come from an elevated spot, but it's way too early be definite on that idea."

Angela looked around. "If you're right that building back there on Secora Road could be the spot. It's the only tall building in the area, but we need to check out your assumption officially," she uttered.

"I sent a couple of my guys to take a look see. Who knows. The perp could still be there watching his handy work."

"That would be way too lucky. Any ID on the victim?" Angela asked.

"Mendel Glick, age, 27. Lives on Maple Avenue in Monsey. Next of kin hasn't been notified. The only other thing we have so far is the projectile. One of the BCI found it in two-pieces. It took them some time to find it. While they were using a metal-detector looking for a projectile, the technician eyeballed it on the roadway. It's marked in yellow, sixteen feet from the body."

"Let's take a closer look," Angela put on a pair of yellow plastic gloves.

Dr. Rush moved with an air of strength and confidence as she made her way to the corpse. Her brown pantsuit under a black leather coat did nothing to advertise her toned figure. Her brown hair was pulled back tightly in an officious bun to the back of her head. No makeup or lipstick and heavy dark eyeglass frames made It seem as if Angela was purposely downplaying her natural beauty. She wasn't trying to turn heads, she just wanted to do her job.

Angela examined the corpse. The plastic Evergreen bags with the groceries and flowers for Hanna were still gripped in Mendel's left hand. She found the entrance hole and moved his head gently to see the damage on his face and forehead. There was nothing much left to see. The front of the young man's head was split open, his eyes seemed to be missing and were now part of the mush that was on the sidewalk.

Angela spoke while looking at the corpse. "Definitely a high caliber projectile. If I were guessing I would say from a high elevated angle. That building looks like the obvious spot. Forensics will break down exactly where the projectile came from."

Angela stood up from Mendel's body and turned to Sassano.

"Could this be a hate crime detective?"

"Way too soon to say that Doctor. We have to do our job now to determine if this young man was singled out randomly or if he was the intended target, or if he got in the way of another target."

A quivering male voice came from behind detective Sassano.

"Excuse me, please. I am Rabbi Kreitzman. Can you tell me what has happened here? I'm wondering if this is a member of my synagogue."

Sassano recognized the Rabbi from the community. "Yes, Rabbi. This young man was evidently shot from behind possibly by a rifle. His identification indicates he is Mendel Glick from…"

"*Oy vey ist mir* … He is a member of my Schul. He is a good person with a growing family. This is a terrible Shanda. A Shanda. I'm sorry, it's a terrible shame, a tragedy for his family and the entire community."

"Rabbi, we have started the investigation asking for any witnesses. If you don't mind, we will be calling on you to ask about the deceased. Please if you wouldn't mind, ask around if anyone saw this happen."

"Whatever you need. Shabbas begins in a few hours. I will not be available on Sunday unless I need to break Shabbas. Of course I will if you need me. I am at your service."

"Greatly appreciated Rabbi. Where can I reach you?"

Rabbi Kreitzman gave his home address to Sassano who jotted it down in a well-used, frayed black notebook.

Kreitzman fought back tears, clearing his throat to speak. "One more thing sir. It is our custom to have a *shomer* with the body from now until the burial the day after Shabbas. I must insist that our *shomer* be with Mendel from here on."

"What exactly is a shomer Rabbi?" Sassano inquired.

"A watchman. A man that will stay with Mendel and say blessings and guard the body in accordance with our religious beliefs."

"Guard the body?" Sassano asked

"According to our ancient tradition the *shomer* prays for the soul and shoos away any animals that will disturb the body. Of course, there are no animals that will bother the body nowadays. This is how the tradition started many years ago."

Sassano replied, "Of course. We will respect your wishes. His body will be moved in a little while and taken to the Rockland County morgue in Pomona. Your watchman can go with the body and certainly be at the morgue the entire time until he is released to a funeral home."

"Thank you. And sir, as a reminder, no autopsy is permitted on the body."

Angela Rush interrupted. "Rabbi, I am the Medical Examiner. No autopsy will be performed. I am well aware of your beliefs and I will only inspect his wounds for additional evidence. I am very sorry for your loss."

"Thank you. This is truly a *Shanda*."

Chapter Six

Hanna Glick was pacing the floors on the first level of her home on Maple Avenue. She knew something was very wrong. Mendel would never be home later than 3:00 p.m. on Friday before Shabbas. He would come home, put his favorite Yiddish music on the house sound system he was so proud of. He loved his collection of old recordings by the famous Russian born Yiddish cantor, Moishe Oysher. He would then shower and dress for dinner. It was now 4:15 with sundown fast approaching at 5:58 when Shabbas officially began.

Seven months pregnant, Hanna was feeling a throbbing in her lower-back from walking on the hard-wood floors in the living room and the stone tile floors in the foyer and kitchen. She was wringing her hands as she walked. Occasionally she would arch her back as she rubbed her strained area.

Hanna's mother tried to alley her fears and spoke to her in Yiddish.

"Daughter, please sit. This is not good for the baby and you will start to upset the children before the candles are lit. Mendel will walk in the door any minute. I'm certain he let the time escape him while study-ing. Please, Hanna, sit down on a soft chair and be patient."

"Mama, not once since I know Mendel has he been this late for Shabbas dinner. Not one time. I hope nothing has happened. Maybe I should call the Schul?" Hanna's face had become flush. Her mother could see the perspiration coming from under her *sheitel*, the wig that most Orthodox Jewish women wear.

With each minute that passed Hanna's anxiety was building. The younger children now sensed something was wrong and stopped playing, and the older ones stopped preparing for Shabbas dinner. The sound of the boys running in their black laced shoes, against the hard wood and carpeted floors was now gone. The older girls remained som-ber near the dining room table, which was elegantly set for Shabbas. Hand-woven linen, the finest china, crystal glassware, sterling silver-ware and heirloom sterling candle holders awaited the family's weekly festivities.

The comforting aroma of chicken soup, two fresh baked *challah* breads, a roast brisket of beef and beef *chulent* simmering on a low frame on the *blach* for tomorrows lunch, which filled the home, was no longer noticed from the worry about Mendel.

It was now 4:45 and Hanna was frantic. As she did every Friday while awaiting her husband, Hanna was dressed exquisitely in her finest below the knee blue and gold maternity dress, adorned by gold ear-rings from Mendel's grandmother and a string of pearls handed down from her own *bubba*. The makeup that she applied earlier in the after-noon had dissipated from stress, perspiration and the few tears that she couldn't hold back, as much as she tried for the sake of the children. Now Hanna's mother could no longer contain her own concern which she was masking for the sake of her daughter and precious grandchildren. She too began pacing the floors, her hands clenched as tight as her jaw.

"I've had enough! I'm calling Jacob!" Hanna shouted as she was standing next to the large granite center island in her new, modern kitchen. Jacob is Mendel's brother who lives nearby in Monsey. Six months ago, the brothers had had a dispute over business and they had not seen one another very much, although the wives and children still got together with one another.

Hanna reached for her cell-phone and started to dial Jacobs number when the doorbell chimed. She dropped the phone onto the tiled floor as her stomach dropped in anticipation. She felt a strong kick from the baby inside her womb. *That can't be my Mendel, he never rings the doorbell,* she thought.

Hanna hurried to the front door, quickly followed by her anxious mother. The children all seemed to be fixed in their places in the dining room.

Hanna reached for the doorknob, her throat seemed to be so blocked from anxiety she could hardly breathe. She began to see tiny spots before her eyes as she felt faint.

Opening the door, her worst fears confronted her. Standing in the doorway was a uniformed policeman. This officer is one of three men on the Ramapo PD who spoke Yiddish in case it was needed. Another man in a suit had a badge draped from his jacket pocket, plus a man wearing the familiar yellow Hatzolah ambulance jacket. The familiar ambulance was parked in front of the house. Her eyes flashed for a second trying to digest the scene. She now saw Rabbi Kreitzman coming up the walkway to the front steps of her home. Hanna's knees buckled as she began to fall to the ground. The Hatzolah man, anticipating this possible reaction was ready and grabbed the pregnant woman before she fell. Hanna's mother gasped but could not speak, throwing both of her hands to her gaping mouth.

The uniformed officer helped carry Hanna into the house and placed her on the living room sofa. She never lost consciousness but simply went limp and seemed catatonic. No words had yet been spoken.

Outside, a group of neighbors, all Hasidic, seeing the police car and ambulance and Rabbi, were gathered out of concern for the Glick family. Word had not gotten to them about the *Shanda*.

A minute or two later, Hanna seemed to regain her senses and stared up at the men standing around her. Her devoted mother sat beside her, holding her hand in hers awaiting the inevitable news.

"Mrs. Glick, there has been an incident," The detective began. "We are very sorry to inform you that your husband did not survive."

Hanna looked at the man as if she didn't understand the words. She looked from person to person, stunned by what she was trying to process. She paused for a moment and looked into the detective's eyes as if she needed to verify what she was told.

"Mendel is dead? You're telling me my Mendel is dead?"

"I'm afraid so, Mrs. Glick. We are very sorry."

Hanna tried to speak but no words would come. Her mother through trembling lips asked, "An incident, what is an incident? I don't understand."

Hanna, looking at the men in her home tried to rise from the sofa. The Ramapo police are trained that a man should not touch an Orthodox woman unless absolutely necessary, so the two men backed away.

Hanna thought better than trying to stand, and remained seated. She cleared her throat and finally tried to speak. As she began to speak only sobs of despair would come.

Finally, Hanna was able to put her words together. She spoke in her native tongue.

Ir kumt shbs tsu mir aun zag mir az Mendel iz toyt.

Ver vet zorgn far mir? Ver vet nemen keir fun aundzer kinder? Ver vet nemen keir dun aundz?

"You come to my home on Shabbas and tell me Mendel is dead. Who is going to take care of me? Who will take care of our children? Who will take care of us?"

Chapter Seven

Chevra-Kadish the Orthodox burial society, was summoned by Rabbi Kreitzman to oversee Mendel's burial to assure a proper burial according to Jewish tradition. They arrived at the scene as Mendel's remains were being placed in a body bag and moved into a white, blue striped Medical Examiners van. Chevra-Kadish was there for a particular reason. All of Mendel's blood, bone and brain matter, spilled on the sidewalk along Route 59, were sopped up into towels for transportation to the Hillman Funeral Chapel. Rabbi Kreitzman selected Hillman for the family, knowing they would approve of his recommendation. All of Mendel's blood and tissue was to be treated with reverence and buried with Mendel on Sunday. By Jewish law, no burials are allowed on Shabbas, and there was to be no desecration of any of the deceased's remains during that time.

As soon as the van left the scene, the crowd, which had swelled to over two-hundred people, had dissipated. Before sundown, only a few non-Orthodox onlookers remained. The Chevra-Kasish workers were allowed to break the strict rules of Shabbas to show the proper respect for the body.

Detective Mike Sassano left when the body was removed and headed directly for the Glick home. When he arrived, Sassano was greeted at the door by Mendel's older brother Jacob. The family was gathered in the living room in stunned silence. The children were sitting in folding chairs and on the floor around Hanna and her mother and Jacob's wife, who sat on the sofa. Not fully understanding the gravity of the situation the younger boys were poking and pushing each other until they were corrected by their grandmother.

Sassano showed his identification. "Sorry to intrude at this time. I'm Detective Mike Sassano of the Ramapo police department. I've come to pay my condolences on behalf of the department. I would like to ask a few questions of Mrs. Hanna Glick if that is permitted."

"Thank you. My name is Jacob Glick. I am Mendel's brother."

Jacob escorted Sassano to the living room. He instructed the children to leave the room so the adults could talk. Sassano approached the widow. He thought of all the times he had to do this with family members of murder victims in his many years on the job. This one was by far the most heart-wrenching seeing the young, pregnant widow and all the young children who were suddenly fatherless.

"Please accept our condolences on behalf of all the members of the police department and the County of Rockland," Sassano began.

Hanna nodded her head and averted her eyes from the male stranger in her home.

Jacob pulled up one of the folding chairs and placed it a few feet from his sister-in-law.

Sassano sat and looked at the pitiful scene before him, breathing in deeply gathering his thoughts for a moment.

"Mrs. Glick, I would like to ask you a few questions. I know this may seem like an inappropriate time. However, the more information we can gather early on, may help us to apprehend the person or persons who committed this terrible crime against your husband."

Hanna nodded her head.

Sassano took out his ragged black book to take notes of the interview.

"Mrs. Glick, would you have any reason to believe anyone would harm your husband? Did you know if he had any enemies?

Hanna paused. After a few moments, her voice raspy from sobbing, replied.

"My Mendel had no such enemies. He was the kindest, gentlest man. A good husband and good provider for his family."

"Of course. Had he recently been threatened by anyone to your knowledge?

"No."

"To your knowledge, did he have financial difficulties?"

"Absolutely no. I don't know much of Mendel's business. Mendel did very well as you can see," Hanna replied. She slowly waved her arm around the surroundings. The large home was well appointed and beautifully maintained. Sassano could tell by the furnishings that the young family was living well.

"Had he had any arguments in the past that may have brought someone to act against him?"

"No. Mendel was never one to get involved with anyone who would do such a thing."

Jacob Glick interrupted.

"Detective, my brother was a good and great man. He and I were in business together since he was seventeen. In the past six-months we had a dispute that was regrettable. I will take this argument to my grave," Jacob's voice quivered.

Sassano replied, "Mr. Glick what was the argument? Did you argue often?"

"Never. This was about business. Our business."

"About money?" Sassano pushed.

"Yes. But not just money. We disagreed about expanding our business."

"Can you explain please."

"Mendel wanted to take our business overseas, to Europe and China. I was satisfied with less. He wasn't."

"I see. We will be asking for financial records and documents in the days ahead. Is that a problem?"

"Absolutely not. We will provide you with everything you need."

"Was your business largely done in cash?"

"Not largely, but there was some cash involved. We split everything fifty-fifty. Neither of us was greedy or jealous of each other. Never."

"I understand. Mr. Glick, was there anyone that you know of who may have been jealous of Mendel or would want to harm him due to business reasons?"

"No. No one."

"Thank you. I will have more questions about your business dealings. Now, can you please tell me where you were this afternoon Mr. Glick?" Sassano queried.

Jacob paused. After a long ten seconds, he responded. "Detective, am I a suspect in my own brother's murder?"

"Everyone is a suspect until we determine what happened to your brother. Please answer my question."

"I was at my office and warehouse. I left at about noontime."

"Then where did you go?"

"I went directly to the shul to pray and to study Torah."

"What time did you leave the synagogue?"

"I left at about two and went directly home to prepare for Shabbas."

"Do you go to the same shul as Mendel?"

"We did for years. After the argument and separation from Mendel, I began going to Community Synagogue."

"I see. When did you see your brother last, Mr. Glick?"

"Not even with the children for Purim a few weeks ago. I think six or seven months maybe."

"Thank you." Sassano returned his attention to the widow.

"Mrs. Glick, when was the last time you saw your husband?"

She thought for a moment, bringing a trembling hand to her mouth.

"Mendel rose every day at 4:30. He would *daven*, then I made him breakfast. He left before six."

"Did you speak to him during breakfast?"

"Of course."

"Can you share with me your discussion?"

"Shabbas. Shabbas is the most important part of our week. Every week. It is a sacred and beautiful day for us and our lives…now I will never have a happy Shabbas again." Hanna covered her face with both hands, sobbing uncontrollably.

Chapter Eight

The sky over Lago Lugano on the Italian-Swiss boarder was a crisp royal blue with a smattering of fluffy white cumulus clouds, making the fifty-eight-degree temperature seem heavenly.

John Deegan and his wife Gjuliana had decided to take a walk to the Italian side of the massive glacial lake. The walk was only two miles long and they had waited for a perfect day like this. The winter was long and colder than normal and the older couple needed to shake out the cob-webs. They had not left their home for what seemed like an eternity, largely due to the Covid-19 pandemic.

"Look at that Lake, Gjuliana. The Italians would say *'un pezzo di paradiso caduto sulla terra,"* John proclaimed.

"Indeed. A piece of heaven falling to earth. It's simply magnificent," Gjuliana replied.

"A far cry from where we grew up in the Bronx."

"I loved where we lived. I guess because that's where we met."

"That's very sweet."

"I'm a hopeless romantic."

"I remember the first time I saw you. I never saw an Albanian before I met you, and it was like being struck by a bolt of lightning. We weren't even in our teens."

"And you made me wait for you almost two-thirds of my life," Gjuliana smiled.

"What can I say? I had my issues. I didn't think I could ever love anyone. Being abused as a small child can destroy a person's soul."

"I'm not complaining my love. Thankfully, I have you until the end."

"Yes, you will."

They walked a bit in silence taking in the beauty of the mountains which surrounds the Lombardy region on the Italian side and the Ticino region of Switzerland. The sun bounced off the lake giving it an almost glistening vista. John inhaled the fresh air deeply into his lungs and Gjuliana held her face up to get the sun on her winter pale face.

"I can tell you are a bit bored. Not by me I hope," Gjuliana offered.

"Never. My mind is restless is all. I enjoy the tough challenges in life. Managing our money from the safety of our home in southern Switzerland is just not enough at times. I need something to do, like I did with Raquel and Vic last year in New York. Helping to solve a major crime is just up my alley. Thinking five moves ahead like a game of chess. Can you imagine, me, an arch-criminal who is being sought by Interpol and the FBI looking to solve crimes. It's a laugh riot."

"Have you heard from them?"

"Who? Interpol and the FBI?"

"No, silly. Vic and Raquel."

"Not in a few months. I called for Christmas. They called for New Year's."

"Well, I'm due for a trip home to see my family. Maybe you can disguise yourself and come along?"

"I think I'll use my Hasidic Jew disguise. I always liked the curls and the hats."

"Funny, I liked the French artist the best. Or the homeless guy. You really looked like a Bowery bum, John."

"Thank you, my love. I try."

• • •

Back in New York, Vic awoke at home in the guest room. He and Pando ate their share of coal fired pizza at Patsy's on First Avenue and 117th Street. Four beers each with the pies, then they bounced a bit. First to J G Melons on Third Avenue and later to the St. Regis Hotel in Midtown. Vic wanted to show Pando the magnificent Maxfield Parrish mural at the King Cole Bar. Pando was impressed. Vic became maudlin. Vic was in no hurry to go home after his blow up with Raquel.

Vic laid in bed trying to focus his eyes on an antique Louis Comfort Tiffany lamp which sat on a mahogany side-board in the antique motif guest room. He was feeling the effect of too much alcohol the night before. Vic was still pissed off at one remark Raquel made. 'Maybe I need my head examined for staying with you.' The comment stayed with him the entire night.

After some time, Raquel appeared at the guest room door. Vic looked at her and looked away.

"You still mad?" Raquel asked.

"Mad? Not mad. Dogs get mad. Upset maybe," Vic replied with a quiet hurt in his voice.

Raquel walked into the room and climbed into the queen-sized bed snuggling up to her man.

"I'm sorry, baby."

"You should be. Maybe I need my head examined for staying with you? That's not very nice."

"You know I didn't mean that baby. You know what happened when I get my Puerto Rican up. The ghetto fighter comes out and my mouth overtakes my brain. I'm so sorry if I hurt you."

"All over this Covid. I think we all have cabin fever."

"Gabriella won't be home until tonight. How about…" Raquel reached down and softly fondled Vic.

Makeup sex is the best sex in life.

Chapter Nine

$\mathbf{D}$r. Angela Rush decided to do the examination on Mendel Glick immediately. She advised her staff that Friday night and Saturday would be on overtime. The Glick family and the Hasidic community could then bury the murder victim on Sunday to comply with strict Jewish law.

Angela waited for Mike Sassano and Assistant District Attorney Mary Jane Cunningham to arrive at the Medical Examiner's office to begin the post mortem examination. Sassano would arrived after he met with the Glick family at their home.

Under the watchful eyes of Dr. Rush and the *shomer,* the M.E . technicians removed Mendel's clothing. All of his flat *platchige biber* hat, his worn shoes, the groceries and the flowers he was carrying and his small prayer book, along with the blood-soaked towels were placed in a black plastic bag. The bag would be transported, with the body, by the funeral home.

The *shomer* was asked to wear protective clothing. He agreed and donned blue cloth operating room gown, blue paper booties, an operating room mask and a face-shield as everyone in the examination wore.

Also in the room was Ramapo Police Officer Banks who was present to identify the body he saw at the scene. Unlike television shows, the Glick family was spared the pulling down the sheet to expose the body. It would be a scene too much for Hanna Glick to take. Office Banks was excused after his ID of the corpse.

The stainless-steel slab table was one of three in the white tiled room. Twelve stainless refrigeration units covered an entire wall in the rear of the room. Scales hug from the ceiling to weigh body parts when needed.

Angela Rush audio taped the procedure noting the victim's name height and weight, and body temperature, the "no autopsy will be performed due to religious belief of the victim" disclaimer and "the body is in rigor mortis" notation. Mendel had been dead for over six hours. His body was practically in full rigor.

Angela verbally notated every aspect of her investigation She asked the technician to photograph the projectiles entry wound when she was examining the victims back. When they turned the body back around, the massive destruction of Mendel's face and forehead were also photographed. The Medical Examiner does an investigation independent from law enforcement and does not rely solely on any of the information gathered at the crime scene.

The assistants and Angela worked on the angle of the bullet into the brain taking into consideration the probable shooters location being the eight-story building on Secora Road, Mendel's height and speed of walking, wind velocity, angle and direction of the shooter and direction were all important considerations.

The investigation was strictly scientific except for the probable location which at this point was theoretical.

"May I probe the victims brain for possible projectile fragments," Angela asked the *shomer*.

"I have no objection so long as all of his tissue is returned for burial. That would include instruments that you will use. That also would include any blood. No samples can be taken... with all respect to your office," the *shomer* replied. In the twenty years that the Chevra Kadish employee did his duty to the dead, he had never seen a skull so ravaged as this.

"I would like perhaps to use my microscope if needed." Angela asked.

"Yes, the slides should be buried with the body as well."

"Understood," Angela replied. *"They don't miss anything,"* She thought.

Angela probed the brain or what was left of it, and the surrounding cranial area and found no bullet fragments. She noticed all the dried blood on his curly *payos* and moved them to access the destroyed skull. Everything was bagged as the *shomer* requested.

The crew worked for almost two-hours, taking notes and additional photographs. They placed Mendel's naked corpse in a black body-bag and into a refrigerator for the funeral home. Hillman would be collecting the body after sundown on Saturday for Sunday's burial.

Finished with the body, Angela called for a meeting in the small, sparsely appointed conference room.

"I know everyone is tired from the long day so I just want to say a few things and hear if anyone has anything on their mind. First, as we have been doing, the Hasidic community does things a bit differently than the secular world. Out of respect for their religious beliefs, we need to do whatever is reasonably requested to comply. Of utmost importance to the police department, and to the community at large, we need to help in any way possible to capture the perpetrator. Detective Sassano, would you like to add anything?"

"I've been asked a few times today if this may be a hate crime. We certainly can't rule that out. We will spare no expense to uncover the full story. Whether it was a hate crime, if indeed that's the case, or if there was some other motive. I have a meeting tomorrow with the District Attorney and Ms. Cunningham to review the steps we will take to hopefully apprehend the killer."

"If I were a betting woman, I would put money on the sniper's location being that building on Secora Road," Angela quipped.

Sassano rubbed his tired eyes before responding. "I tend to agree with you on the surface, but we are looking for some evidence to verify the theory. That building is the Esther Dashew Apartments. I dispatched detectives to the location soon after the shooting. We will canvas the area tomorrow and Sunday. There are a lot of Orthodox people living in that building, so getting information on the Sabbath will be an issue tomorrow. It's a low-income senior citizen building so we are hoping someone saw or heard something that will help. Older people tend to stay at home, especially now during Covid."

"Detective, have you had a chance to look at the projectile?" Angela queried.

"I did. I have to tell you that I've never encountered this kind of bullet. It was in two pieces, and it will be brought up to the New York State Police Laboratory in Albany tomorrow morning for testing and determination. I don't expect an answer on that until Monday at the earliest. We were very fortunate to find it so quickly."

"Yes, I agree. It's something I haven't seen before although my experience in ballistics is very limited compared to yours." Angela winked at her old coach.

Chapter Ten

"There will never be Shabbas again, Mama, never," Hanna Glick said weeping to her mother, who herself was overcome with grief for her son-in-law whom she loved for his kind and gentle spirit, and the way he treated her daughter and grandchildren.

It was early Saturday morning, the day after everyone in the Glick home, and likely many other Orthodox homes in the Jewish communities from Williamsburg, Brooklyn to Kyrias Joel, in Orange County, were in mourning over the recent murder. The Satmar sect in Monsey and in the next-door community in New Square in New Hempstead, New York seemed to be reacting with a sense of despair and fear. After all, one of their own was brutally killed as he was preparing for a good Shabbas.

Hanna's mother replied. "Daughter, your job as a Jewish mother did not end at Mendel's death. You still have a responsibility to teach your children the proper way to live. To teach them Torah. As much as it will hurt, you must still light the Shabbas candle every Friday at sundown. You still must follow and teach the rules of Judaism. Without women, there would be no Jewish faith. We are the backbone of our great and sacred religion. *Hashem* will be the answer for you. He is only giving you another life, another chance to prove yourself to Him."

"I can never be with another man. Mendel was the *mench* of all *menches*. A true man in so many ways. How do I go on mama, how?"

"You must!"

The Glick house was so quiet, it had become surreal. The dishes and silver remained on the fine linen covered dining room table. The fresh, golden challah breads remained on the marble side table, with the bread knife aside of them. The ceremonial bread remained whole and uncut. Jacob, before he left for his home, had covered all of the mirrors in his brother's house. This time in a Hasidic home is for personal reflection and not on vanity. The scent of the food, all prepared by Hanna and her mother, which had permeated the entire home the day before was less obvious. Only the aroma of the still, slow cooking *chulent*, whiffed through the mourning home.

No visitors would be visiting today, on *Shabbas*, for sitting *shiva*, the solemn seven days of structured mourning, would commence after the burial.

For anyone who had an appetite to eat, the chulent, the beef, bean and potato stew would have to do today. The children remained in their rooms, the younger ones not yet fully understanding that their father was gone from their lives forever.

Hanna's mother continued her lesson. "You will go on by putting one foot in front of the other as many Jewish mothers did dealing with a tragedy since the time of Abraham. And tomorrow, which will be the hardest day of your young life, you will ask Hashem to guide your soul and to be strong for the sake of everyone around you, especially the children."

• • •

"I'm told I should no longer say 'Good morning ladies-and-gentlemen', or Okay guys listen up'. It seems these days my old school has burned to the ground," Mike Sassano opened his remarks at the conference room at the District Attorney's office at the Rockland County Courthouse in New City. This was Sassano's way of protesting the new cancel culture in America. Sassano's personality, age and the respect he had from everyone in the County allowed him to step aside politically incorrect ideas and language. Everyone chuckled at Sassano's wisecrack including Mary Cunningham and her boss, District Attorney, Edward Welch, often thought of as stone-faced and humorless man in the courtroom.

The conference room was large. A dark colored cherry-wood desk and fifteen swivel chairs was surrounded with a standing room only assemblage of uniformed police officers, detectives, attorneys and a stenographer who was also in charge of audio taping the meeting.

Sassano continued, "The entire Orthodox community is in mourning after one of their own was shot dead in broad daylight yesterday. I don't know about any of you, but I had a hard time sleeping last night. I don't think I'll have a good rest until we catch this killer."

"So, I made some notes last night that I would like to share. I'm not too great with the computer so my twelve-year-old grandson put my thoughts down on this bullet point thing."

One of the uniformed officers worked the lap top and the conference room screen came alive.

"Ok, here we are. Number one. Hate crime or vengeance or random act? You will see your names next to the assignments. I met with the family and there seemed to be an issue with the deceased and his brother about six months ago. We need the records of cell numbers and home and office phones going back at least a year to see any patterns. I briefly interviewed the brother, Jacob Glick, and he has agreed to provide us with business documents and bank accounts. We also will be looking at all license plate readers with our people and NYPD for the brother and the victim to track their movements for the past few months, both here and in Brooklyn."

A hand rose from the side of the room alongside a wall spotted with photos of District Attorneys from the 1800's

Sassano pointed to a detective who raised his hand. "Mike, I'm not sure if a Hasidic man could be so good with a high-powered rifle, if we are to assume that information on a rifle is correct."

Sassano sat back in his chair before he commented. "Jimmy, first off you are probably correct, although I take nothing for granted. Perhaps the Hasidim are not good with sophisticated weaponry, but you have to agree that they have the cash to pay someone that is."

D. A. Welch gave a slight smile and nodded his head in agreement.

Sassano continued, "Next point. Hate crime? No one knows at this point but the odds are in that direction. So, Jimmy, Carl, you two will be looking at anything we have on threats to the Jews on file, prior attacks, Nazi graffiti and that kind of thing. Also, I'd like you to get your contacts to find out if that white supremacist group in Sloatsburg are possibly celebrating. Anything is possible."

D.A. Welch raised his hand.

"Yes sir," Sassano pointed.

"Mike, have you played with the idea that Mr. Glick wasn't even the target? Perhaps he just got in the way?"

"Yes, we have. Our unit will be going around tomorrow to collect every video recording from the Secora Road spot up and down Route 59. We will be looking at anything and everything. Maybe we can spot the shooters vehicle."

"Next point. Starting tomorrow there will be two men assigned to the Secora Road building until every single tenant is canvased. Did they hear anything? See anything? Any strangers walking or driving around? Also, two men are assigned to the Evergreen Super Market. Get the store video. I want to see every move Mendel Glick made while he was in that store yesterday. Was anyone following him? Did he seem nervous or upset?"

"Next point…his synagogue. I want every one of his prayer buddies canvassed. They may be resistant because of their culture but explain that we are trying to help the community. Two men are assigned there."

Sassano continued, "Next point, please." He pointed to detective Phil Alesio. "Phil, as of today you are Mendel Glick. I want you to find out everything about him. You will know him as good as you know yourself. I want you to work with everyone here to gather their reports. I want you to know the victim like you know yourself. Anything that happened from a year ago until yesterday. Know him like you know yourself. His routine, his business dealings, his doctors…everything." Alesio nodded his understanding of his assignment.

"Next point. I will be working with the Crime Lab on the results of ballistics tests, to know everything about the possible gun and projectile. I'll follow up leads on the kind of equipment that was used.

"Final point. Do everything by the book. Cross every T and dot every I. No shortcuts, no assumptions. Stay within the law so we don't fuck…I'm sorry, so we don't screw up on any legal loopholes so the shooter can skate. And one more thing, I will be going up to Kyrias Joel to meet with Rebbe Teitelbaum to see if has any thoughts on the case, and let him know we are diligently seeking justice."

"Good move, Mike. I will join you." Welch replied. Sassano nodded. He thought, *"Typical politician. He wants to run for governor."*

"Any questions or comments?" Sassano asked.

Welch stood from his chair at the head of the conference table.

"Thank you, Mike. It seems as if you have most everything covered. Everyone is to think outside the box. If you have a suggestion, bring it to Mike. At this point, we will keep things inside of Rockland County law enforcement. If it's determined the homicide was a hate crime, and Mendel Glick's civil rights were breeched, we have the option of calling the FBI into the case for help."

A low murmur of discontent from the police who were present filled the room.

Chapter Eleven

Vic Gonnella woke to a beautiful, spring-like morning in Manhattan. The sun was shimmering on the East River and the chirping birds were a comforting, welcome sound. It seemed that the worst of winter was finally over.

Vic ambled down to the kitchen and made a cup of strong Café Bustello in the DeLonghi espresso machine, adding some cream, he popped it into the microwave. Vic liked his morning coffee piping hot. Raquel smelled the lovely aroma from their bedroom, threw on her jogging outfit and joined Vic.

"Good morning baby." Raquel whispered. She kissed him softly on the side of his neck."

"Buon Giorno, seniora."

"Breakfast? Should I get some bagels?"

"I'm good at the moment. I thought I'd make some French toast and sausages when Gabriella and your mom get up."

"Hmmm, sounds great."

Vic sipped his coffee while he looked at the East River from the kitchen window.

"Want to do anything today?" Vic asked. It was almost like a challenge.

"Like what?"

"I thought it would be a great day to drive up to Arthur Avenue, walk around a bit, have lunch at Dominick's, sit outside of the Parisienne Café and people watch. Maybe get some cannoli at Delillo's for tonight."

"Baby, it sounds great but I'm just not ready," Raquel uttered.

"Can I say something without starting an argument?" Vic gently inquired.

"I know. I'm still neurotic about Covid."

"Well…we've both had the two vaccinations. We can wear our masks. Most people are out and about. You know…the herd immunity theory the are talking about. The restaurants are at fifty-percent capacity. I'll call Charlie. He'll put us upstairs at Dominick's away from everyone."

"Let's just maybe take a walk along the river instead."

"Listen to me. Olga was up in the Bronx for a few days. How do you know if she wasn't exposed to Covid from her lady friends?

"She had the vaccines, too." Raquel retorted.

"My point exactly. I think you need to break the ice and get out a bit."

"Maybe in a few weeks. I'm just…just still worried."

"Okay. I'll go up there alone and bring back the food for all of us," Vic offered.

"I have a better idea. I'll make your mothers Sunday sauce and your favorite rigatoni. I have all the stuff. You can help me make the meatballs."

"Braciole, too? Vic asked.

"Of course. And the hot and sweet sausage and pork. It'll be fun."

"Sounds like a plan. And I can watch the Yankees pre-season game. Maybe a college basketball game or two." Vic thought, *"I tried. Don't push her anymore. This too shall pass."*

• • •

Mendel's body was ready for burial. Hillman Memoria funeral home worked in the early morning hours to meet the 10:00 a.m. funeral which is steeped in ancient tradition. His body was ritually washed, the *tahara,* in warm water, the *shemira,* having the body watched by someone until he is buried would soon be fulfilled. Mendel was clothed in a white linen shroud. His shoulders were draped in a white *tallit,* a prayer shawl and a white *yarmulke* was placed upon what was left of his head. Mendel's un-embalmed remains were gently placed in a plain pine box with the bag of his body parts and bloody towels placed at his feet. A small bag of Palestine soil, *eretz yisroel,* land of Israel, was placed behind his head.

The Glick family arrived at Hillman Chapel at 9:30. There were hundreds of Hasidim already waiting, showing a unified community for the murder victim.

Hanna, wearing a dark dress and a black head-covering arrived with the children, her mother and Jacobs family. Monsey Trails, the local bus company donated a vehicle to transport the family. Friends and other family members were already inside, awaiting the widow and children. The immediate family, waited with the coffin in a large room, in silence. No one was permitted to see the body.

The weather was beautiful. The sun was shining and the sky bright blue much like the last day of Mendel's life, but without the wind.

As the time for the funeral arrived, there were well over a thousand Hasidic men standing outside the chapel. Synagogues generally are not used for a funeral. Rabi Kreitzman arrived and made his way to the young family. He read from scriptures, reciting several Psalms in Hebrew and Yiddish. Within fifteen-minutes, the service was concluded.

At the cemetery, Hanna felt as if she was going to pass out, but overcame the feeling with pure determination. She blocked out the large crowd, not even hearing the Mourners Kaddish. Rabbi Kreitzman cut a bit of cloth from the clothing of the immediate family members.

After lowering the coffin into the grave, the box was slightly opened to expose the body. Some male mourners used the convex side of the shovel to carry the soil directly onto Mendel's body so he will return to dust quickly. The shovel is not passed from hand to hand but rather placed into the earth for the next person to use. The flat side of the shovel is used to symbolically show the reluctance to say goodbye.

The funeral was over. The murder victim was buried according to Jewish law and tradition. Shiva would begin at the Glick home immediately. No one in the massive crowd of mourners wore masks of socially distanced as mandated by New York State decree.

Chapter Twelve

While Mendel was being buried, Mike Sassano and his team hit the ground running. The two detectives assigned to 20 Secora Road, the potential sniper's nest, were going door-to-door asking the apartment building residents if they saw or heard anything unusual on the past Friday. This kind of canvasing is painstaking and done on a regular basis in crime investigation.

Tenant after tenant had the same things to say. They saw nothing, heard nothing or were not at home. Some were shopping for Shabbas, some others would be at a senior citizens center or just were not interested in talking.

From nine in the morning, the detectives were frustrated by the boredom of not getting a nibble. One elderly woman, who was collecting her mail in the lobby, thinks she saw a young man with a large carry bag waiting in the vestibule to be able to get into the building. He made access into the building by someone, despite the tenants being told not to open the door to strangers. The aged woman said she didn't remember whom, and that the young man went quickly to the stairwell door. She couldn't describe him, nor guess at his age other than to say he was young. He was white was all she could additionally offer. Another woman in the building recalled a car alarm going off briefly on Secora Road, which didn't seem important.

After their lunch break, at 2:00 p.m., the two detectives, returned to the building and were assaulted by the aroma of cooking cabbage, chicken soup and other foods being prepared for the elderly people's early dinners.

The detectives canvasing would continue into the evening without success. A young man without any description wasn't much of a start. Even the building superintendent and porter, who spent his day doing repairs in the apartments, and the porter, who was mopping the black tile floors in the hallways and common areas, were of no help.

Late that afternoon. Mike Sorrano received a call from the New York State Police Laboratory in Albany on his cellphone.

"Sorrano," he answered.

"Detective Sorrano, this is Captain Matt Morresy at the State Lab."

"Nice to meet you Matt. Is Tony Cerillo still with you guys?"

"Tony retired last year after thirty-five years. I worked with him since the day I started here. I suppose you knew him."

"Yea, he helped me out on cases a few times over the years. Nice guy."

"He truly is. He moved to Myrtle Beach."

"Good for him. Nice meeting you, Captain."

"Matt, please."

"Thanks, I'm Mike."

"We have a report for you on the projectile you guys collected on Friday. I'll be sending a full report via e-mail but I figured you would want to talk about it."

"Great Matt. What do you have?"

"The report will break down in full detail what I'm about to tell you. This is an interesting projectile. It's very uncommon for a few reasons. It's made out of tungsten carbide with a copper wrapping. This kind of alloy is generally used by the government and not for anti-personnel applications. It's more for anti-material usage. Just to give you an idea, if a diamond is rated a ten on a hardness scale, tungsten carbide would be rated a nine point five. I can't think of another bullet with this hardness. We are certain that this bullet was homemade and here's why. The weight of the projectile you sent to us is 307 grains. We checked with our contacts at Lehigh Industries of Pennsylvania and a couple of other manufactures this morning. They tell us these projectiles are made, by computer at a constant 300 grains. After firing and hitting a target the weight should be lower, say 287 to 291 grains. Not 300 or higher. That weight indicates a non-manufactured projectile. Someone made this bullet. We call it homemade."

"Interesting," Sassano replied.

"Now to the kind of firearm. Taking into account the data you shared, the potential distance being 548 yards to the target and the damage done by the photo's you forwarded, we are ninety-five percent suggesting it was a .338 Caliber. We took into consideration the temperature and the wind that day. We checked with the weather people and determined there was a ten-mile an hour wind. That would not have made the shot from that building easy. Matter of fact, the wind was a considerable factor at that distance. Don't get me wrong, whomever took that shot is pretty proficient to make a direct head shot. A body shot under those conditions would have been less difficult. Now, let's assume he was shooting from the roof-top. The shooter would have had to know the elevation hold and the wind hold. Most hunters for example could not make that head shot."

"So, the shooter knows his stuff, Sassano added."

Captain Morresy paused. "He was either lucky or he is good. We think he is very, very good."

"Let's get back to the homemade concept. What would the shooter need to make this type of bullet?"

"Good question. First off, he would have to source the tungsten carbide. Then he would have needed a grinder to be able to shape it into a projectile. He would have to know how to plate it with copper and use a reloading press which is fairly easy to obtain. Whoever did this, knows his way around the machining tools needed and had access to expensive equipment," Morrisey informed.

"So, making this kind of projectile is difficult?"

"Extremely. This shooter didn't just go out and buy this bullet. He made it. For sure."

Chapter Thirteen

It was now a week since Mendel Glick was shot and killed. The family sat *shiva* in the traditional manner of sitting on boxes, lower than other chairs to signify the family mourners and not adding to their personal comfort. A *yahrzeit*, a memorial candle, is lit for the seven days and visitors do not ring the doorbell or knock to make entrance into the home during visiting hours.

Hanna and the children and the rest of the immediate family was doing the best they could to hold up during *shiva*.

Plenty of food was brought by or delivered on a daily basis from the community and friends. No further visits from the police department were made out of respect for the mourning period.

Another Shabbas was here and the Orthodox community began preparing for sundown.

. . .

The shooter was again on the prowl. New Square, was his next intended location. In the Town of New Hempstead, in Rockland County next to Monsey and Spring Valley, New Square is a totally Hasidic, densely populated community.

Entering New Square from Route 45 is like going into a community like no other. For the uninitiated, it is like going into another world, filled with Hasidic men, women and children. The men, some gathering on street corners, all dressed in long black coats, white shirts and various black hats, chatting, as many of the women wearing dresses with opaque stockings, long sleeved blouses or jackets and well combed wigs, pushed their baby carriages and prams going about the preparation of *Shabbas*.

Young boys released from school seemed not to be concerned about the few cars that passed by. They ran into the streets pushing one other and, seemingly wild, ignored any vehicles that slowly drove through the community.

The homes and apartments are close together, on many of the streets named after United States presidents. Teenage girls dressed similarly as the married women but without wearing wigs walked in packs of five-to-eight after school. They were no doubt all going home to help their mothers prepare for the Sabbath dinner, and all lighting the *Shabbas* candles at sundown.

Empty corrugated boxes were strewn on almost every block making New Square look like an unkempt dump. The few homes which had tiny grass patches in front were not trimmed or otherwise cared for. A landscaper would starve in New Square.

The men noticed any strange cars, and stared at the driver or other occupants. Anyone who looked like they didn't belong would often be approached by the men and questioned as to their need to be inside the community.

The shooter quickly noticed that there would not be a flat area where he could take a shot with his high-powered rifle. Going on top of a home or building was out of the question. However, he intended to shoot from the rear of his van through a gun-port which he had made for this purpose. Twice he was approached by the men dressed in their various Hasidic hats and their long black coats. Rather than interact with them, he simply drove on, nervously exiting New Square as quickly as he entered.

He drove north on Route 45 toward Spring Valley, then west to New Hempstead Road, looking for a flat area where many Hasidic people would be walking. He was looking for a spot to take a long-shot on his next victim. The killer was hunting.

He drove to Route 306. The road had no lack of men walking to their synagogues to pray or to study or on their way home for their preparation for Shabbas.

Finally, he spotted what he thought to be an ideal spot to pull his van over to the side of the road. Next to the van was an undeveloped piece of land, filled with trees. The opposite side of the road was also like a tiny forest, without any homes or stores. He noticed the stream of traffic along 306, while sporadically busy, was good enough for him to wait out a break in the traffic, when fewer cars drove by.

Like any good hunter, he was patient. His rifle, which he hid under some boxes in the van, was unsheathed and at the ready. No one seemed to notice the van on the side of the road. He spotted a potential target from the rear of his vehicle. A Hasidic man wearing a *shtreimel*, a high fury hat two- hundred-yards from where he waited, was walking in his direction.

The shooter noticed a break in the traffic coming in his direction. He opened the gun port, aimed the weapon, calculated his distance and wind speed, which was negligible and shot, his suppresser killing the sound of the discharge.

The shot was off the mark, perhaps because he was still jittery from the New Square experience or because he was rushing to take the shot in traffic. Instead of a direct hit to the victim's head, the victim was hit in his throat, opening a huge gap in the rear of his neck. The shooter saw the massive spray of blood in his scope. He was certain the victim could not survive.

He was correct.

Chapter Fourteen

Heshe Weissman was only twenty-two years old. He just had his first child, a boy, who had his *briss*, the Jewish rite of circumcision three weeks ago.

When he was shot and killed, he was hurrying back to his home minutes after a minyan at his synagogue. Heshe was a member of the Hasidic Satmar sect, the same as was Mendel Glick.

• • •

Mike Sassano immediately knew he had a problem that was bigger than his department. A second Hasidic man was killed on back-to-back Fridays, just before the Jewish Sabbath, and the notion that the first killing was a random act had evaporated.

The thought that this was a serial hate crime was now in the forefront. The Ramapo Chief Tom Frank conferred with Rockland County

District Attorney Edward Welch and it was agreed the FBI needed to be contacted.

Chief Frank called Special Agent Rob Wright at the FBI Field Office in White Plains, New York. Things would be different for everyone from today forward.

The projectile that took Heshe Weissman's young life took some time to find. The forensic unit searched the sidewalk and the roadway of Route 306 without success. The exit wound was so profound the bullet would not have lodged somewhere in the body. Finally, after almost an hour of inch-by-inch combing, the projectile was found by the forensic unit in bushes in front of a home, nine feet from the body.

Sassano took a look at the bullet with the forensic technician. It looked identical to the tungsten carbide, copper covered projectile that was used in the previous murder. It seemed obviously the work of a potential serial killer.

Noting that the bullet trajectory seemed as if it was from street level, the forensic team fanned out along the now closed Route 306. Roughly 200 yards down the road from the body, fresh tire tracks were found on the stubble of grass side of the road. Molds were taken to be sent to the crime lab for analysis. This could be a break that hopefully would lead to the shooter.

Special Agent Wright and two FBI agents whom he assigned to the case met with Sassano at the Rockland County Medical Examiner's office to witness the analysis of Weissman's body.

As Angela Rush did the second Shabbas murder examination in the past seven days, the same *shomer* watchman who sat with Mendel Glick's body was present to fulfill Jewish law.

Angela noticed that Sassano seemed more uptight about this murder.

The detective asked a question, to anyone within earshot in the crowded room.

"Do we have a serial killer on our hands?"

Wright gave a text book answer. "By definition, a serial murderer is typically someone who murders three of more victims for obviously abnormal psychological gratification."

Sassano didn't want to bet there would not be another murder on his watch.

"Why is three the magic number?"

"Just a guideline, Mike. We can classify this as a serial with the information we have at hand. I'm sensitive to not waiting around for the next victim, but the truth is, if the shooter is inclined to act again, there is just so much we can do to prevent it. Right now, we are here to represent the victim's rights based on the federal Hate Crimes Prevention Act of 2009."

"Hey, we need all the help we can get," Mike replied.

"I will contact Quantico to begin the process of building a profile of the killer. I think we have enough information to get things started. I have to tell you Mike, in our experience there are seven serial killers doing their killing in the United States on any given day. We have plenty of experience in this arena."

• • •

Grand Rebbe Aaron Teitelbaum got word of another of his Satmar followers being killed by a sniper in the Monsey area as he prepared for *Shabbas*. Teitelbaum was at his headquarters in Kyrias Joel.

He immediately ordered a shutdown of the one square mile community of Kyrias Joel with permission for a posse of armed Hasidic men to break Shabbas to protect the entire community. There is one road, Satmar Drive, that dissects the small, generally crime free community. The men were ordered to block the road and investigate any vehicles they deemed suspicious.

The Village of Monroe Police Department has jurisdiction over Kyrias Joel but the word of the Grand Rebbe would not be countermanded. The Rebbe has significant political clout in Albany as his followers vote as one at the Rebbe's discretion.

This order was made indefinite by the Rebbe, who also contacted the Satmar Rabbis within Williamsburg, Brooklyn and Monsey, ordering that security be tightened around Orthodox Synagogues and community centers.

Word was quickly spreading from household-to-household, from synagogue-to-synagogue, to every *minyan, davening* throughout the entire Hasidic community. There was a madman shooting people.

A new name was being passed around within the Hasidic world.

"The Shabbas Killer" was on the loose.

Chapter Fifteen

After an uneventful week at their private security company, Vic and Raquel had no plans for the weekend largely because of Raquel's obsessive fear of catching the Covid-19 virus. Business was way off from the prior year due to the pandemic and the company was on auto pilot. Few employees came to the office opting to work from home as Raquel did. Vic went in every morning at 7:30 as usual but would leave by two in the afternoon.

On Saturday at noon, while Vic was pacing around like a caged lion, bored to tears waiting for some college basketball to air, Raquel was scanning Gabriella's pictures from birth until now to make a video CD to the child's favorite music. Gonnella was trying to be patient with Raquel's neurosis and his mood was beginning to become dark. The *"This too shall Pass"* mantra was starting to get on his nerves, big time.

Raquel's cell phone rang. She saw an unfamiliar number flash on her screen. It was from Switzerland. It had to be John Deegan. He used a variety of throw away phones to keep whoever was still looking for him, if they even were anymore, off his back.

"My darling, how are you?"

"John, so nice to hear your voice," Raquel almost sang.

"At the risk of sounding like a Jewish Mother in Miami, you never call, you never write…oy vay…So how are you Raquel?"

"This Covid thing is awful. Otherwise, we are safe and sound. How is Gjuliana?"

"Poor thing. She's desperately in love with me, but very well."

"And my favorite niece?" Deegan inquired on Gabriella.

"Growing up quickly. I'll send you a CD when I'm finished."

"And mama?

"Oh, she's still Puerto Rican…but she's very well."

"Can I be lucky enough to get you and that dunce on the speaker?"

Vic walked into the study as he was pacing the floors. He heard Raquel speaking to John. She always had a different tone in her voice when she spoke with him. Somewhere between respect and concern.

Raquel pressed the speaker symbol on her screen.

"Hello Mr. Deegan, how are you?" Vic asked. He was sincerely happy to hear from John. He would be happy to hear from anyone today he was so zoned out with boredom.

"I guess I'll be coming to New York soon. I see a new case on the horizon."

Vic looked at Raquel, shrugged his shoulders and made a quizzical face.

"You have a new case? Is the FBI and Interpol aware of this?" Vic joked.

"No, you two have a new case. Aren't you aware of your surroundings?"

Raquel smiled into her phone. She adored Deegan's playful, mysterious antics. "What are you talking about this time John?"

"I just love it when you roll those beautiful brown eyes Raquel."

"Okay Deegan, spill the beans. St. John's and Seton Hall are playing in an hour," Vic blurted.

"My contacts tell me that someone is using Hasidic Jews for target practice. You mean to tell me this hasn't been all over the news over there?"

"First I've heard. Vic, do you know about…"

Vic interrupted Raquel, "Nope, not on our radar. Anyway, what does this have to do with us?"

"Two dead, forty-five minutes from your lovely home. Shot by a sniper. Both Satmar Hasid's. Your phone will be ringing any time now," Deegan offered.

"Oh, hold on while I transfer you to the dead Hasid department. Are you insane, Deegan?" Vic replied

"Matter of fact, in certain circles, I could be classified as such."

"No shit?" Raquel blurted.

"Ok, how many times have I told you both to think four-to-six moves ahead? Here goes. Two men in their twenties, both Satmar sect Hasidic. Both shot dead up near Monsey, New York. Both on the eve of the Sabbath. FBI has been called in to profile. Any day now the governor or some other limp wrist will be calling you two for help."

"C'mon will ya? Just take Gjuliana to see her family and we will meet up," Vic said.

"Here's how it will work. This killer will not be found without us. The State and the FBI know it and, like it or not, you two are the go-to people to get whomever this is off the streets. Of course, it goes without saying, I'm also in the mix," Deegan announced.

"Hmmm, I think we will pass on this one John, but. Thanks anyway," Raquel declared.

Deegan cleared his throat "Excuse me, it will play out like this. The Hasidic community will be in sheer panic. Especially if he shoots another one. The FBI will say it's a hate crime, the news media will be all over this like stink on shit, maybe a copy-cat or two, then your friend the governor will get the call from the Rabbis reminding him who is really in charge with the votes, then he will cry uncle, call you and I'll already be up there figuring things out."

"Okay Deegan, what's that two, maybe three weeks? I'll have time to paint the inside of the townhouse and shampoo all the rugs," Vic replied.

"Nope. If I'm right, which as you know I usually am. Well perhaps in the ninety-percentile, I'll be seeing you within ten days. In Monsey."

Deegan pushed the end button.

Vic spoke first. "Well, that was very interesting. Just in case, I'm going to Google this Monsey shooter thing and see what's going on."

"I knew you were going to say that. I'm going to tell you right now, there is no way I'm going to Monsey or any place up in that mess. I just read about those people. Covid is rampant among them. Only seven percent of that population has been vaccinated. That's the lowest in New

York State. These people are crazy, absolutely insane. They don't respect the disease or the people around them. They don't wear masks, they don't socially distance, nothing. They have weddings with thousands of people attending in spite of state laws. In Brooklyn, they disrespect the police and ignore orders to socially distance. You think they are washing their hands multiple times a day? Or using hand sanitizers? I saw on the news that one of their Rabbis died from Covid and there were thousands of men packed into a synagogue for his funeral. They have a death wish I guess. They are dropping like flies Vic. No fucking way will we be going anywhere near those messed up people."

Vic just stood there staring at Raquel.

"What?" she screamed.

Vic seemed dumfounded.

After a few seconds, he finally responded.

"Do you hear yourself? You're judging a whole community by what they do with masks and social distancing. First of all, this is John Deegan, a certified maniac telling us we are about to be drafted into another search for a serial killer. And you go off half-cocked into a tirade about Covid. Look, to me a case is a case and if, in any unlikely event we are called into a case like this, we are going. Business is business. I don't want to hear another word about it!"

Raquel said nothing but she thought, *"No fucking way!"*

Chapter Sixteen

S*habbot* is considered the most important of holidays in Judaism. Every week there is a celebration and reflection of the creation of the heavens and earth and how the creator rested on the seventh day. It is a joyful time that also looks forward to the return of the Messiah.

Instead of joy and happiness, this *Shabbas* brought concern and fear. As the word spread so did the rumors. The Nazi's are returning was prominent among others. The White Supremacists and Alien Nation were unhappy with the results of the presidential election and they were staring a civil war, and the Orthodox community was where it was all to begin.

Everyone was concerned for themselves as well as their loved ones. Who can stop a madman or a group of maniacs from picking off people off as they went about their daily lives?

An unsettled feeling turned this *Shabbas* into a gut-wrenching, nerve wracking time for everyone, but especially for Grand Rebbe

Teitelbaum who took his position of leader of the Satmar as a father to all his people. Mendel Glick's murder was a terrible *Shanda*. Now, the Heshey Weissman murder had turned the community into virtually an armed camp. Many of the community were armed in some fashion and most have illegal firearms for personal protection. Many of the Hasidim have cash businesses which goes along with protection of their bread and butter.

The Satmar sect is not following the way of letting anyone—no organization, no government and no person—to tread on them and take advantage of their seemingly peaceful manner. The days of pushing around the helpless Jew has been ended among the Satmar.

On Sunday morning after the horrible murder on Route 306, The Rebbe was driven down from Kyrias Joel to the second funeral of a murdered follower in two consecutive weeks.

This time, the heart-wrenching event was covered by a few of the New York affiliates of network television, several major newspapers, and local television stations. Interestingly, outside the funeral home and the cemetery as well, there were many people taking cell phone photographs and videos to post on social media. The Orthodox community are mostly forbidden to use the internet. However, there are curios reform and non-Jewish residents still living in Rockland County, in spite of the visual in the big box stores such as Cosco, in nearby Nanuet and BJ's Wholesale Club in West Nyack, every Sunday. The stores are like a sea of Orthodox families doing their big bulk shopping.

After Heshe's burial, which was attended by at least a thousand more mourners than Mendel's, likely ordered by the Rebbe to show no fear and display communal unity, Teitelbaum met with Rockland

Officials at Hillmans Funeral Chapel, in a large room where coffee and Kosher Danish was served.

The meeting was set by the Governor of the State of New York who also attended the funeral, more than likely pressed by the Rebbe. This Democrat governor knew which side his bread was buttered on.

Everyone who was anyone in Rockland politics wanted an invite both for the media exposure, a possible ten second sound-bite or a chance to rub elbows with the grad poobah from Albany himself.

However, the Rebbe selected those who would be permitted to attend. The Governor of course, seven prominent Hasidic Rabbi's from the upstate communities and from Williamsburg, District Attorney Welch, Police Chief, Frank, FBI Special Agent Wright, Detective Mike Sassano and Yiddi Rosenberg would attend.

The Rebbe was the Rebbe because he is brilliant. Not only in matters of religion but in matters of money. Yiddi Rosenberg was arguably the wealthiest Satmar in the world from his global real estate empire. He is a major benefactor to the Satmar community and a close personal friend of Rebbe Teitelbaum. When the Governor saw Rosenberg, he nearly swooned.

"Gentlemen, of course, I thank you for attending. We are a community in crisis. Not only here is Monsey but also in Kyrias Joel, Williamsburg, Montreal and anywhere a Satmar walks in the world. There is a target on us and only Hashem knows from whom it is coming. Is it a hate group, perhaps just a lone maniac, perhaps as many of the followers are saying, the Nazi movement has maybe returned? I will say one thing in front of our illustrious Governor, who we as a Hasidic community helped to elect, and I'll say it in front of the law enforcement people here today. We will not be intimidated, we will not be forced into a ghetto and shot, we will not run and hide like in Warsaw, we will never be led to our deaths by anyone ever again. I say to you here and now, enough is enough already. I have not allowed the media into this room as you can see. They are not welcomed. There will be no interviews or speeches after this meeting. There will be no written communication from us to the outside world. I will do nothing and say nothing to the outside world that would sound incendiary or further endanger our people. I am calling upon the people in this room to help us find who has killed these men, and to help protect our community at large.

"Furthermore, the Satmar community are not a vigilante group. We are not looking to capture and bring the culprits of these heinous killings to justice. That is the job of the law enforcement people in this room. However, we will protect ourselves which is our given right from Hashem."

"Now go. Go find who killed these innocent men. And I leave you all with a challenge. Ask yourself, have I done today my best, have I done everything within my power to solve these crimes and protect the people?"

Chapter Seventeen

The Rebbe and the Rabbis left to go and pray at the Satmar Synagogue where throngs of followers would be awaiting their arrival.

The Governor, with his best somber look and ignoring the calls from the media for a few words, bid farewell and shook the Rebbe's hand with both of his. Good optics, but useless if the Rebbe told his community to vote for someone else. Their strength was always in voting as a block.

The law enforcement group hung back at Hillmans' for an impromptu meeting.

The D.A. spoke first.

"The governor told me we have the New York State Police at our disposal. That is comforting but I think we can handle things ourselves, of course, along with the help of the FBI field office and their profiling expertise in Washington. If it's okay with everyone, I would like to have debriefings at my office every day. We can do this early each morning or after 6 p.m."

Sassano thought, *"There he goes again. Typical politician looking to control the information."*

Welch continued, "Okay with you Chief? Mike?"

"Fine by me. I'll leave the timing up to Mike here."

"I'll report to you every morning. I just want all my men to be out there pounding the pavement."

Welch paused. "Sure…no problem." Welch knew that Mike Sassano was not a fan of his, but with the Chief's acceptance he would get his way.

Special Agent Wright raised his hand as if he were asking for permission to speak.

"The Rebbe's words hit me pretty hard. Are we doing everything we can? Look, I have the strength of the entire FBI and Quantico at my disposal. And please forgive me for being bold, but if we can use investigators from the State police, we should put more boots on the ground and forgo any jurisdictional nonsense. Beyond that, I've spoken with our New York City Field office this morning. My colleague Inspector Sean Lewandowsky whom I've worked with on several serial killer cases reminded me of the best serial murderer group around."

"You may all know them by the names Vic Gonnella and Raquel Ruiz. I suggest we bring them in to look over our shoulders. It's money well spent. I understand they are quite close with the governor if you need his approval."

Sassano jumped in. "They broke that John Deegan case and a few others. I think we should reach out today. There is no ego with this old soldier. I just want to catch this mother…" Sassano stopped himself from finishing his thought.

Chapter Eighteen

"**A**nother Sunday morning in Covid prison," Vic thought. He had asked Raquel if she thought it might be safe enough to take a ride? A ride anywhere, somewhere just for a change of scenery, just to get out of the townhouse. Maybe Mystic Seaport in Connecticut, Cold Spring, he even tried for Arthur Avenue in the Bronx again. No matter what he suggested Raquel gave him the same answers, followed by various statistics on new Covid cases, new hospitalizations, new deaths, and news of new side effects from the virus, even though the mortality from the pandemic was dropping, On and on. Raquel even quoted stats from Europe.

"You want to go out and catch this thing after being cautious all these months? Listen to me baby, my friend Lisa has family in Italy. She told me as of yesterday Italy was on total lockdown again. Her cousins told her they have to have a document to even leave their house. This thing is not even close to being gone," Raquel rambled.

Vic gently replied, "So why are airlines flying people to Florida? It's almost spring break. I hear…"

Raquel interrupted, "Do you think that's not adding to the spread of Covid? I'm just amazed at the stupidity some people have. So now you want to go to fucking Florida?"

"I was just pointing out things are starting to loosen up a little."

"I'm going nowhere and neither is Gabby or my mom. I had words with mom yesterday. I put my foot down. No more trips to the Bronx to see her lady friends for her until the coast is clear. Until I say so."

Vic knew he was fighting a losing battle. He was retreating into himself and getting increasingly annoyed. Not so much during the week when there was business to keep him occupied, but the weekends used to be exciting and fun. There was always so many things to do in the Metropolitan New York area. Now his wife has retreated, way off the rails, into a cocoon of fear.

Vic raised his hands in mock surrender to avoid an argument that had the potential to explode into a skirmish and then into a war. His looked at his cellphone to check the time and momentarily pretended it was a transporter from Star Trek and he could ask Scotty to beam him up somewhere.

The phone rang. Vic was taken aback for a second. The screen read Sean—FBI.

"So, what's it been, a year since I saw your Irish mug?" Vic started.

"That's Polish-Irish to you bud."

"How you been, pally?" Vic asked. He had a wide smile on his face.

"All good under the circumstances. It seems the last year went by like a bad dream."

"Bad nightmare. If I get to see you one day, I'll tell you my tale of woe."

"You okay, Vic?"

"Yea… yea… just feel like a prisoner is all. This too shall pass, I keep telling myself."

"I have something for you. Have you heard about those shootings of the Hasidic men in Rockland County?"

"Shootings? As in more than one? I heard something about it. Didn't pay too much attention," Vic fibbed.

"Second one two days ago. The locals are calling it the *Shabbas Killer*. Two weeks and two dead Satmar. I'm told panic is setting in."

"Holy shit, how does he do it?" Vic mumbled. He was talking out loud asking how John Deegan figures out these things.

"With a high-powered rifle," Sean replied.

"What…oh…ok. Like a sniper."

"Exactly. Listen, I gave your name to my guy in our White Plains field office. Wright is his name. Decent guy. We went to the academy together. He reached out to me a couple minutes ago. They need help."

"Of course. I'm interested."

"Vic, this isn't a freebe like that pipeline bombing case you were on with your buddy the governor. I'll get the agency to guarantee payment. The Agency is tighter than a crabs-ass when it comes to a buck.

"Whatever you say, my friend. How many more years until you get your pension and get over here with us?"

"I appreciate it more than you know Vic. After you nail this shooter we're going out." Sean laughed.

"Yea, like I can wave a magic wand. I'll wait for Wright's call."

"Good luck, see ya." Sean ended the call.

Vic started talking to himself.

"He said see you in ten days. How the hell does Deegan know this stuff? Like a clairvoyant, ESP some kind of gift? He comes in and out of my life like an old family member that I only see at wakes and weddings."

"Who was that you were talking to, baby?" Raquel asked. She came out of the study into the French Country decorated living room. Vic was sitting on the edge of a beige and brown show-wood sofa.

Vic drew in a deep breath and let it out slowly. "You'll never believe it. Sean just called. The FBI is calling us into this Hasid shooter case. I'm expecting a call on the details."

"Just like John said. My God, that's scary." Raquel put her hands up to her mouth, her wide brown eyes sparkled in the light from a double bay window.

"Ya think? How does he figure out these scenarios? He's way the fuck somewhere in Switzerland and this is going down practically in our backyard."

"Genius. That's what everyone always called him. John Deegan the genius serial killer."

"Guess so. The White Plains FBI Field Agent will be calling any minute. I'm calling Phil from the office. We are going to need a primer on the Orthodox community. He can do it in an hour and we'll be up to speed.

"Vic, I'm going to help for sure but I'm letting you know now. I'm not going anywhere near these people," Raquel announced.

Vic was at the end of his patience.

'Ya know, you talk about 'these people' like they have leprosy. Yes, they don't follow what they are told to do except what the Rebbe tells them. They're in danger from more than fucking Covid. This shooter and bigotry because they are dressed different and worship differently is a bigger danger in my eyes. You have some nerve. It wasn't that long ago that I remember Puerto Ricans being 'these people' but I guess you forgot that or you were sheltered from it."

"I don't care. I'm not dying from Covid!" Raquel screeched.

"Get it through your think head Raquel. You are not going to die from Covid. Even if you get it and the chances are less every day, read my lips… you… will…not…die…from…Covid. You are young, strong, healthy and have zero preconditions. Get over yourself, will ya!" Vic hollered.

At the moment Raquel was going to start a torrent of curses toward Vic, Gabriella and Olga walked into the room.

"Mira Raquel, Listen to me. Do you know what you two sound like? This is terrible. You can't keep arguing like this."

Gabby looked scared. She ran into her mother's arms.

Olga looked at Vic with her lips pursed and her hands on both of her hips. Vic took it as if she were blaming him.

"So, it's me Olga? I'm to blame?"

"No, it's not just you. It's both of you. Settle your differences without upsetting the entire home. Find a compromise.

The bell went off in Vic's head.

"You know what Olga? You are one-hundred-percent right. I have the solution.

At that moment, Vic's cell phone rang. A 914 White Plains number. Like Deegan had predicted, the FBI was calling.

• • •

Everyone in Monsey was on edge. Some had already left to visit family and friends and flee for safety, at least for the time being.

Hadassah Twersky married well. As they say in Yiddish *Shep Nachos.* Pride and Joy.

At seventeen, upon deciding to live the life of wisdom, comprehension and knowledge, the three pillars of Chabad-Lubavitch philosophy, Hadassah decided to see a renowned matchmaker, a *shadchanit* to help her find her *Bashert*, her soul mate for her life ahead.

Such a beautiful young woman with extraordinary musical talents, a teacher, with a profound knowledge of Torah and the daughter of a prominent Chabad-Lubavitch Rabbi, Hadassah would have no problem finding her pick of eligible young men within her religious community.

Her first meeting with Zvi Kessler was kismet. Zvi and Hadassah were destined to be future leaders in the two-hundred-and fifty-year branch of Hasidism.

They had similar religious training, similar interests in music and more importantly, they both wanted a large- family.

At first, when she heard of the potential match, Hadassah was a bit apprehensive about one thing that Zvi had in his background. She was very troubled by it. Zvi and his family were enormously wealthy. Hadassah did not desire this kind of life but instead preferred a simpler life that her family was always comfortable with. The matchmaker assured her the Zvi was a good man and not at all affected by his money. "Just meet him. One heart will reach out to the other if it's meant to be."

Kessler S.A. is a global diamond giant with significant mining operations in South Africa, offices in Zurich, Antwerp, Tel Aviv and Manhattan. Zvi would be managing sales in NYC so Monsey was as good a place to start his family as any. Hadassah was born and raised in the same modest house as all nine of her siblings. She would prefer to stay near her family.

Within a year after their marriage ceremony which drew six thousand guests and was officiated by the Grand Rebbe, Hadassah Kessler became a mother of a beautiful baby girl whom they named Eliana a Hebrew name meaning 'My God has answered me.'

The two shootings in Monsey rattled the entire international Hasidic community.

Zvi's father called him from Durban, South Africa insisting on he and his young family returning to his birthplace until the killer or killers were apprehended.

Strong willed and independent, Zvi told his father, "We are all in Heshem's hands. Everything will be fine. As you taught me father, I must be my own man."

Eliana is now nearly six-months old and her parents are already discussing the next child. Every single Hasidic family, anywhere in the world but especially in Monsey were awaiting this Passover with great anxiety and apprehension. Hadassah was no different from everyone else.

She was preparing her home for the sacred and special holiday but at times felt something strange stirring in her spirit. She decided to discuss her feelings with her husband.

"Zvi, I think a change would be good. I would like to see South African and the home where you were raised. Perhaps we should listen to your father and go."

"Esther, our home is here. My responsibility to the company is here. I have no fear. *Baruch Hashem,* bless His name, we will raise our family to know that running away from trouble is not the answer anymore. My family... your family was forced to flee from the Nazi's. So many of them were slaughtered. I refuse to run."

Hadassah replied, "I am your wife I will respect your wishes. I just feel you are a target. I will do all the shopping, all of the errands for *Shabbas,* to keep you from walking around. Who knows what can happen to you with a maniac roaming around. When you go to *daven,* I pray that you will be coming home. Zvi, the thought of being without you is making me very anxious and upset. I'm even having trouble sleeping. All of the women I talk with feel the same way. I know a cousin of Mendel Glick. She said the entire family will never, ever be the same after this *Shanda.* I feel like I'm living in a nightmare."

Zvi smiled at his wife tenderly. "Have faith, Esther. Whatever is meant to be, will be. We must go about our lives without fear. You will see, this will soon pass."

Chapter Nineteen

Carl Schuster looks like a skinhead. At six-foot three, two hundred thirty pounds, a blonde crew cut and piercing blue eyes, and a gold earring in each ear, he sat at the Crossroads bar in Mahwah, New Jersey. He is dressed in worn jeans, brown work boots and a white and red Trump t-shirt.

Mahwah is a large town on the boarder of Sloatsburg, New York in Rockland County. Crossroads is a typical dark, shot-and- a-beer joint with a long wood bar and a smattering of four top, uncovered wooden tables and cheap wooden folding chairs. The bar is a known hangout for seedy, white supremacist types who are not very friendly to new faces, unless those faces looked like Shuster. A person of color would find himself in a bar-fight almost immediately.

There were three other men, all wearing jeans, work boots and vests that resembled those worn by bikers. There were no motorcycles in the parking lot. Two dirty Ford F 150 pick-up trucks were out in front instead.

Schuster quietly nursed a bottle of Heineken, no glass.

"Hey bud, you new around here?" one of the three called over.

"Pretty much. Lookin' for a place to rent nearby."

"Where you from?" another of the three asked.

"Upstate. Near Phoenicia."

"Wanna join us?"

"Why not?" Schuster grabbed his beer and ambled over.

"I'm Tommy. This is Lefty and Rob."

"Carl." They all shook hands.

"Nice to see a man who shakes hands and doesn't wanna do that silly knuckle bump Covid thing," Tommy stated.

Carl replied, "Yea, this whole Covid bullshit. The way I look at it, if you get it you get it. I'm not wearing that stupid mask either."

The three regulars raised their beers in a salute to Schuster. They all clicked bottles.

"Hey Vera, set up some shots for us will ya?" Lefty called out to the dissipated blond bartender. Her ample breasts were crawling out the top and the sides of her wife-beater, black tank-top. It helped with tips.

They shot the shit and drank for almost two hours.

"I'm not familiar with the area. My boss wants me down here on some construction site. Anything going on around these parts?" Schuster asked.

Tommy laughed, "Yea, we was just talkin about it. Jews are being picked off. You know, the filthy ones with the big long coats and hats and curls."

"Fuck those slimy ass Jews," Rob added.

"Pickin them off?"

"Yea, shooting them dead. A sniper."

"Who the hell would do that?" Schuster followed.

"I'd like to shake the guys hand." Lefty laughed.

Schuster added, "Yup, we should have given Hitler ten more years."

They all laughed and toasted again.

"I'd like to pick a few off myself," Tommy added.

"You got these Jews up by you Carl?"

"From time to time. They like to buy up property."

"Those sleazy fucks don't even pay property taxes. They make their house into a church or something." Lefty blurted.

"No shit? Really?' Carl asked.

"Yup. And get this. They ain't even married according to the State of New York and they go on welfare. Get six- hundred a month for each little Jew kid. Do the math. Ten kids, they get six-grand," Lefty added.

After a while of similar conversation, Carl announced.

"Hey guys, I gotta go. See you again I hope." He threw a fifty on the bar. And a twenty for the blond.

"We're here most every night. Gets crowded. Some broads too."

"I'll be back. Good to know you guys."

"You are one of us. Come back anytime buddy," Tommy said.

Shuster got into his gray Dodge Ram pick-up. He took his cell-phone out of his pocket and made a call as he drove away.

"It's me. I made contact. Just what we imagined. Going back tomorrow night." He ended the call.

Chief Tom Frank took the Governor's offer.

Carl Shuster an undercover narcotics detective, drafted from the New York State Police by the Ramapo PD to break the ice.

Chapter Twenty

Vic had spoken with the FBI and after a lengthy discussion, he agreed to help with the investigation. His fee was high and not questioned.

Vic then poured a Jefferson Bourbon over three ice cubes and sat in his study to look over some data and relax.

He began prepping for his visit to Rockland County. He planned to read up on everything on the Hasidic community that was prepared for him by his administrative assistant. He needed to pack a large suitcase later on. Getting away for a few days would do him good he thought.

Thirty-minutes later, John Deegan called Vic from yet another throw-away phone from an undisclosed location.

"Have you received the call yet?" Deegan asked.

"You were a few days off," Vic responded.

"I suppose you should have bet me on the over."

"I have no idea how you figure this shit out from across the Atlantic."

Deegan laughed aloud. "I'm a genius, or hasn't anyone told you?"

"Yea, I've been told that by you many times."

"So, what are your plans Vic?"

"I'm going up to Rockland County tomorrow morning. Have an early meeting."

"And Raquel?" Deegan asked. Vic could tell he was fishing.

"She's going to stay in Manhattan and work the case from there."

"Hmm. I could tell something was off when I spoke with you both the other day. She has this anxiety about Covid, I suppose."

"How the hell do you know?"

"I listen very attentively, Vic. She said a few things and the stress in her voice told me the story. Vic, free advice. You need to be patient. She'll figure things out and come around. You'll see."

"Hope so. Her fear has become a real phobia. It's not fun," Vic replied.

"Well, I'm nearby. I'll see you tomorrow."

"Deegan, listen to me. Rockland will be crawling with law enforcement. Local cops, FBI, state police and the blood sucking media will be all over the place. You show one hair on your skinny old ass and a Supermax prison will be your home address till you die. Unless of course you're going to use that Hasidic Jew disguise you have," Vic chuckled.

"The last time I used that was in Brooklyn when you were trying to track me down remember? I slit that pedophile Rabbi's throat for him right in the Synagogue office."

"You sound very proud of your work."

"I am, I really am. He needed more than that but I was in a hurry."

"Stay away Deegan. I'm not going to walk away from your advice mind you. You were a big help on the last few cases."

"That's encouraging. I can recall you wanted nothing to do with me, Vic," Deegan offered.

"I've learned not to kick a gift horse in the mouth, or something like that."

"It's look a gift horse. but that's okay. So here is some pre-investigation advice. The Hasidic community is already thinking the shooter is gunning down Satmar followers. The killer has no idea which sect they belong to. The killer sees an Orthodox Jew, he aims and then he fires. And he's a decent shot at that which is a good start for us. Gives us more clues to figure out who he is. However, I haven't figured out the why yet. Now, he will strike again and likely this Friday so plan to hunker down in Rockland County."

"The profilers will say that you need three killings over a period of time. Likely the shooter will take a break," Vic added.

Deegan responded, "This is a serial killer for sure. Not exactly textbook but he is. If it were a one off, trust me we wouldn't be talking. We are a long way from figuring the shooter out but we eventually will."

"Where will he kill next?" Vic queried.

"Anywhere there are Hasidic Jews. My guess is around where he has killed before. Not sure about that though. That's just a guess."

"I always thought you guessed a lot."

"That's an insult my dear Vic. My guesses are made from thoughtful consideration. Remember the chess moves I always tell you about? Not just guessing…more like advanced planning."

"So, you are ruling out a hit on these two homicides?" Vic fished.

"No hit. There is a hatred. Why, I don't know yet. Too soon to develop a logical path. Look, its way easier to shoot at a larger mass. This guy isn't going for a body shot. He's a head guy. To me that's just added hate. Fuck up the victim's head and neck. More gore."

Vic paused. "Hmm, interesting. It will be good to see you again Deegan."

"Wow, what a turn around. I'm getting a tear in my eyes. Anyway, I gotta go now. See you soon." Deegan ended the call.

Vic looked at his phone.

"I've befriended a maniacal serial killer. Who would have ever thought," Gonnella blurted aloud.

• • •

After Vic spoke with Deegan, Raquel and Vic were in their study pouring over everything they had on the Hasid community that was sent to them. They were working in silence.

"Are you looking forward to starting this case?" Raquel questioned.

"Yea"

"Looking forward to getting away from me?"

"No, what makes you ask a silly question like that?

"I'm just feeling you are a tiny bit distant."

"I'd be happier if you were coming with me, but I'm told to have patience with your Covid thing"

"Patience. Who told you that?"

"Deegan."

"Deegan told you to have patience with me? How does he even know?" You told him?" Raquel was getting herself into a frenzy.

"No. He heard it in your voice when we spoke with him."

"How did he know?"

"How does Deegan know anything?"

"What did he say about me?

"No judgement. Just that I need to be patient is all. Hey, sometimes a short- separation is good."

"Oh, it's a separation now?

"Not in that sense of the word Raquel. A few days away and…"

"And what?" Raquel raised her voice looking for an argument."

"Just listen for a second. Everything we ever did, every case we ever had, we were together. This Covid thing is just screwing up everything. I love you more now than ever. I'm just frustrated."

Raquel jumped from her chair and into Vic's lap.

"Well, that's a nice thing."

She kissed him deeply, rubbing her hand into his crotch.

Vic became aroused.

Raquel licked his ear, then whispered, "Let's go upstairs. I'm going to drain you. I'm jealous of those Hasidic woman,"

Vic picked her up and began walking to the stairs which led to their bedroom.

"Would you help me pack?"

"Sure, tomorrow morning"

"I'm getting up at four-thirty"

"I'll get up at four, Raquel purred."

• • •

The Glick family finished their last night of *shiva* at sundown. Jacob Glick seemed very anxious, pacing back and forth. His behavior was a bit out of character for Jacob and certainly not in line with custom and tradition.

The first three days of shiva are the most difficulty. The last four are meant to reminisce about the deceased and settle into the finality of life.

Jacob leaned down to Hanna. She was staring up to the ceiling, thinking of tomorrow and what she needed to do for her family.

Jacob whispered to his sister-in-law.

"Hanna, I will come by tomorrow. There are some things I need to discuss with you about Mendel's business affairs."

Hanna looked at Jacob incredulously. She nodded yes, but thought, *"What do I knew from Mendel's business? What is this about?*

Chapter Twenty-One

There was no tremor in Edward Olsen's hands. Not when he crafted the bullets, and certainly not when he gently squeezed the rifle's trigger.

He worked silently in a twelve by twelve, windowless, dusty room, in the basement of his dead parent's home. The room was solely his domain. Not even his late father would enter the room for fear he would go into a solitary depressed funk.

A dozen hunting magazines shared the space on an old and battered light-brown table along with several stacked textbooks. The books were graduate school level—Applied Physics, Advanced Chemistry, Ballistics and Engineering—from the time he spent at the University. He never got the degrees. Didn't need them. Whatever Edward read he would be able to recall, word-for-word, with an acute understanding of how to apply the book knowledge to his work. His only focus, what he lived for, what enveloped his everyday thought process, other than his work at Lamonia and Company, was target shooting. Long range target shooting to be precise.

On his fifth Christmas, his parents gifted Edward with a Remington .22 rifle. What turned from a little boy's want into a twenty-two-year obsession as a sniper was the result.

On his workbench, in total silence, a six inch by six-inch solid piece of tungsten carbide and a long strip of copper would soon be turned into more bullets to fulfill his obligation. Friday, his day off, would be here in just five days.

• • •

The drive from Manhattan to Suffern, New York took only fifty minutes.

Vic was the first to arrive at the Ramapo Police Department at six-twenty Monday morning. One of the officers offered coffee and bagels. Vic poured a cup of black coffee and waited for the Chief to arrive.

Soon after, Chief Frank arrived wearing his dark blue police uniform and white shirt with a dark blue necktie. The shirt had two stars on each collar and a gold shield on the left side of his jacket. As they walked toward his office, Frank couldn't help but display his enthusiasm for meeting Vic for the first time.

"Mr. Gonnella, I can't tell you what an honor it is to meet you. I've been following your career since you were a detective with NYPD and on that John Deegan case. I was a detective myself back then, and I followed the case like a groupie."

"Chief, just do me one favor, my name is Vic. When someone says Mr. Gonnella, I still look around for my father," Vic chuckled.

"Sure thing Vic, thank you."

Chief Franks office was sparsely decorated indicating the kind of no nonsense man he is. No awards on display, no photos of him with various politicians, no sports memorabilia on the walls. Only a couple of photographs of his two grandchildren were on his desk.

"You ever have a serial killer case up here before?" Vic asked.

"No, this is a first. Murder cases of course but nothing ever like this. We did have that Brinks armored car robbery in Nanuet back in '81. The Weather Underground. They killed three people including two Nyack cops. I was too young to be on the job. With this one, we have our work cut out for us."

Vic replied, "These are never easy cases. I will help you any way I can."

"Greatly appreciated. I expected to see your partner, Miss Ruiz with you. You guys got a lot of publicity on that water pipeline case last year."

"We certainly did. Long story about why she's not here. Anyway, Raquel, will be working on the case from Manhattan. We have a pretty good staff and she will be laying out all of the evidence we gather and help tie up any loose ends. We work off a computer-white board and she will share what we compile on a virtual basis with you and your department. As you know, most times, the devil is in the details."

A light tap was heard on the Chief's door. Detective Mike Sassano and FBI Special Agent Wright arrived for the meeting at the same time. At precisely seven o'clock.

Introductions were made all around. Everyone was cordial and perhaps a bit star struck by Vic Gonnella. Chief Frank started the meeting.

"Gentlemen, I must tell you that so far all we have is evidence that indicates the shooter has used a unique, home-made projectile that is made of tungsten carbide with a copper coating. I'll be handing out fact sheets in a moment. We are early in the investigation as you are all aware. There is a person of interest in the case. The brother of the first victim had a falling out over business months ago. Mike would you elaborate please."

Sassano piped in, "I questioned the brother myself. He was the one that actually brought my attention to the riff they had. I'm pretty certain he was not the shooter but people are capable of a lot of shit when things involve money. The brother has no priors and nothing indicates that he ever owned a registered fire arm. I'd classify him as of interest but my gut tells me otherwise." He continued," We are sending a forensic accountant to his office this morning and the office of the victim to dissect the books."

Vic spoke up, "Was there a reason you waited a week to get this information looked at?" Vic asked. His tone was friendly and not at all accusatory.

"The family are all Hasidic Jews. We allowed them their mourning period to be sensitive to their faith and traditions. Trust me, their Rebbe has a direct line to the governor and if we make a move to upset them he's not embarrassed to play that card," Sassano replied.

Chief Frank followed up. "Rebbe Teitelbaum is convinced that the shooter is going after members of his Satmar sect. Both victims are Satmar Orthodox. We are tracking down if the two victims have any other commonality. Did they know each other? Any business dealings, any personal issues? So far we're comeing up with nothing but we need more time on this."

Vic sipped the rest of his now cold coffee before responding.

"The assumption that the shooter is after only Satmar followers, while plausible is just that, an assumption. Barring any new evidence to the contrary, it's likely the shooter is simply shooting at men with black hats and long black coats." Vic felt a bit guilty from taking this supposition from John Deegan.

The FBI's Wright jumped in. "We are awaiting a preliminary profile from our serial killer unit in Quantico. It may lead us to some other assumptions."

"We've worked with them in the past on a few cases. They are simply amazing. Quantico has a lot of expertise when it comes to serial murderers. The data they have and their analysis is second to none. Let me ask you, is Gail Green still there?" Vic inquired.

"If you mean G.G., the answer is yes. She's brilliant," Wright retorted.

"She is as brilliant as she's eccentric," Vic added.

"I see you do know her, Vic."

"She worked on the Deegan case with us. Very interesting person to say the least."

• • •

Jacob Glick got to his brother's home a little after ten that Monday morning. He rightfully figured that Hanna would need some time to get the older children to Yeshiva and the younger kids into Hebrew pre-school.

Hanna and her mother sat together on the sofa, Jacob in a high-backed chair. It is not acceptable for a woman to meet with a man alone, even if that man was her late husband's brother.

Jacob seemed nervous. He was looking down at his shoes.

"Jacob, what is bothering you?" Hanna asked.

"Hanna, did Mendel ever tell you about a large sum of money he may have lent to someone in the community?" Jacob asked. His voice was unsteadied.

"Why would he tell me such a thing. Everything inside this house, I took care of. Anything outside was my Mendel's responsibility. I know little to nothing about his business."

"My brother left me a sealed envelope which was given to me by his lawyer. There was a letter to me expressing how badly he felt about our breaking up." Jacob paused holding back his tears. "But also, he told of a large sum of money which was taken from our business, that is to say, when we were together in business. This money was in cash and was lent to a man to help start his own business."

"Who was the man? Do I know him?"

"Avi Nussbaum. Do you know of him?"

"No. Mendel knew so many people."

"He is from Williamsburg."

"Jacob, I just told you I don't know from this man. Are you trying to say my Mendel stole this money from your business…impossible," Hanna blurted. Her mother reached for her hand and held it.

"No. Mendel may have been doing a *mitvah,* a blessing for someone, and was expecting to be paid back. I never…Mendel…he would never take for himself. This money is mine and now yours Hanna."

"So why come tell me? Why not go to this Avi Nussbaum and get the money?" Hanna asked.

"I did Hanna. I did go to him. He denies it. He said he once spoke to Mendel about a loan but never took the money. Mendel left me no signed papers. I have no proof. Even if I went to the Rebbe I have nothing."

"How much is the money?

"One hundred thousand."

Hanna gasped.

Jacob asked, "And he never told you about this man like he never told me?"

"Jacob, no he did not!" Hanna shouted.

"Hanna, no need for this. Jacob is trying to do what's right for you," her mother said.

"Hanna, I asked around about this Nussbaum. He did start a business when Mendel and I were still in business. His business failed and he closed down. I'm just wondering if I should take this to the police."

"You take it to the Rebbe. If he says take it to the police…then you take it to the police," Hanna replied.

• • •

Vic spent most of Monday examining evidence which was collected from the murders of Mendel Glick and Heshe Weissman. Ballistics reports, photos of the crime scenes, the bodies, post mortem examinations, background information on the deceased, everything and anything attached to the killings were turned over by the Ramapo Police. In turn, Vic was sending the data to Raquel for her white board, laying out the evidence. Rob Wright was sending the same information to FBI Headquarters in Quantico.

The race to find the killer was on. Even though all of the law enforcement agencies, along with Vic and Raquel, were working together, there was still a competitive spirt, looking for the one or two items that would lead to the resolution of the heinous murders of the two innocent men. The ability to say their organization solved a crime like this was a feather everyone wanted for their cap.

Vic called Raquel just before suppertime.

"Hi baby. All good?" Vic asked. He was mentally preoccupied with the case and searching a lab report while he called.

Raquel was also enveloped in the case. "Yea, everything is fine. I'm all over the information you've been sending. I've going over the geography of the shootings. The killer seems to want some space to make his shot. Two-to- five-hundred plus yards. I'm looking on the satellite maps and Google Earth to see an area where the Hassid's walk in that area that gives the shooter his next opportunity."

"So, you are convinced he will strike again?"

"No, not convinced. Just looking beyond the evidence we have so far. Trying to anticipate his next move."

"You sound like Deegan and his chess game now...that's a great idea baby."

"It's a very densely populated area. It's as if a lot of Orthodox from Brooklyn have moved up to Rockland County. Whoever the shooter is he's picked two places so far to avoid being seen. I'm trying to figure out if I were to take the next shot, where would I do it?" Raquel said.

"I like it. How about any connection between the victims? I know the FBI is screening that but what have we discovered?" Vic asked.

"So far, no good. We are pretty sure they prayed together but that's about it. No paper trail, no big friendship."

"These Hasidic are an interesting group. They don't really want to talk to cops. They agree with a handshake and cash. Very little on the paperwork. One guy told me today that if a Hasid screws another Hasid on a diamond deal at ten o'clock in the morning on 47th Street in New York, by suppertime in Antwerp, every diamond dealer shuns the bad guy. These are a very tight people."

"Getting them to talk to a *shiksa* Puerto Rican investigator would be a real challenge," Raquel joked.

"I'd love to see that. A gentile woman who looks like you. Their hats would spin like a top. Think about coming up here, just for shits and giggles."

"Gotta go now." Raquel ended the call. She was annoyed at Vic's try. Just once she wanted Vic to lay off her Covid phobia.

• • •

The Crossroads bar was busy for a Monday night. After work, from about four-thirty to nine, there was plenty of action. Lots of women who worked in the surrounding industrial parks who liked cheap drinks, construction type bad boys and twangy country music, attracted the guys, married or single.

Carl Shuster arrived, leaving his aviator sunglasses sitting on top of his head strictly for effect or just in case he recognized someone he'd locked up further upstate.

The undercover cop got more than a couple of smiles and a few winks from women at the bar, some who knew how to use their straws as a phallic symbol. Shuster had a job to do. He wasn't looking to meet a bed partner. He scanned the bar until he saw what he termed the three stooges: Tommy, Lefty and Rob.

There they were talking to a bleached blonde and a brunette with purple stripes in her hair. The moment one of the guys saw Shuster it became like old home week with the loud 'yo dude' high fives and chest bumping that somehow makes men look like twelve-year old boys.

"Yo, Carl say hi to Cindy and Melissa. Girls, meet our new best buddy Carl," Tommy announced.

Pleasantries went all around the group. Cindy was especially friendly as she put herself between Carl and Melissa with a stupid question about whether or not his sunglasses were Ray-Ban or Maui Jim.

Lefty blurted, "Check it out, Cindy tell Carl what you were just telling us, you know about the dead Jews,"

"I will for a second drink you cheap-ass fuck," Cindy replied to Lefty. "Old alligator arms over here still has his communion money, wrapped in his baptism money. He was the cheapest guy in high school. Hell, I even had to buy the condoms once." Everyone roared with laughter, so loud that almost the entire bar took notice.

Schuster waived to Vera, the dissipated blond bartender, getting her attention and pointed to the girls.

"They drink on me all night."

Cindy went with the moment, "Hey, thanks Carl, I may still have some of those condoms in my purse." More booming laughter.

Cindy felt like she was the center of attention and she adored that position.

"So, there's this guy I met here a few times. Real quiet. Nice looking. I know you guys have seen him. Sits on the end of the bar over there. Looks like that movie guy...what's his name...the actor in....ya know...that movie...American Psycho.

Mellissa shouted, "Christian Bale!" as if she were on a game show.

"Yup, that's who he looks like. Like an older Christian Bale. Kinda scary looking. So, anyways, sometimes he's here for days and days then he vanishes for like a month or six weeks. Well, he was kinda nice the other night and asked if I wanted a drink. I had a drink already but I sat next to him at the bar. He was telling me what kind of gun the guy used to shoot those two Jews. Told me how the scope had to be set up, the distance, the wind, the whole nine. The way he described it, I thought I was watching the whole thing myself. He's a strange dude. Never married, hates everyone from gays to blacks to Jews to anyone that ain't as white as us."

"Did you ask him if he was the guy who shot them." Schuster asked.

"I sure did. I said, 'Dude you sound like you were the one who offed those suckers,' and he just looked at me, smiled, put the beer bottle up to his lips and drank it down, the whole time looking at me and never blinking an eye."

Chapter Twenty-Two

Raquel read to Gabriella from an ongoing story they visited every night. It was Gabby's bedtime and her mom tucked her in and kissed her goodnight. Raquel read to Gabby every night since she was two-years old.

Olga was in the kitchen, making a cup of Café Bustello for herself. She didn't turn around when Raquel entered the room. Raquel felt a coolness coming from her mother.

"Mom, what's wrong?"

"Nothing."

"Don't say nothing. I can tell something is wrong. Are you feeling all right?"

"I'm feeling just fine," Olga said coldly.

"Mira, deja la jodienda."

"There is no bullshit with me. Maybe the bullshit is with you, daughter."

"Okay, now we are getting somewhere."

"You want to hear what I have to say or are you going to tell me to mind my own business?"

"Yes, I want to hear you."

"Let me tell you something. You are a fool. Vic is a young, good looking man. If you want to push him away, keep doing what you are doing. He's working a case and you are burying your head in the ground like that ostrich bird. You should be with him. All because of this Covid bullshit of yours."

"Mama…"

"Quiet. Let me finish. What if you didn't have all this money? All of these things? All this fame and popularity? What if you were still a cop, with a child, like Gabby, working for a weekly paycheck? Would you tell your boss you have to hide in your house for more than a year? Would you risk losing a good man like you are doing now? I can't believe I raised a daughter who has no faith in God. So many people have to go to work every single day, but Princess Raquel wants to build a wall around herself out of a stupid fear of getting sick. Look, you are young and healthy and have no sickness. Even if you caught the Covid, you will survive. Talk about bullshit? The way you are behaving is total bullshit in my opinion. I'm your mother and I have to tell you this. You can lose a husband. I can tell he is fed up with you making us watch you imprison yourself and us, too. Now you want me to stay inside and not visit my friends. I am afraid of nothing. If I am meant to die and the Lord wants me, I will die. That's it. I hear you arguing with your husband. He says you may need to see a doctor and you go crazy on him. I say you need to grow up and forget this Covid. Live your life, my daughter. We have one life and we are only loaned to each other by the grace of Jesus. Above all, you need to have faith." Olga's lower lip began to tremble and tears filled her eyes. She took a kitchen towel and sobbed into it.

Raquel held onto her mother and held her close, patting her on her trembling back.

"Thank you, mama. I love you so much." Raquel was crying, too.

Chapter Twenty-Three

Vic Gonnella and Detective Mike Sassano drove up to Orange County to call on Rebbe Teitelbaum at his office in the main *Schul* at Kyrias Joel.

As they entered into town, a group of armed Hasidic men, seeing that they were not locals waved the car onto the side of Satmar Drive.

Sassano kept his hands on the driver wheel to show compliance with the men who all wore the traditional black hats and long black coats. The detective identified himself as a police officer from Rockland County and was here on official business to see the Rebbe. He was asked to show identification and he slowly displayed his gold shield and credentials.

A car with two Satmar men escorted the car to the Rebbe's office. A second car followed behind them. After some discussion on Sassano and Vic not agreeing to surrender their firearms, another Hasidic man appeared with an AR 15 semi-automatic rifle strapped on his shoulder.

"Do you have an appointment with the Rebbe?" the man asked quickly in a thick Yiddish accent. He was well over six-feet with a pale white complexion like many of the Hasidic men have.

Sassano replied, "We are here to discuss the two homicides of Satmar men in Rockland County. I understand and respect your need for security. I'm Detective Mike Sassano of the Ramapo Police Department and this is private investigator Vic Gonnella. You are free to call my Chief of Police or the Rockland County District Attorney to verify our identity."

"So, why no appointment?"

"Didn't know I needed one on an ongoing homicide investigation," Sassano replied.

"You wait. Stay in your car."

The jittery Satmar disappeared into the large stone and wood synagogue with many Hasidic men walking in, out and around the temple.

Ten minutes later, a short, overweight Hasidic man came from the building followed by the AR-15 carrying man.

"I'm sorry for the delay. The Rebbe will see you both. You can follow me," the chubby man said in a rapid, accent- free voice.

Sassano and Vic were ushered into a dark wood paneled room where two other long bearded men Hasidic men stood in front of a large bookcase which was filled with rows of dark blue and maroon books with Hebrew lettering.

A short, portly dark man with horn-rimmed glasses, a scraggly white beard and a short-crowned Sierra hat entered quickly into the room. His white and gray curls fell from under his hat, half-way down his beard. He had a pleasant look on his face. Not a smile or a scowl, but an affable demeanor about him. He was escorted by four other men, also on the short side, whose beards were darker as they seemed considerably younger. All of the men wore eyeglasses.

The Rebbe sat low in a high-back leather chair at the head of a long table in the room. Vic and Sassano were offered to sit in smaller leather chairs close to the Rebbe.

The short overweight man who brought Sassano and Vic into the temple came into the room. He stood next to the Rebbe and the two detectives.

"Gentlemen, I will act as the interpreter for the Rebbe."

Vic and Sassano had no idea if the Rebbe didn't speak English or didn't want to.

"How can the Rebbe help you gentleman?" The interpreter asked in a quick, rather loud voice, as if he wanted everyone in the room to hear him.

Sassano began, "Let me start by saying we are sorry that two members of your community lost their lives in our jurisdiction. We will do everything in our power to get this killer."

The Rebbe understood what the detective was saying, nodding his head and looking intently at Sassano. He didn't wait for the translation and replied in Yiddish. His voice was sharp and strong.

"We thank you for doing whatever is necessary for justice. Our community is in danger…we have been in danger for many, many years because of our beliefs. Terror is nothing new to us. Nothing will change our determination to follow our faith," the Rebbe replied. Vic immediately knew that the Rebbe was a man of strong character with an even stronger personality, a true leader.

Sassano followed the Rebbe's answer. "Rebbe, we are here to tell you at this time, we have no trail to the killer. No hard evidence except for some data on the bullet and an assumption on the weapon used. The FBI and all of the state and local law enforcement agencies are working hard to track down the killer with the little we have."

Vic jumped in, "Rebbe, may I ask a direct question?"

Teitelbaum shook his head in the affirmative.

"What do you think about these killings? Could there be an outside force known to you, that is behind these homicides? I know for example that there is an ongoing feud with your group and the Satmar group in Brooklyn. Could these murders be a result of that dispute?"

The Rebbe stroked his beard and looked at Vic over his eyeglasses. He looked as if he were sizing up Vic, trying to figure out this *goyim's* sincerity.

He spoke quickly and directly and the interpreter followed. The Rebbe went into a speech like response, raising his voice for emphasis at times.

"Let me be clear to you. Our problems with Williamsburg and their problems with us is strictly between the Satmar community. I will not elaborate on that except to say violence is not coming from our own. However, it is very possible that Zionists are behind this *Shanda* to send upheaval and fear through our people. Zionist know that we are opposed to the state of Israel. To us, Israel does not exist. They have no right to exist. Until the messiah returns and leads us into the promised land, as scripture tells us, there is no Jewish state. The Jewish state does not exist. So, even Trump, when he was president made a big deal out of Jerusalem. Yes, Jerusalem is a holy city. Zionism is the opposite of fearing God and Torah and has absolutely nothing to do with the holy city of Jerusalem."

Every man in the room was captivated by the Rebbe's words. Vic paused before responding to the Rebbe.

"Rebbe, do you actually think the Zionists would resort to murdering innocent people in broad daylight?"

The Rebbe went on, "Satmar is opposed to the State of Israel. The Zionist are capable of anything including murder. So why not in broad daylight? Does it need to be dark outside to kill?"

Vic was momentarily taken aback.

"This guy is actually serious," Vic thought.

"Rebbe, with all due respect to you and your position, I was expecting you to say this is a hate crime, and…"

"Of course, this is a hate crime, the Rebbe interrupted. "Hate comes in many disguises. Zionism is built on politics, not on faith. We, the Satmar people, prefer to pray and study and be observant of the six-hundred and thirteen commandments until God sends us the Messiah to restore the Jewish government to the Land of Israel."

Sassano thought, *"What happened to ten commandments? Now there are six-hundred and thirteen, holy shit."*

Vic replied, "Yes, Rebbe, I am aware of your many commandments and I respect them; however, to blame Zionism, will be difficult if not impossible to prove. I prefer to look a bit closer to home."

The Rebbe went on for a ten-minute speech about how Zionists want to eradicate the Hasidic world for their own political motivation. Vic and Sassano began to glaze over and both realized the Rebbe was lecturing them on his theory. There would be no revelation or clues coming from the Satmar leader. The meeting ended cordially.

As they were leaving the Rebbe, being escorted back to their car, Sassano saw a familiar face, who recognizing him turned his back to hide his identity.

It was Jacob Glick.

Chapter Twenty-Four

"**A**ny good places to eat up there in Rockland County?" Raquel asked Vic. It was four o'clock in the afternoon and Raquel was calling from her cell-phone.

"I guess so, why?"

"I'm in the car with Pando, heading up there now and I'm starting to get hungry."

"What? You're coming here?"

"I heard the Sparkill Steakhouse is the bomb."

Vic called the hotel, traded-up from a single room that he was staying in to a suite at the Pearl River Hilton Hotel in the Rockland County town of Pearl River. The fee they were getting from the Feds covered reasonable lodging. To Vic, the exclusive Hilton was more than reasonable. He wanted Raquel to be as comfortable as possible.

Some things are better left unsaid so Vic never mentioned the Covid phobia that Raquel had developed and that they all had suffered with for a year. He also made no mention of the fact that Monsey, where they would be doing their investigation was a hot-bed of the Covid virus and she would have much rather had stayed in the sanitized safety of her townhouse.

• • •

Even with the wide black mask covering the lower portion of her face, Raquel turned more than a few heads as the couple were brought to their table at the Sparkill Steakhouse. She wore her hair pulled back into a tight bun. Her high cheek bones and shiny chestnut brown hair pulled back in a tight bun, her button-down blouse and short beige skirt finished by brown knee-high boots made everyone, women and men alike, take notice. She was a hot item to say the least.

The couple dove into the case with renewed vigor. The fact that they were together on a case had its own magic.

"Tell me more about your idea of predicting where the next shooting will be. I'm not sure there will be a third event. Time will tell. Regardless, I'm intrigued by your theory," Vic stated.

Raquel had studied the street-by-street map of Monsey. She had Pando drove around before she met with Vic.

Watching the Hasidic men and women walking around Monsey almost sent her into a true panic attack. Raquel tried hard to put the Covid pandemic out of her mind, but the thought that this community was rife with the virus kept creeping back into her mind.

Raquel presented her concept. "These are urban people. They like to walk. They walk everywhere. To the stores, to the synagogue, just walking the baby to visit one another. When was the last time you saw one of those big baby carriages? I counted twelve today and saw at least ten strollers. They make plenty of babies. I can attest to that."

"Now, I see the Mendel Glick shooting clearly on the map. That building is the highest point around and perfect for a sniper shot. The second one, the Heshey Weissman killing on Route 306, was also a fairly long, but relatively easy shot. Both of these locations have a common denominator…a lot of people walking around. My bet, and of course it's only a gut, is the next busy spot that he will go with is Maple Avenue. The shooter wants targets and he's making a statement. He'll get you where you like to walk so everyone goes into a panic."

Vic took a sip from his martini. "Makes sense. I'm going to recommend to Chief Frank to put extra patrols on Maple Avenue on Friday. I remember when I was in uniform one hot summer in the 43 precinct in the Bronx. Crime was soring with no let-up in sight. It came from upstairs, from Borough Command that we drive around with top lights on the squad cars on at all times. The brass said it psychologically tells the community we are there. You know, police presence. I don't think that's a bad idea for Monsey at the moment."

"Good idea, it may help," Raquel replied.

"I have a question. What about the possibility that the shooter goes back to that building on Secora Road, picks off another victim near that Evergreen store?" Vic asked.

"Do you think so? I don't know. People will be watching for a stranger, listening for noises, shots, something! But, on the other hand, there are a lot of targets walking around that entire area."

"I think we should go there. See what's up at that place. Do you think they're open now?" Vic inquired.

Raquel took her cellphone out and Googled, *Evergreen Monsey,*

"Open 'till Midnight," Raquel announced.

After dinner Vic and Raquel drove from Sparkill, to Monsey. As they drove down Route 59 and as they got closer to Monsey, they started to see the black hats bobbing up and down on the side of the road. Even in the evening, there were plenty of men walking around. Some were alone, some walked together in a group of two or three, perhaps to shul to pray or to study or maybe just to get some fresh air and get away from all those kids at home.

Vic parked in the large store lot at the Evergreen just down from where Mendel Glick was murdered. He pointed to the building with its lights on and then pointed to the approximate location of the killing.

Once inside the Evergreen the world changed. Raquel wore a long brown raincoat to cover her sexy self. Her modern look, a short, above the knee skirt, no wig, sleeveless blouse and not wearing opaque nylons might have caused an accident or worse. She immediately noticed that virtually every inch of the store had merchandise piled high and deep. Most of the signs were not in English.

Vic pointed out that the voice over the stores loudspeaker system was a male speaking only in Yiddish.

As they walked further into the store, on the right was a busy delicatessen like counter. Four Spanish male workers were busy filling orders from mostly women customers but there were a few men as well. The men did not wear masks but the women did. Raquel now wore a double mask.

"Ola!" one of the deli men saw Raquel and knew she wasn't from around there.

Raquel smiled through her masks.

Next to the counter, across from where the people stood to order their dinners and tomorrow's lunch, stood a stainless steel self-serve, hot food unit.

"That looks pretty good baby," Raquel said pointing to one of the steaming dishes. "What is it?" She asked.

"I can tell you what it isn't. It ain't Italian food that's for sure." Vic picked the ladle that was resting in the stew-like food and held it up. They looked at it with interest."

"No idea!" Vic added.

"Chulent. Beef Chulent." A heavy accent came from an old man on the other side of the steam-table. He was filling a small plastic container with another unknown food.

"Why thank you," Raquel replied. Vic didn't look up going on to look at the next hot food.

"Usually we eat the chulent on Shabbas. Mime great-grandmutter made for us in Romania. And mine grandmutter and mine mutter."

Raquel though the old guy was sweet and he seemed like he wanted to be of help.

She pointed to the next tray.

"And this?" She asked.

"Chicken mit noodle soup. Jewish penicillin," the old man laughed. His teeth were stained yellow. His long black coat was rumpled and seemed stained with food. His hat was crooked on his head.

"Raquel, look…a pickle barrel." Vic grabbed a large container and picked up the prongs to grab a few."

"So, what this has to do mit people getting shot?" the old Hasid asked.

"Sorry? Excuse me? What did you just ask?" Raquel said.

"You are detectives buying pickles. *Oy vey* what a *meshugana* world."

"Excuse me sir. How do you know what we are?" Raquel said with a bit of a tone in her voice. Vic started to chuckle.

"Only because you two chased me over two continents until I allowed to you find me."

"Fucking Deegan?" Raquel blurted.

Vic replied. "The one and only. I though you retired that yid disguise Deegan?"

"I did but mine vife said it vas sexy."

Chapter Twenty-Five

"I'm really bugged about seeing Jacob Glick up there with the Rebbe." Mike Sassano shared.

Vic answered, "Why is that? He's a Satmar isn't he?"

Sassano, Vic and Raquel were having an early breakfast at the Hilton in Pearl River. The hotel resembles Versailles in a strange way. The view from the dining room was special. It looked like a French estate and it felt so calming that Raquel had forgotten about Covid for a while.

"Not so much that he was there to see the Rebbe. It was the way he looked away as if he didn't want me to recognize him. There is something up with that guy, Vic. And believe it or not, just between us three, I don't trust that little Rebbe one bit. That bullshit about the Zionists... c'mon will ya?"

"From all the reports, the forensic accounting on the businesses, background checks, personal financial information, Jacob checks out fine," Raquel added.

Vic added, "That doesn't mean he didn't kill his brother or know who did."

Raquel nodded.

"I think we should go see him or call him in before Friday and it gets crazy around here," Sassano offered.

"No time like the present," Raquel blurted.

After breakfast and a conference call with their office in Manhattan the three detectives were on their way to Jacob Glick's office in Monsey.

Jacob ran his company on the second floor of a two-family house just off Route 59. There were no fewer than eight women, all Hasidic, all wearing the *sheital* wigs, traditionally and, conservatively dressed, working in a bullpen of open sectional desks. Three Hasidic men, working in a glass enclosed cube to the rear of the office, the book keepers and office manager, moved rapidly all around the office with papers in their hands. Jacob's glass enclosed office overlooked the entire operation and was to the left of his accountant's cube. Nobody joked, smiled or otherwise looked like their work was enjoyable.

The three detectives rang the bell at the front door and were immediately bussed in.

The girl in the first desk in a slight Yiddish accent asked, how she could help the *goyum* three-some.

"I'm Detective Sassano with the Ramapo Police Department. We're here to see Jacob Glick," he said. Sassano showed his identification.

You could hear a pin drop. The girls stopped working, taking their focus off their desk-top computers. The girls were naturally all looking at Raquel. They were not accustomed to seeing non-religious women. The men looked at Vic and Sassano. Not that the men didn't notice the pretty *shiksa*. The gentile woman. They noticed all right, then they quickly averted their eyes to prevent thoughts that were unacceptable.

Raquel noticed how beautiful each of the girls were. The lead girl had amazing features. High cheekbones, full lips, a perfect nose and large violet eyes.

"Do you have an appointment?"

"Please just tell Mr. Glick we are here. Thank you," Sassano answered with his cop authoritarian voice.

Before she could walk to Jacobs office her phone beeped and she was told by Jacob to show them to his office.

When they walked into Jacob's office, the look of anxiety on his face was obvious to the trained detectives. He was guilty of something.

"Jacob, it's nice to see you again," Sassano offered. Jacob made no remark. He looked like the proverbial deer caught in the headlights.

"This is private investigators Vic Gonnella and Raquel Ruiz. They are here to assist the department with the murder of your brother."

No one in the office was wearing protective masks. The three visitors all had masks. Raquel had two. Her palms were wet with moisture from her anxiety of being near the Hasidic people. Luckily, Jacob couldn't shake her hand because its improper to touch a woman who is not your wife.

Jacob offered the two chairs in front of his desk and one of the men hustled in a folding chair. The man with the chair never picked his head up to look at anyone.

"So, what can I do for you detective?" Jacob asked. His voice was unsteady.

"We are working on some interesting leads on this case. We are interested to know what you were doing at the Rebbe's office the other day."

Jacobs eyes fluttered and he looked frightened. He folded his arms into himself. He looked down and didn't respond at first.

"*This guy has a lot of lying tells, here we go.*" Vic thought. Mike and Raquel read his body language as well.

"I…I was… seeking spiritual guidance," Jacob lied.

"From the Grand Rebbe, not from your Rabbi at your local synagogue?" Mike followed.

Jacob was nonplused. He pulled his folded arms closer to his chest.

Vic instinctively went into bad-cop mode.

"I want you to listen to me, Mr. Glick. And listen very carefully. I'm not here to waste my time. Withholding information and evidence or aiding and abetting a criminal is a felony in the State of New York. Now before I read you your rights and advise you to call a criminal lawyer, I suggest you make it easier on yourself and tell us what you were really doing at the Rebbe's office." Vic was stretching the truth and betting on the come.

Jacobs already pale complexion went ashen. He put both of his hands up, covering his head, which he lowered down almost to his desk. He recovered quickly. He sat upright in his chair and removed his eyeglasses.

"I did not kill my brother. I've done nothing wrong."

"But you have an idea who did, don't you?"

Another long pause from Jacob.

"Rebbe reminded me of one of our commandments. Do not accuse anyone falsely. Do not tell lies," Jacob uttered.

"Lies? It's also a lie not to tell what you know about your own brother's murderer," Vic pressed.

"My brother loaned money to someone. That doesn't mean that person murdered him," Jacob was near tears.

Raquel took a chance, "It also doesn't mean he didn't. That's what we do. We investigate and determine if that individual is a person of interest. Tell us what we need to know Jacob."

• • •

Carl Schuster went to the Crossroads bar late that same afternoon. It was around three-thirty and the place was empty of patrons. He wanted more information on the guy who spoke with Cindy. Cindy had no idea who he was or even his name. Carl knew this lead could be a dead end, but it also could be something that may lead to the shooter.

The blond bartender Vera remembered Carl as a big tipper. Plus, she thought he was hot. Carl ordered his bottle of Heineken and put a fifty on the bar.

"There is a guy that comes in here once in a while. Quiet guy sits over there. I think I went to high school with him but I forgot his name. He was into guns last time I saw him," Carl stated.

"You must mean Richie. Good lookin' guy but not as good lookin' as you sweetie," Vera flirted.

"Yea Richie. I forgot his last name," Carl fished.

"I have his number if you want to call him."

"You have his number? How did you get his number sweetheart?"

"He was pretty drunk one night. He said if I ever wanted a good time I should call him. He put the number into my phone. I'm never called him, but if I was horny I was gonna call. Sometimes a girl has to keep her options open, ya know. Especially at closing time." She took her phone out and showed Carl the number. "Here it is. You want it?"

• • •

At the Satmar synagogue where both Mendel Glick and Heshe Weissman prayed and studied every day, a *minyan* of seventeen men was formed and met for prayers.

Each man rocked back and forth with a bit more emphasis than usual. This motion is called *shuckling*. It comes from the book of Proverbs. "The soul of man is a candle of God." The candle's flame constantly sways and flickers as it attempts to tear free of its wick and ascend on high. This is the way prayers are concentrated and focused on God Himself, to bring the believer closer to the creator.

The worry and anxiety from the killings were palpable among the praying men. The *davening* seemed more fervent than ever.

After the *minyan* was concluded, the men agreed to meet and discuss the horrible events of losing friends and fellow Satmar followers. They stood around in a meeting room, each holding their prayer book in dark blue or black velvet pouches. The conversation was in Yiddish with an English word or two added.

"I will admit, even though I have faith in Hashem, I am terrified by this Shabbas Killer. How can any one of us feel safe as we walk here and there? Especially to *Schul*," Eli Adelson, a diamond merchant stated. Adelson is a third generation of diamond dealers at New York City's Diamond District on West 47th Street.

He continued, "When I come off the bus from New York, I'm worried I will be shot and killed. This is no life for me. For anyone."

Levi Blout, a cousin of Mendel Glick added, "I told my wife to prepare to pack to go stay by my brother in Toronto. I may completely relocate my entire family just to feel safe."

"We are none of us safe so long as we look the way we do. Will we be forced to abandon our traditions? Is this freedom?" Mordechai Bauer, a Bronx landlord blurted. "I'm already carrying a gun. So, what? I carry a gun and someone shoots me dead from a mile away. What good is this gun?"

"Most of us are carrying a gun now. Most of them are not registered. We can go to jail for this," Adelson added.

"Will the Rebbe allow us to break Shabbas and not come here? I doubt that!" another man yelled.

"My grandfather told me how life was in Europe. He ever knew from one day to the next if he was going to be shot down in the street.

This is no different. I ask you all, who are we hurting being good, religious people?" another asked.

"I have eleven children. I work hard for my family...we all do. I haven't been able to sleep or take in a good meal. The Rebbe is trying to help with security but he cannot put a bubble around all of us," Yiddi offered. He is an insurance man known to everyone in the community.

Levi Blout was near tears. "My cousin Mendel...a good man. He *davened* with everyone here. He is gone from us...forever. His wife is with child. That boy or maybe it's a girl, will never know a father. What can be done? Are we all just waiting to be picked off until they find this...this...Hashem, forgive me for my bad thoughts."

Adelson lamented. "So, what to do? Do we talk about it or move away like Levi here or do we stand and fight? And who are we fighting?"

"The Rebbe thinks it may be Zionists, killing Jews... their own people. I am not one to go against the Rebbe but I can't imagine one Jew wants to kill another Jew because of our religious differences," a younger Satmar announced.

Adelson. A respected leader among his group raised his arms high in the air.

"We all have many questions without clear answers. We must be strong and stay strong as a group. We don't know what next Shabbas will bring. We don't even know what tomorrow will bring. I say to everyone here and now. We must pray harder. The answer will come from Hashem."

Chapter Twenty-Six

V ic and Raquel rose early and went to the Ramapo Police Department Headquarters in Suffern for a seven o'clock meeting.

They picked up three dozen assorted- bagels, butter and three kinds of cream cheese at Zimi Bagel Café in Nanuet as a treat to everyone for the day ahead.

Raquel was bravely fighting her feeling about the Covid virus, especially being in the Monsey area. She washed her hands multiple times, used hand sanitizer like an obsession and wore double masks. She was trying very hard to fight her phobia. She already took the first step realizing her behavior was over the top.

The tension in the Ramapo PD conference room was intense. After all, it was another Friday morning. The last two Friday's ended in tragedy for two Hasidic families and the Orthodox community as a whole.

Special Agent Wright had arranged for a Zoom meeting with Gail Gain at the FBI Quantico Serial Profiling Unit. Along with Wright, Vic and Raquel, Chief Frank, Mike Sassano and seven of his detectives were in the tight room.

Wright worked the lens on the computer, trying to center the FBI Logo on the screen. He wasn't having much luck.

Raquel got up from her chair and adjusted the large screen. She was wearing black leggings and a Columbia sweatshirt that rose a bit when she stretched high to fix the image, exposing the bottom of her tight, slightly thick butt.

"Wow, what an ass," Chief Frank thought.

"Very nice, milf, I'd do it, and Gonnella's a lucky fuck, were among the thoughts of the men in attendance. The two women detectives were noticing her gorgeous hair and her white Nike sneakers that were stylishly an inch below the bottom of her leggings. They noticed the great butt too.

Special agent Wright had a more sinister thought. *"These two want to take all the glory. For them it's a fucking big paycheck and a bunch of publicity and more fame. I'll be lucky if I get a promotion out of this case. We'll see."*

The FBI image flickered once and the screen went black. The next image, was Gail Gain in a cloud of her own cigarette smoke staring into space. *"What the hell!"* Chief Frank contemplated.

Wright paused for a moment to take in the image of G.G.

"Hello, Ms. Gain. Are we connected?"

G.G. at first looked startled and tried to focus her attention onto the screen. However, when she did look at the lens it seemed she was looking above the camera and her eyes seemed to look in different directions.

"Yes...I can see you all."

"Great. Ladies and gentlemen, please meet Gail Gain. As I have mentioned to you all, G.G. as she is known in Quantico, is the authority on serial killer activity. She has been instrumental in solving and uncovering some of the most well-known serial murders in the United States and other countries. I know that G.G. worked with Gonnella and Ruiz in the past."

Excitedly, and to Vic's surprise, Raquel practically yelled out "Hi G.G." as if she were saying hello to a high school friend she hadn't seen since graduation. To make it even more awkward, Raquel was waving her hand like she was on the platform at a train station waiting for her long-lost cousin."

Vic looked down at his note book hoping the pain of embarrassment would leave quickly.

G.G. responded like she had never even heard of Raquel Ruiz. She didn't respond but simply stared ahead. Hoping for recognition and getting nothing, the smile on Raquel's face turned to neutral in a nanosecond.

Without further introduction or a segue into the meeting's agenda from Wright, G.G. began.

"We have reviewed all of the evidence on this case. It's my opinion that the shooter will continue his or her spree. I'm going to go out on a limb and say he will strike again every Friday until Passover and then potentially take a long break or possibly disappear completely."

G.G. looked at the camera as if she were awaiting applause. She was already zoning out, her comfortability, some would call it anti-social behavior clearly came through.

Raquel noticed that G.G.'s hair was grayer than the last time she saw her, which was five or six years ago. She doubted that G.G. washed her matted, greasy hair in weeks. The rosacea she had during the Deegan case had now spread to her forehead and chin. The skin on her puffy cheeks were nearly purple from the skin condition. Several cans of Coca Cola with straws sticking from their tops along with two full ashtrays were prominent on G.G.'s desk. A crumpled red pack of Pall Mall unfiltered cigarettes stood beside an open container of a past meal. Likely Chinese food by the look of the long brown noodle hanging on its side.

Wright asked the first question.

"What makes you believe that he will strike again?"

"You said he. First of all, I always say he or she until it is determined and verified that it is a male shooter. I will go with a male at this point because the bullets that were used are made with specialized and sophisticated machinery. Likely aided by a computer. Women are not generally adroit with machinery of this kind. The tungsten carbide projectile that was used is likely from a chunk of that alloy, or potentially molded from a tool of that same metal. Either way, the person, again we will say a male as an assumption, has a good working knowledge of making ballistics from metals. An assumption that a woman is not familiar with this kind of tooling and bullet manufacturing is sound. The copper coating verifies my hypothesis of self- manufacturing."

G.G. took a long draw on her cigarette which was now a nub. Her dark yellow, nicotine stained fingers were evident even on the screen. Her already bulging eyes widened further with the draw on the Pall Mall.

Mike Sassano was sitting next to Vic.

"Mencia, monga brodo, sciamannata." Sassano said almost to himself, in a voice slightly above a whisper.

Vic nearly laughed out loud. He remembered his mother's father using phrase like that in Sicilian when Vic was a boy. Instead of a laugh, Vic stifled his laugh and pursed his lips. Sassano was alluding to G.G. being a disgraceful mess who couldn't even make herself soup. It sounds better in Italian.

G.G. continued. "Now, is this a true hate-crime? It very well could be. Or it could be for another reason only known to the killer. We know that he is angry about something, going for the gory head shots when a body shot is easier and effective with that kind of ballistic. Whatever his reason, he is an expert shot. I would look to shooting ranges, outdoor ranges especially due to the distances he selects. Look for people who use a high-quality scope on a .338-caliber rifle. The assumption that he also uses a suppressor in valid in that no one at or around the building where he shot the first victim heard a discharge. Likewise, with the second shooting."

G.G. awkwardly stared into the camera.

Wright spoke again.

"We are going through countless thousands of names of registered owners of high caliber rifles, with special attention to .338 calibers. We are cross referencing that data with known anti-Semitic and known white supremacist individuals. As you know, this is tedious and time-consuming work to say the least. There are an awful lot of rifles like this out there. We have also checked with the manufacturers of tungsten carbide ammunition. So far, nothing."

G.G. inhaled deeply again on another cigarette which she lit from the nub of the first one. She ignored Wrights report.

"Are you eliminating a hate crime?" Vic asked.

G.G. once again stared, then looked up to the ceiling. She didn't respond for a long ten-seconds.

"I don't thing I said that. If you were listening attentively I said it could be but there could also be another reason. If you want to look at anti-sematic individuals, I certainly would not rule that out. But it could very well be a much wider field. Also, I don't believe the killer has a psychosexual motivation but I will not yet rule out that possibility. Frankly more information is needed to formulate an accurate profile on this killer."

Some more uncomfortable moments ensued during the call. G.G. seemed to pick something out of her rats-nest of a hairdo and looked at it before flicking it away. During another question, she clearly was picking her nose.

Wright and the rest of the group were looking at the screen in quiet disbelief.

• • •

The Zoom call ended and the group shared information and ideas until after nine a.m. As they were breaking up the meeting, Chief Frank's secretary came into the conference room.

"Mr. Gonnella, there has been a shooting in Williamsburg, Brooklyn this morning. I have an NYPD inspector on the line for you," she announced.

Chief Frank took the call and put it on the speaker for everyone to hear.

"Vic Gonnella," Vic answered.

"Vic, Inspector Mike Roma, NYPD. The Commissioner asked me to track you down. Thought you would want to know there was a shooting of a Hasidic male on Division Street in Williamsburg early this morning. The assailant shot from the rooftop of a four-story building. He was apprehended leaving the scene. He used a Remington 770 rifle which we've handed over to CSI. The victim was shot though his shoulder and brought to the hospital by Hatzolah. He's expected to survive."

"Inspector, this is Special Agent Wright, FBI. I'll notify our field office in Brooklyn to assist. This is a Federal Case as you know."

Vic rolled his eyes.

Inspector Roma announced, "Already done. Your guys are here. They're of the opinion it's a copy-cat, and not your guy, based on the kind of weapon and the fact that the assailant is a local, and a just released mental patient. He was at Bellevue Hospital, when the shootings in Monsey took place. Needless to say, the community is in a total panic."

"Thanks, Mike. Tell the boss I appreciate the information."

"Vic, he wanted me to tell you he's already taken a call from the Governor."

"Thanks again."

Vic rubbed his eyes. "This is all we need. Crazy people with guns shooting at the Hasidic," he blurted.

• • •

It was now one o'clock that afternoon. News of the shooting in Williamsburg ran through the Orthodox community in Monsey and Kyrias Joel. Rebbe Teitelbaum ordered more men at the entrance and exits at Satmar Drive in Kyrias Joel. Shabbas was just a few hours away and the Hasidic people in Monsey nervously went about their Friday rituals of preparing for sundown.

The police cars were patrolling all the highways and byways of Monsey, with emergency roof top lights of all vehicles ablaze as ordered. There was thought of shutting down Route 59 in both directions in Monsey but the idea was scuttled so as not to produce panic and confusion by diverting the heavy traffic.

On the corner of Maple Avenue and North Saddle River Road, there is an old cemetery. Historic Monsey Cemetery was established by the Dutch Reform Church. It has graves of veterans of the Revolutionary War, the Civil War and the War of 1812.

Rows of old gray and reddish headstones, worn from the centuries of being battered by the elements, are in poor condition. The graveyard is hardly noticed by the Orthodox community as they hustle to and from their schools and *shuls*.

Hidden among the gravestones, totally unseen from the passersby, wearing complete hunting camouflage gear, is a man with a rifle in a prone position. His rifle is also camouflaged so not to reflect any sunlight and attract attention to his position.

The temperature was an unseasonably warm seventy-one degrees. The sun was beating down, the trees casting helpful shadows to further shroud the shooter. Beads of perspiration formed on his forehead just below his camouflage beret.

He waited patiently, for precisely the right moment to take down his target, as if he were hunting deer in the woods,

In the crosshairs of his scope, Edward Olsen saw a tall Hasidic man, carrying what looked like a velvet-like portfolio. The pouch contained his prayer books. His head curls were almost as long as his dark beard. The man looked very thin, almost anemic. He wore horn-rimmed glasses and had a protruding Adams apple. The assassin slowly adjusted his scope but the thin man was not his target. He wanted the person behind the thin man and waited for him to move a half-foot to the left or to the right to take the shot.

Suddenly the killer could see the flashing of red and white lights in his scope. He patiently held his finger off the trigger, placing it along the rifles chassis directly above the trigger guard. He waited for the police cruiser to pass. The vehicle turned to the right, away from the target and out of the shooters line of fire.

In the center of his scope was the magnified image of his third victim, a mere two-hundred and-thirty-yards away, clearly in his sights. He knew he could easily make a center mass shot from three or four times that distance. There was not even a small breeze that he needed to calculate for wind variance for his shot.

He slowly placed his finger on the trigger, centered his target, inhaled smoothly. As he exhausted all of the oxygen in his lungs, he stopped breathing for a second while he pressed lightly on the trigger between his heartbeats.

Through his scope he saw the targets chest explode, sending a whoosh of blood into the air behind the mark.

Hadassah Kessler fell back behind the dark blue, Silver Cross Baby Stroller she was pushing. Her heart burst upon impact of the tungsten carbide projectile.

Chapter Twenty-Seven

Hadassah Kessler had just started her new life as a married woman. She was born and raised in Monsey, followed the two-hundred and fifty-year old Chabad-Lubavitch branch of Hasidism faithfully. Seven months ago, at eighteen years old she had her first and only child. She would never fulfill her dream of having a large Hasidic family.

Vic and Raquel visited the family of Hadassah Kessler on Monday, the day after the third Hasidic person was buried after being gunned down on the streets of Monsey.

It was the first day of *shiva* for the large Chabad-Lubavitch family. The fact that Hadassah was a woman and not a Satmar Hasidic male showed that John Deegan was surprisingly not correct.

The shooter didn't care what sect his victims belonged to. Hasidic Jews, any one of them, for the time being were his targets.

Vic and Raquel agreed there was no time to wait until the Kessler family finished their mandated seven days of mourning. They hoped that the family would accept them and share some insight on Hadassah's life. Perhaps there was a connection to the prior two murders.

Raquel was terribly frightened. She had attended many *shivas* in the past. None of them were for Hasidic people and none were during the worst worldwide pandemic since the Spanish Influenza one-hundred-and-three years ago. Raquel felt as if she were going into the mouth of the lion among the Hasidic community in Monsey, who had among the highest Covid infection rates in the entire country.

Vic could tell she was terrified from the slight tremor in Raquel's hands as they approached the front door of the Kessler home. He almost called off the visit but wanted her to face her demons nonetheless.

The home was large for a young couple. Zvi Kessler, Hadassah's husband's family, giants in the Diamond business in South Africa and New York City, gifted the home to the newlyweds. Zvi is a vice-president of sales for the firm.

Vic wore a dark suit and tie. Raquel, trying to be as respectful of the family's religious beliefs and traditions wore a black pantsuit, with a long sleeve blouse under her jacket and a traditional head- covering. Just before visiting that morning the couple went into Monsey and purchased Raquel's scarf and a black Yarmulke for Vic.

The two private investigators opened the front door without knocking as is the *shiva* tradition.

Hadassah's husband, her father, Rabbi Yitzchak Twersky and her mother Sima Hagar among others were all seated on low benches in a huge living room.

Raquel noticed the covered mirrors and an oversized dining room table that was filled with platters of food. Two women, in long Hasidic style dresses hustled around the table serving food to the mourners. Vic stopped guessing how many people were in the home as they walked into the packed living room.

Sima Hagar noticed the two *goyum* and recognized them from a photo in the Yiddish newspaper. She took Rabbi Twersky by the hand and approached Vic and Raquel. Mrs. Hagar introduced her husband and herself.

"We normally do not speak much during the first days of shiva. I'm sure you both understand. The entire family is broken-hearted," Sima said. Her voice was strained from grief.

Vic let Raquel make the introductions. Vic held his eyes steady on the grieving parents. No explanation of sorrow is to be given in this tradition.

"Rabbi, Mrs. Twersky, we are aware of your mourning period. However, I hope you understand that we have precious little time to end these tragic events. We thought we needed to get a fast start on our investigation."

The Rabbi, a short stout man with crystal blue eyes and a long white beard was dressed in the simple black Hassid garb as all of the men wore. He spoke in a clear, strong voice, averting his eyes from the female stranger and in a slight Yiddish accent directed his words to Vic.

"There are times when our traditions have to take a backseat to logic. Our entire family will assist you in any way we can. This has to be stopped. What you are doing for our community is greatly appreciated."

"Thank you for understanding," Vic offered.

Raquel got right into things.

"Mrs. Twersky, what can you tell us about your daughter Hadassah."

"My Esther. That's what we called her. We have nine children, she was the next to the youngest. *Baruch Hashem,* bless His name, until now. She was the most gifted of our children in school. Especially in music. She was offered to go to Julliard but she decided on being a wife and mother. Her daughter…"

Sima could not go on. She nearly collapsed from grief and was taken into the room by two women who stood by her side.

"Please, come with me into a quieter space," Rabbi Twersky said.

The Rabbi led the way into a smaller room off the side of the dining room. The Rabbi closed the door behind them.

"None of us are as strong as we pretend. My wife is doing the best she can under the circumstances. Let me tell you some things about Esther. She was brilliant. I must tell you among many Hasidic people, education for women is not embraced. In Chabad-Lubavitch we have intensive Torah education for our women. Esther, even at her young age, was a leader in the community. She worked tirelessly with the children of our community, teaching them, nurturing them, and guiding them into a good and happy life based on the teachings of Torah. To you, not being of our society, it is a difficult thing to understand how we are steeped in Torah and faith. My daughter, believe me when I say this, she could have been anything she wanted to be. She had a genius level I.Q. yet she chose to be a mother and wife, to pass our culture and religion onto her family, and the families of others. So, this genius young woman, my daughter, last week, Esther started scrubbing her home in preparation of *Pesach,* our Passover. She scrubbed her kitchen clean of *chameitz,* let me explain how intense our religion is and why my daughter was so devoted. There is a passage in Exodus, in our Torah that states;

'Seven days you shall eat unleavened bread; on the very first day you shall remove leaven from your houses, for whoever eats leavened bread, (this is the *chameitz,* I'm referring to), from the first day to the seventh day, that person shall be cut off from Israel.'

Esther was the best of the best. Not an enemy, not a foul word ever, a good wife and mother. So now she leaves a seven-month old daughter without her mother and why? Because of hatred?"

Vic and Raquel sat in stunned silence. Finally, Vic shook his head as if to wake himself from a nightmare.

"Rabbi, I've seen hatred over my entire career. I've also seen a lot of jealousy. Forgive me, but could someone in the community, or maybe in your son-in-law's business, have a reason to want to see your daughter dead?"

"Mr. Gonnella, I know to both of you our religion may seem very strange, as do our customs, what we eat, how we pray, even the way we dress and mill about in a secular society. But, I must tell you in all candor…we love just like everyone else in the world. We hurt just as deeply as everyone does. We mourn, we cry, we laugh, we even have fun. To answer your question, is anyone in our world capable of such horror? Of course. We are just people. We are just like every human being on this planet."

Chapter Twenty-Eight

As a favor to Vic Gonnella, Sean Lewandowski, now an Assistant Director of the FBI's New York City office, jumped in to help with the Shabbas Killer case. Sean and Vic went back to when Vic was an NYPD detective on the Deegan case.

Sean went with one of his Special Agents, Sal Colangelo to pay a visit to Avi Nussbaum at AN Trading Company on Clinton Avenue in Williamsburg, Brooklyn. The entrance to his office was in the rear and in the basement level of a two-story, red brick residential house. In the driveway of the home was a dirty and battered Honda-Odyssey mini-van.

Colangelo, a Brooklyn Street kid who was snatched up by the FBI after he finished his law degree at Fordham University, looked through the grimy windows of the Honda just to be snoopy.

"What a mess! No wonder with all the kids these folks have," he thought.

Sean and Colangelo rang the outside bell and were let in without hesitation. They walked down a flight of wooden stairs which led them to another door which had a large glass cut out. The two men could see into the busy office. Two long rows of Hasidic women were on their desk top computers. They all wore headsets over their wigs, their fingers moving rapidly along their keyboards. Several Hasidic men, in their four-cornered linen *tallit,* prayer shawl over their white shits hustled around the office with boxes and paperwork. Attached to each corner of their shirts were long *tzitzis,* specially knotted ritual tassels.

Colangelo opened the unlocked office door.

After introductions, a very short wait and having to pass the gauntlet of women who would only steal a peak at them, Sean and Colangelo found themselves seated in front of Avi Nussbaum.

"It's not every day I get a visit from the FBI. Do I need a lawyer?" Nussbaum asked.

"That depends Mr. Nussbaum. There is plenty of time for that. I suggest we just have a conversation first. We are here to ask a few questions about your business dealings with the late Mendel Glick," Colangelo offered

"A Shanda. What kind of *mashuganas* are out there just shooting people like that?" Nussbaum was the nervous type. He spoke very rapidly which is not unlike many Hasidic men. His accent was not as badly affected by Yiddish as most. He had long blond hair and the mandatory long side curls, with deep set dark eyes. His beard was reddish blond and scraggly. Bushy blond eyelashes added to a look of being unkempt.

Sean cut to the chase, "Mr. Nussbaum, what can you tell us about the unpaid loan which you received from Mendel Glick?"

Nussbaum was taken aback by the direct question. His eyes blinked rapidly before he answered.

"I…I was having a rough time in my business. Actually, I closed it down and started another business… this one, we trade…"

Colangelo interrupted, "We know what you do, Nussbaum. Where were you the afternoon Mr. Glick was shot?" Colangelo knew when to expose his tough guy Brooklyn accent.

"I…I was in *shul*, like I always am before *Shabbas*."

"I'm sure the men in your prayer group will be willing to attest to that," Colangelo followed.

Sean jumped in. "You see Mr. Nussbaum. We have looked into your business dealings very closely. We had you followed for a good amount of time. I don't think you had anything to do with killing Mendel Glick, but agent Colangelo here has his doubts."

"I could never kill another person…never!"

Colangelo moved to the edge of his seat. He pointed at Nussbaum's face.

"But you could forget a hundred- thousand-dollar debt and have someone else kill him."

"Never!"

"And never repay the family? A widow with a lot of children? No, Mr. Nussbaum, I'm not convinced you are a totally innocent man. People have been known to do stupid things over money," Colangelo insisted. He was playing the bad cop.

"*Baruch Hashem*, I am doing well now. Yes, I feel guilty about not paying the loan. I will pay back the loan to Mrs. Glick, I swear."

Sean waved his hand in the air. "Mr. Nussbaum, we are not here to get you to pay a debt. However, that is the right thing to do."

"I don't care about the loan Nussbaum. I want to find out if you know anyone that would have Mr. Glick murdered.

"I swear on my family, my children, I would never know anyone…"

Colangelo interrupted again, "Save it Nussbaum. You thought with Glick dead, you erased the loan."

"I think maybe I now should call my lawyer."

Sean replied, "I don't think that's necessary. We are keeping you as a person of interest. The FBI will keep this matter open with you until we find who shot Mr. Glick."

Colangelo stood from his chair. "Did you borrow money from Heshey Weissman too?"

"I didn't even know him. No, I did no such thing," Nussbaum protested.

"Agent Colangelo, I'll meet you outside," Sean said. The 'bad-cop' left Nussbaum's office.

"Mr. Nussbaum, I hope you are not lying to me. Tell me again. Are you certain you had nothing to do with these shootings…nothing at all?" Sean asked. He lowered his voice to just above a whisper.

"No. Nothing. I'm sorry I didn't pay back the money. I will pay today. I don't want my reputation to be destroyed in the community."

"I'll be back in touch with you Mr. Nussbaum. Let's see what we find about the shooter. I appreciate your time today."

"I don't think he's lying. Scared shitless but not lying," Colangelo said to Sean outside the house.

"If for nothing else he will pay the widow the money. I felt like a mob enforcer collecting on a loan. He's as innocent as you and me," Sean replied.

• • •

As he removed the magazine from his rifle and prepared to clean it Edward Olsen spoke aloud to himself.

"Two men, one woman. They need to suffer like I have. My father is gone because of them. The women have the babies. They all need to be stopped."

Edward, alone in the world, could only think of his own loss with no regard for the random people whom he had murdered. All he knew, all he cared about was they were Hasidic. They took his father from him. He wasn't even aware they were Jewish. Edward had no conception of God, religion or anything of the sort. Nothing else mattered to him but his father was dead because these strangely dressed people gave him Covid 19.

Chapter Twenty-Nine

"When you have peanuts, you make peanut butter," John Deegan announced to Vic and Raquel.

The three of them sat in the rear dining room at Broadway Bistro in the Rockland County town of Nyack. John, disguised in a thin gray beard, wore his artist Basque beret, a blue denim shirt with a gold ascot and John Lennon rose colored round sunglasses. No one would have ever suspected the short old artist was one of the most notorious international serial killers, still at large.

"I guess we are in for another Deegan lesson," Vic spouted. Gone was the normal sarcasm in Vic's voice when he spoke with his once upon a time serial murderer.

"We have shit on this case. We all know it. Those FBI jokers couldn't get laid in a Louisiana whore house with a fist-full of fifties, so forget them. The Ramapo PD are way over their heads. That leaves the three of us and we have nothing but a lick and a promise. So, peanuts…we have that at least. I've done some research on homemade tungsten carbide

151

projectiles. Whomever is doing this, making these bullets, knows his stuff around machinery. Right now, until this guy shows a hair on his ass, this is all we have. Let everyone else look at hate groups, ties to the Hasid world and that Rebbe with his Zionist insanity. Unless we find the bullet maker, we will be talking about the fourth dead Jew on Friday."

"You were right about the Satmar angle John. The woman was from the Lubavitch sect," Raquel added.

"Try to put yourself into the shooter's mind. For whatever reason, he wants Orthodox Jews. He sees them all as one," Deegan offered.

The old man continued, "Hold on a sec. Would you allow me the honor of ordering?" Vic and Raquel pushed their menu's aside knowing John was going to do the ordering anyway.

Deegan called the owner of the Bistro with a wave of his hand. In perfect Italian, Deegan ordered, squid ink fettucine, two large Caesar salads with extra anchovies, eggplant parmaggiano, layered with chicken cutlets and a whole, roasted Bronzino. From out of a two-bottle wine holder bag he was carrying came two bottles of 1997 Sassicaia super Tuscan wine.

Vic's eyes opened wide. "Sassicaia! You spare no expense Mr. Deegan."

"Forgive me for spending lavishly. I don't get to see you two very often."

"Anyway, this particular alloy is not your garden variety bullet. Our job is to figure out where it's being manufactured, and find the someone who has access to specialized machinery and equipment that can mold metals into projectiles."

"The State Police have a beat on a guy who indicated he may have knowledge or may actually be the shooter," Raquel offered.

"In that case, I'll fly back to Switzerland with Gjulianna after her family roasts the baby lamb this weekend," John laughed. "I hope it's that easy."

"Failing that?" Raquel asked.

"We hit the pavement looking for machine shops, tool and dye makers, gun shops, that kind of thing," Deegan replied.

"Shouldn't be too many in this area," Vic stated.

"Assumption." Deegan replied as he opened the first bottle and poured the wine.

"Divide and conquer," Vic blurted.

"You pick up fast my boy. I imagine it's someone that can drive here. Tri-State area I say."

"I'll have our office give us a list of those kind of...." Raquel started.

"Already done. I've broken it down to eighty-three possibilities. We start tomorrow," Deegan replied.

• • •

From the cell phone number obtained from the Vera, the blonde bartender at Crossroads Bar, Carl Schuster and a team of New York State Police Detectives ran down Ritchie and followed him for the better part of a week.

Richard G. Gebhardt was a jack of all trades and master of drinking. Among his many jobs, Gebhardt drove long-haul tractor trailers, did some masonry, home repair, worked for a moving company and did some tool and dye work. The latter is what the joint task force of FBI, New York State Police and The Ramapo PD was focused on. If he knew how to make bullets, Gebhardt could be their man. The fact that he belonged to a white supremacy group in Sloatsburg added to his person of interest status.

At four o'clock in the morning, armed with a no-knock warrant, fourteen members of the task force approached the six-apartment house they had been surveilling. A neighbor's barking dog woke Gebhardt who grabbed the Glock 9-millimeter handgun that he kept under his mattress.

The tactical officers overtook their prey without firing a shot, instead using their loud and repeated shouted warnings that they would blow Gebhardt's fucking balls off. They took the dazed Gebhardt from his filthy dump, cockroach infested apartment, in a pair of tighty-whities and a red Make America Great Again t-shirt.

The only weapons found were the Glock 9-millimeter pistol and a Colt AR-15 rifle. Boxes of ammunition were stacked on a table next to Gebhardt's refrigerator in his tiny kitchen. The pistol was unlicensed. A worn poster of Adolf Hitler was Scotch taped to a paint peeled wall behind the suspect's bed. Two Nazi armbands and other German World War II artifacts were found throughout the one room unit. A copy of Hitler's *Mein Kampf* with many dog-eared pages lay on a metal snack table with an ashtray full of cigarette butts and doobie roaches.

Shuster read Gebhardt his Miranda rights in the hovel, and FBI Special Agent Wright read them again to him at Ramapo Police headquarters.

"Mr. Gebhardt, do you know why you are here?" Wright asked.

Gebhardt, hands and legs cuffed with a cigarette in his mouth, puffed a plume of smoke into the air.

"No fucking idea."

Wright starred at him for a long moment.

"I see you're a Hitler fan."

"I'm also a Tom Brady fan."

"I didn't see a Brady poster in your room."

"Yes, I like the Fuehrer. So what?"

"How do you feel about Jews, Mr. Gebhardt?" Wright queried.

"Hitler was right. He just ran out of time."

"Your handgun is illegal, are you aware of that?"

"Yup."

"According to the laws of New York State, you can do jail time. We know you have a police record for similar charges and already did some time."

"That would suck."

"So, let's talk about what other guns you have Mr. Gebhardt. We have the AR. Do you own a .338 Caliber rifle by any chance?"

"Nope. Wish I did."

"I see you have store bought ammunition in your apartment. Ever make your own ammunition?"

"Too much work. Is that a crime too?"

"Not unless you use it in the commission of a felony. Tell me, Mr. Gebhardt, you've done some tool ad dye work. Ever have access to machinery that can manufacture your own bullets? Ever work with copper?"

"I worked for a time in Paterson, New Jersey. Made drill bits, stuff like that." Gebhardt lit another cigarette.

"I guess if you can make drill bits, you could make bullets, right?"

"Guess so. I didn't"

"So, have you heard about the shootings of Jewish people up here in the county?"

"I have. It's all over the news. The Shabbas Killer. Is that why I'm here?" Gebhardt laughed in Wright's face.

"We have someone's testimony stating that you led that person to believe you possibly knew who the shooter of these people is."

"I wish I did."

"Why is that?"

"To shake his hand and buy him a drink."

"Did you shoot these people, Gebhardt?"

"No. And I have no idea who did so if you want to charge me for this shit, have at it or let me the fuck out of here. I know my rights. I can sue, you know."

Wright ignored the threat.

"So, let's cut the bullshit. Why would you tell the bartender at Crossroads Bar that you knew about these shootings?"

"I never said that. If that ditzy bitch said that she's lying through her teeth."

"And you don't lie? Everyone lies Gebhardt." Wright countered.

"If you have anything on me, bring it. Maybe I didn't answer her question and she just ratted me out."

"So, you admit that you lead her to believe you were the shooter or you knew the shooter?"

"Maybe I did. Maybe I was just trying to get laid."

There was no real evidence to hold Gebhardt for the shootings. Wright held him under suspicion for forty-eight hours and pressed charges on the unlicensed handgun. He would be arraigned on the fire-arm issue and released pending a hearing.

Wright knew better than to believe the word of a low-life like Gebhardt.

Chapter Thirty

"This is what we are living with at the moment," Special Agent Wright pronounced. He was on a Zoom call with G.G. at FBI Quantico, Vic, Raquel and Mike Sassano from Chief Franks office at Ramapo Police HQ.

"G.G. look at the headlines of the New York Post," Wright held up the tabloid to the camera.

"See it? 'Shabbas Killer Strikes Again.' Every local television and radio station is asking what the FBI and local law enforcement is doing to protect the citizens. And get this, the head Rebbe of the Satmar sect is going around saying it's a Zionist conspiracy. Passover is coming up and there is a betting line out there that the shooter will strike again this coming Friday. Three to one odds that he does. Forget about the Facebook crowd where the anti-Semitic stuff is off the rails. We are the butt of all jokes. I'm hoping against hope you can help with an updated profile model and narrow down the field.

Gail Gain looked at the camera like she was just caught shoplifting at Walmart.

Raquel couldn't help but think, *"I don't think she's even showered since the last Zoom meeting. She's wearing the same clothes."*

After another awkward pause and a long drag on her cigarette, G.G. looked sideways at the camera.

"First of all, forget that whole concept of a Zionist conspiracy. The Rebbe has his own agenda to promote his narrative. Total bullshit."

G.G. continued. "It's obvious to everyone the shooter killed a woman to send a message. The female represents the future of any society. In this case, in the Hasidic community, procreation to grow their community is paramount. I've read that they want to replace the millions that were lost to the Nazi's. At any rate, this reminds me of the Atlanta Child Murders in the early eighties. Wayne Williams was sentenced to life for killing two young boys but we know he killed almost thirty people. He just kept doing what he did best even though the agency had him in its grasp. Finding him was the needle in that haystack and he finally got stopped by local PD which led to his capture. I believe this will be the case with this perp.

He will make a mistake. I believe it's a white male. I'd be guessing if I said he was an anti-Semite, but it's very likely he is, guessing if he is ex-military which is possible. His knowledge of weaponry and the physics of long range shooting points to that possibility."

"He likely lives alone and is socially awkward to the extreme. We know he drives a van like vehicle by the tire tracks he left at the second murder. He is bold. How else does he go to crowded areas to take his shots in broad daylight. Frankly, he would be capable of shooting a child unless he has mommy issues and that is conjecture at this point. In short, he will likely miss a few weeks and plan another shooting, probably on the afternoon of the Jewish Sabbath again. He likes to disrupt the tradition of the Jewish faith."

G.G. stopped to take another drag.

She waited for a response.

Vic cleared his throat and spoke. "So, we have to let him do his thing and hope he makes a mistake."

"I'm afraid so." G.G. took a few gulps from her canned Coca Cola.

"It certainly is not a sexual attack as with most serial killers. I'm sorry, I have to go to the toilet now."

G.G. stood and walked away from the Zoom camera. Wright dropped the connection.

"Talk about socially awkward," Raquel blurted.

"The line between genius and insanity is very thin," Wright added.

• • •

Vic and Raquel decided to get back to the hotel for a bit of afternoon delight. After a steamy session that left her relaxed and Vic falling asleep, Raquel spooned her man.

"Baby, I have to get home for a day or two."

"I hope you 're not getting spooked again with the Covid thing." Vic worried.

"Again? It's never left me. It's not that. I want to get home and see Gabby and mom. Don't worry. I'll get Pando to bring me back up here before Friday. In the meantime, I'll check out a few of the places on Deegan's list. There are three of four in the Bronx and Brooklyn."

"Okay my love. I think Pando should go with you."

"I can handle it. You forgot I was a cop when we met."

"Bring Pando anyway," Vic said.

They waited for a few more minutes before they started round two.

As they dressed, Vic put on the television and tuned into Channel Twelve, the local New York City news station.

The reporter was reviewing the Covid pandemic and the statistics on the spread of the virus.

The reporter spoke as footage of Hasidic Jews moving around in the county were on the screen

"The risk of exposure to Covid-19 in Rockland County is extremely high. There have been fifteen reported deaths In the County in the last two weeks. I'm told by the local Board of Health that the test positivity rate at a fourteen-day average is at eight percent while total number of new cases is one hundred and seventy, indicating that total cases are likely undercounted. Only seventeen percent of the total population have been fully vaccinated. Total reported cases so far in Rockland is nearly forty-four thousand cases. The Hasidic community in the county has not embraced the warnings of public officials to socially distance and wearing masks is not being adopted by many of the residents of Monsey and New Square," the reporter announced.

Raquel stood in her underwear, her mouth agape at the report.

"See? I fucking told you so Vic. This place is a cesspool."

"Wait a minute Raquel. Think for a minute. Of late the Hasidic community has seen a lot of criticism aimed at them for the spread of Covid in their communities and elsewhere. What if the shooter is angry, just pissed off at the Hasidic typical non-conformity with orders to contain the virus. What if he got sick, or someone in his family did, or maybe died and he's blaming the Jews? Look, historically the Jews have been blamed for everything from killing Jesus to the bubonic plague to destroying the German economy and the advent of Hitler.

It's may be a stretch but certainly within the realm of possibility

Chapter Thirty-One

Avi Nussbaum took the Monsey Trails bus from Williamsburg, Brooklyn to Monsey. The coach was much less occupied than normal. The Hasidic community were not enthusiastic to go into the land of the Shabbas Killer. Fewer visits from family and fewer business trips for the time being was the smart thing to do.

Only a few women were on the bus. In the past, the Orthodox women were separated from the men by a green curtain, so the men could pray and not be distracted. Now, that curtain is gone, the result of a lawsuit eliminating the old religious dictate. Gender equality had broken the barrier of Hasidic tradition.

Nussbaum placed a brown leather carry-on bag with one-hundred-thousand in cash on the empty seat next to him. He *davened* practically the entire way, praying hard that his guilt would soon be relieved.

When he arrived at the grieving Glick home, Avi Nussbaum handed the heavy bag to an astonished Hanna Glick. With few words other than saying his name and offering blessings, the flustered man quickly turned from the home and walked back to the bus-stop, praying every step of the way that he would not be the next victim.

• • •

In a small, four store strip-mall on Main Street in Monsey, Jewelry by Esther has been a staple in the Orthodox community for over forty-years.

In the narrow shop, Esther is behind the long display case of glimmering jewelry, greeting her customers with her beautiful, friendly smile and her well-coiffed auburn *sheitel* wig. Three other sales people assist Esther with items from exquisite diamond rings, rare stone broaches, and high-priced watches, to affordable ear rings and costume pieces. It's not unusual for Orthodox as well as *goyum*, non-Jewish patrons, to wait for close to an hour to be served.

While a young, non-Jewish couple from just across the border in nearby New Jersey were looking at engagement rings, Esther was with an older, Hasidic woman who needed her watch repaired.

"Esther, who can sleep? My David was walking two minutes behind Heshey Weissman when he...*oy* I can' even speak of it I get so *farklempt*," Riezl Hoffman stated.

"Terrible. Who could have ever imagined this happening right here in Monsey?" Esther replied.

"And *Shabbas* is almost here already."

"Please, my heart is pounding just thinking about it. Those poor widows and the children without husbands and fathers. And the mothers, oy." Esther held her hand to her ample breasts, tears welling in her light blue eyes.

Riezl leaned in closer to Esther to tell a story. "So, Esther, I know a woman who said she saw a van driving around New Square a few weeks ago. The man looked at her with such a hateful look on his face, you shouldn't know from it."

"Did she tell someone in the community? The security people maybe?" Esther asked.

"Her husband told her not to spread rumors. Not to get involved. She told the other mothers and they are all very nervous. All she remembers is the van was with not with New York license plates. Not even the color can she remember."

"But she should report this. They always say if you see something, say something. Maybe it was the *Shabbas* Killer, go know," Esther warned.

The young man with his fiancé who were looking at rings overheard the conversation. He wanted to say something to the older woman but thought she would think him rude. He works as a dispatcher for the Bergen County Sheriff's department just over the Rockland County boarder in Mahwah, New Jersey. He made a mental note to discuss what he heard with his supervisor.

Chapter Thirty-Two

Back at his home workbench, Edward was in total solitude. He counted the bullets which he made by hand, lining them up in a row like tungsten carbide soldiers.

On the kitchen table, along with a half-empty can of Broadcast Corned Beef, were unopened utility invoices for the past two months. His father used to pay the house bills, along with his business bills online. At twenty-seven years old, Edward had no idea how to do a wash, never mind how pay a bill.

But from the time he was a boy, his dad taught him how to use the lathe and make metal parts in the unattached garage shop.

Edward thought about a few things as he worked the lathe. *"I get only two days off every week. Friday and Sunday. This Friday they want me to work. Double overtime. I could use the money for food and gasoline. I want to drive up there and shoot the fourth one, but now I have to work.*

Maybe I can get one this Sunday, but I always visit my mom and dad's grave on Sunday and I wind up crying a lot that day. Especially for Dad."

• • •

On Friday morning, the governor took a frantic call from Rebbe Teitelbaum asking why he hadn't called out the national guard to protect the streets of Monsey and Kyrias Joel. In truth, the governor was seriously considering doing just that. However, the way the murder rate was climbing in New York City, he would have been severely criticized for not having a military presence in at least three of the five boroughs. He would have been accused of pandering to the Orthodox community for votes. Truth is, like any politician in New York, pandering to one of a hundred groups was a constant.

By noon, the Evergreen Supermarket in Monsey was virtually a ghost-town. Instead of lines at the deli section and at the row of check-out cashiers like every Friday afternoon, the store had only three or four shoppers. Most of the community did their Shabbas shopping on Thursday night to gather what was needed for the Friday feast.

The normally active public-address system in the store, announcing sales and specials in Yiddish was silent.

Even the poor, begging for some help outside the store, were gone.

The normal hustle and bustle on the streets of Monsey was gone. Most men decided to work from their homes rather than chance getting a bullet in their heads as they walked to *Schul* or to the stores. Indeed, it was near impossible to find a minyan of ten men at any of the Orthodox shuls in the community.

Children were quickly ushered home from schools before noon by their near panicked mothers. The corners where the men met to chat were empty, and no women were seen pushing their baby carriages and strollers on Maple Avenue and Route 306 or anywhere else in Rockland County.

Esther closed her jewelry store at noon. Not one customer entered the store past ten o'clock that morning.

The Ramapo police, still driving their RNP's (Radio Motor Patrol) cars, with their emergency lights on, reported no traffic to speak off on the major roads. Police were in full force, slowly driving around every development in Monsey, in every available vehicle, including their own personal cars at the departments disposal.

The fear of the *Shabbas* killer lurking somewhere to find his fourth victim had touched each and every family in Monsey and New Square.

The Rebbe ordered his armed Satmar security teams to stay in their cars at the entrance to New Square on Route 45 and were instructed to be extra vigilant against strangers, especially those who were driving vans. Rumors of a van had emanated from gossip mongers.

Monsey Trails buses were empty from passengers' fears of walking from the bus stops and being gunned down.

The normally vibrant community was in lockdown. The wonderful weekly festive *Shabbas* celebrations were now hampered by a maniac with a rifle.

Three families and their extended families grieved for their loved ones that were torn from them by a mysterious, hateful sniper.

The singing and the laughter around the Shabbas tables would now have a damper from the anxiety and concern of the celebrants. The elders would remember the breaking of the beautiful tradition during the dark days of World War II in Europe.

Little did the community know that the *Shabbas* Killer had to work his day job.

• • •

Raquel returned to Rockland County late that morning. Pando dropped her off at the hotel in Pearl River. Her investigation of three locations that could possibly have someone making tungsten carbide bullets came up empty.

She and Vic had a quickie before they drove to Ramapo Police HQ for an update meeting with Chief Frank and Mike Sassano.

"This is so sad, baby. These good people have a nice life they created and they really don't bother anyone. All they want to do is live their lives in peace and follow their religion. Now it's a freaken ghost-town." Raquel uttered.

"I wonder what the kids are thinking. This kind of stress can really screw with their minds. This can have long-term effects on them."

Raquel replied, "Can you imagine if Gabby had to go through something like this in her life? I'm worried about catching a virus and these poor people are worried about taking one in the head."

"We have to find this fucker," Vic whispered.

Chapter Thirty-Three

On Saturday morning, a huge collective sigh of relief came from the law enforcement agencies involved with the Shabbas Killer case.

There wasn't even a traffic summons issued the day before. Hatzolah was busy with their usual chest pain and kidney stone cases but other than a cut finger from cutting the *challah* bread, no blood was shed in the Hasidic community.

• • •

That morning, Ray Ali, the young police dispatcher who overheard the two women at Esther's jewelry store, mentioned the conversation to his supervisor.

At first thinking it was just two old Jewish women having their way with the Monsey rumor mill, the supervisor called the Ramapo, PD with the, 'ya never know' proviso.

Saturday during the day was not the time to barge in on religious Jews to question them about a murder case, but after sundown it would be fair game.

Chief Frank asked Vic and Raquel if they wouldn't mind chasing down the lead as his men were pretty much at their exhaustion point.

"I couldn't think of anything I'd rather do on a Saturday night," Vic laughed.

Chief Frank looked at Raquel and thought, *"I know what I'd be doing if I were him."*

Vic and Raquel drove the short five- minute drive from Suffern to the Bergen County Dispatch in Mahwah, New Jersey, to interview Ray Ali to get a full report on what he had overhead.

They had expected to see someone with an Islamic background. Instead Ray Ali was obviously Latino.

Raquel said hello in Spanish and said a few things that Vic didn't understand except that Ray said he was from the Dominican Republic.

"Ray, how did you get the name Ali?" Raquel switched to English for Vic's benefit.

My real name is Ramon Ernesto Ali. My great-grandfather was from Turkey. Muhammad Mustafa Ali was his name. But I'm also a mix of Filipino and Spanish from Spain," Ray said. Ray had a distinct Dominican accent.

Raquel replied, "Interesting. I'm boring, one-hundred percent Boricua. So Ray, can you tell us what you heard the other day when you were in that jewelry store in Monsey?"

Ray recounted, almost word-for-word, what he had overheard between Esther and her customer.

Vic jumped in, "Every lead is important Ray. You're reporting this was the right thing to do."

"Thank you. I hope it isn't just a waste of your time," Ray followed.

Raquel smiled, "We have nothing but time at this point."

Raquel researched Esther's home address from the emergency contact numbers of store owners in the district from Ramapo PD. At eight o'clock that evening, thirty minutes after sundown she and Vic went to interview Esther at her modest Monsey home.

At first, Esther was taken aback by the two private investigators who flashed their identification at her door. Raquel put her at ease, assuring her that they were only following up on leads regarding the recent tragedies. Esther invited the couple into to her home for tea.

Vic noticed a plate of *rugelach* pastry horns on the kitchen table. He was thrilled when Esther offered the treats. Vic took off his mask. Raquel left hers on.

"Esther, there was a woman in your shop that was overheard by another customer telling you that she knew someone, perhaps a young woman, who saw a strange van in New Square. We would like to speak with that woman."

"Yes, I remember the conversation. Do either if you know what a *yenta* is?"

Vic laughed. "I think so but I'm not entirely sure what it means."

"A gossip, a busy body. Someone who likes to sometimes pass rumors around. She is a very good person with a heart of gold but a real yenta, and a customer since I'm in Monsey."

"Can we speak with her?" Raquel asked.

'She lives in New Square. Don't scare her. She is a widow and has heart trouble. Her name is Riezl Hoffman. I have her address at the store if you need," Esther replied.

"You are so kind. I'm sure we can find her address," Raquel smiled.

"Esther, Raquel and I will stop in one day to look at rings," Vic blurted.

Raquel gasped. "You're kidding me right now, right?"

Esther roared with laughter, her beautiful smile beaming.

"I think it's about time, don't you?" Vic asked.

"We never even discussed this, Esther. It must be you!" Raquel announced.

"If you don't see what you like at the store, I can make whatever you want," Esther answered.

"I can tell you one thing, Vic. I'm not changing my name," Raquel laughed.

• • •

Vic thought it best to see Riezl Hoffman on Sunday morning. He and Raquel had breakfast at the hotel and drove to New Square. Raquel wore her double mask and dressed conservatively in a brown pantsuit, flat shoes and a head covering. Vic wore a pair of black chinos and a golf shirt with a tan sports jacket. He carried his mask in his jacket pocket.

They entered New Square and were immediately surrounded by a group of long coated, bearded Hasidic men. An old, banged up Buick regal blocked their entry into the community.

"Vus machsta?" A short chubby Hasid asked in Yiddish after Vic rolled down the car window.

"We are here to visit someone," Vic announced.

"Who someone?" The man replied abruptly.

"We are investigating the recent shootings in Monsey. We are private investigators. Just so you know, we are licensed and are both armed."

"So you are carrying guns and you expect us to let you into our community? Who are you here to see?" the man said in a strong Yiddish accent.

"I think we need to protect the person's identity at this point. You can call the Rebbe and tell him who I am. I'm Vic Gonnella and this is my partner, Raquel Ruiz."

The man barely looked at Raquel.

"You can leave your guns here with us."

"Absolutely not. I can call the Ramapo Police if you like and they will escort me," Vic answered with a testy voice.

The man thought for a few seconds and waived the blocking car away.

"Good luck with your investigation. Thank you for helping us."

"Not a bad guy after all," Raquel offered.

"They mean business. I'm glad they're are taking this seriously and not sitting on their asses," Vic replied.

Vic drove through the winding streets of New Square until they found the address they wanted with the help of the car's GPS.

"This place is a freaken mess. Look at it. Empty boxes and garbage and litter everywhere. Reminds me of the South Bronx," Raquel blurted.

"Yea, without all the Puerto Ricans," Vic joked.

Raquel glared at Vic.

Riezl Hoffman answered her door in a flowered housecoat, slippers and her head wrapped in a triangular scarf *babushka*.

"Mrs. Hoffman, please don't be alarmed. We are friends of Esther the jeweler. She helped us find you."

"Ahh, Esther. Such a dear. What is this about?"

"We hope you can be of help regarding a witness who saw a van come in here a few weeks ago."

Riezl replied, *"Oy vey ist mir* please come in."

As messy as the neighborhood was, Mrs. Hoffman's home was impeccably neat and clean. Polished silver glimmered in an antique dark mahogany breakfront. There was a dining room table with a lace runner topped with silver candle stick holders and a silver bowl which saw many Shabbas dinners. In the kitchen was a vintage 1960's kitchen set that included four immaculate vinyl chairs which looked like they just came out of the box.

"What is that amazing aroma?" Raquel asked.

"What, Pine Sol?" Riezl replied.

"No…no, the cooking."

"Oh, that? *Motzo Brei*. Eggs and motzo. I made for breakfast. Come, I have some left over. Come, eat!"

"I'm gonna be five hundred pounds if this case goes much longer," Raquel thought.

Riezl made coffee in an old percolator pot which Vic hadn't seen since his grandmother was alive.

"You are so gracious, Mrs. Hoffman," Raquel stated.

"Tell me *bubbala,* how can I be of help?"

Riezl put some sugar on the *motzo brei* as she spoke.

"We understand that you may know of a woman who saw something here in New Square that she was reluctant to report. We would like to speak with her," Raquel said. Vic was liking his second breakfast. He pointed to the *motzo brei* with his fork. "Baby, we have to make this," he muttered.

Mrs. Hoffman watched Vic as he sipped his coffee. "Such a handsome man you have here," she said to Raquel.

"Anyway, I told her it was important to speak up but her husband said not to carry on what she saw. Feiga Aberman. Such a wonderful young mother. She lives right next door.

After you finish, I'll bring you. I warn you she will not go against her husband's word."

Chapter Thirty-Four

John Deegan disguised himself as a businessman. He wore a blue pin-stripe suit with a white shirt and a sincere reddish tie. An American flag button in his lapel made him look more like a pandering politician.

Deegan's shoes were black and highly polished. He also wore a disguise of a salt-and-pepper goatee and moustache. The thinning hair on his head was the same color as his facial hair and was worn slicked back. Clear framed glasses partially hid his false, bushy eyebrows. Deegan looked nothing like himself in case at the outside chance some-one would recognize him.

He started off at several machine shops in Paterson and Passaic Counties, in New Jersey. The neighborhoods were awful and deserted. Those conditions could be dangerous for an older white guy in a suit and tie, however, Deegan knew how to plan for the worst. A .45 caliber SIG Sauer P 220 Nightmare, in a flex holster was tucked into the small of his back. His back up was a Recoil five-inch partially duel serrated switchblade knife in his front pant pocket. Deegan was trained to be deadly with a tablespoon, so he was in effect heavily armed.

Deegan was looking for leads to discover the who, what's and where's on homemade bullets in the region.

When Deegan stopped at a machine shop he would say he was looking for shops that could make a variety of projectiles from various metals. If he was able to tour the work area, Deegan would keep his keen eye out for anyone who looked suspicious or strange which was about eighty-percent of the workforce. In this case, however it took one to know one. Deegan could smell a killer from six blocks away.

Not until he got to B & A Lathe and Millworks, in Totowa, New Jersey did Deegan actually find someone that was friendly and willing to chat.

B & A's Lathe and Milling's best days were long behind them. The two thousand square foot shop looked like it hadn't seen paint, a broom or a good dusting in years. There was a lone ceiling lightbulb that cast an eerie shadow at the rear of the shop. The lathes looked like they were shut down for good at the turn of the century. The smell of lubrication oil lingered in the dusty air forcing Deegan to sneeze four times in a row.

Sitting in a large office at a bettered wooden desk with a lamp barely illuminating the space, sat a scruffy man in his nineties who looked as if he were lost.

Deegan knocked on the office door. The startled old man looked up and smiled widely.

"I hope you are here to buy this place."

"Well, I wasn't looking to buy an entire shop. I was just looking for someone who could manufacture some items for me," Deegan announced.

"I own this place. Well, I used to own it. We were very busy back then. I'm Antonio De Mazzo. Who do I have the pleasure of meeting?"

"Jack Roach. I'm from New York City. Looking for a manufacturer of bullets and other ordinances.

"My pleasure, I'm sure. I think we did that years ago. Some government work when my partner was with me. Can't remember his name anymore. He died right here in this office. I can remember back to 1950, but can't remember where I live right now. My son drops me off for a few hours just to get some errands done and get me out of house. He's a policeman, I think in Paterson…not sure."

"What kind of bullets did you make?" Deegan asked.

"We worked mostly in copper. Copper coatings. We were very busy, you know. The copper on the…," Antonio drifted off in his thoughts.

"How old is your son? Is he still on the job?"

"He never worked with me. He's a cop."

"He'd be pretty old to still be a cop, I think," Deegan stated.

"He's thirty or maybe forty."

"Oh, you must mean your grandson."

"Yes, that's what I said."

"Ok, Antonio. I have to be going now." Deegan said. He realized the old man was either demented or a pretty advanced Alzheimer's victim. He wanted to get out of the place and move forward.

"If you want bullets go out to Pennsylvania, Lehigh Defense, 130 Penn Drive, Quakertown, PA.

"You remember their address?"

"Of course. They made armor piercing tool steel and armor piercing tungsten carbide bullets.

"Yes, I know that company. Read all about them during my research. Big company. Let me ask you, Antonio. Anyone else you know deal in that tungsten carbide stuff?"

"Not with bullets but with other things. There is a small guy. I really do not remember his name right now. He used to come around a while back. He has a small shop in Pennsylvania. Nice fella. Younger than us."

"Do you know his address, Antonio?"

"I can't even tell you my own address right now, but I know where I lived in 1956. Three-sixteen Valley Road, Clifton, New Jersey."

"In Pennsylvania you say?

"Yea, Broomall. Near Philly. Would ya look at that. I remembered. Were you in the war?"

"Yes, I was. In Central-America," Deegan replied.

"That was a popcorn war. I was in the big one. WW II. In Burma. First Infantry."

"Thank you for your service."

"You look like a guy I served with but he was killed. Phil Leonettti. We were with Merrill's Marauders.

He lived in New York City, too. Maybe you know him?"

"Sorry Antonio, I don't know him. Thanks for the information. I have to go now."

"Say hi to Phil would ya?"

• • •

Riezl Hoffman led Vic and Raquel to her next-door neighbor's house. They could hear Feiga Aberman's children running around playing when the young mother opened the door. The welcoming aroma of chicken soup filled the air.

"Feiga, these nice people are investigating the shootings. They were just by me for a while. I think you should talk to them," Riezl announced.

Feiga starred at the two *goyum* before opening her door wider for them to enter. Like any good *yenta*, Riezl Hoffman walked in with Vic and Raquel. Feiga gave her a look of disbelief.

The home was clean, but messy from children's toys and books littering the floors. The children came to see the strangers and looked at them in wonderment. It wasn't often they saw non-Hasidic people in their world. The oldest boy, about six-years old already wore the *payot* curls twirling down his head under his yarmulke. He wore clear framed eyeglasses. The ages of the four kids ranged from six to six-months.

As usual with Hasidic women, Raquel took over the questioning. Her voice was muffled under her double masks.

"Mrs. Aberman, thank you for letting us speak with you. We are asking around the community to see if anyone saw anything out of the ordinary in this development within the last few weeks. We understand that you may have seen a vehicle that was out of place in New Square."

Feiga looked at Riezl and spoke to her inn rapid Yiddish.

"Why did you bring these people to me? You know very well my Aaron said I shouldn't speak about this."

"You owe it to the community to speak up. It's probably nothing."

"I will not go against my husband. You should know better."

Riezl translated Fiega's words to Vic ad Raquel.

"I'm sorry, I cannot help you," Feiga said in English.

"Then perhaps we need to speak with your husband," Raquel answered.

"Let me call my husband. He works in Monsey."

After a few minutes of Yiddish between husband and wife, Feiga said her husband would be here in ten minutes.

Vic, Raquel and Riezl sat in the living room, Riezl on a club chair, the couple on a long sofa.

One of the little girls, blue eyed with long sandy hair, as pretty as a porcelain doll, walked to the sofa and reached for Raquel to pick her up. She wanted to touch Raquel hair. Raquel enjoyed the child and allowed her to stroke her head. The girl then looked at Raquel's painted nails in amazement, touching them with her fingertips.

After a few minutes Aaron Aberman walked into the home in a flourish, his black coat waived behind him in his wake. The children, except for the six-month old ran to their father in glee, each one being patted lovingly on their heads by their smiling father. He led them to a playroom and returned. Feiga suddenly seemed jittery.

Vic took over. It was understood Aaron would rather speak with a man. He stole only glimpses of Raquel.

"Mr. Aberman, information has come to our attention that your wife may have seen a strange vehicle in the neighborhood a few weeks ago. We are looking for a man that may have some connection with the recent shootings," Vic announced.

"I don't think she should be involved with any of this. What if this *meshugana* comes after her next. We really don't want to be…"

Vic interrupted. "I understand your concerns, however, if we are to stop these killings we need the help of everyone in your community. Mr. Aberman, whatever your wife saw could possibly lead us in the direction of the shooter. Perhaps it was nothing, but I have one question for you. If the killer strikes again, are you going to wonder if your wife's help could possibly have prevented another tragedy? Another loss of a Jewish life?"

Aaron heard Vic's words. He looked at his wife with loving eyes.

"I must protect my family, and at the same time prevent innocent Jewish blood from being spilled. I'm sure my Rabbi would agree."

He turned to his wife and shook his head in the affirmative.

"Thank you, Mr. Aberman," Vic responded.

Raquel addressed Feiga whose face became flushed from nerves.

"Don't worry, Mrs. Aberman. Your response to my questions are confidential. Please try to relax. Now, can you remember what you saw with respect to a man who was driving around here that made you have some concern?"

Feiga looked down at her hands for a moment.

"I was walking the baby in her carriage. The other children were at home with my mother-in-law. This man, not one of us, was driving by slowly. He looked at me. He looked to me like something may have been wrong with him. A strange look I can't explain. Like he was looking through me, or maybe like he was looking for someone. I stopped walking, thinking maybe I should turn the carriage and run back home. He almost stopped, then he went forward. That's all I can remember."

"How old would you say he was?"

"It's hard for me to tell the age. Young, messy hair."

"About your age you think?"

"Yes, maybe a little older."

"So maybe mid-to-late twenties?"

"Yes, maybe."

"Was he heavy set, thin?"

"Very thin. His eyes seemed to me to be sunken in with dark circles around them."

"Did he smile at you, Mrs. Aberman?"

"No, just a blank look. No smile, nothing."

"Can you describe the vehicle, please?"

"A van. It was a van. Not a car. It had windows in the back only."

"What color was the van?"

"I can't remember."

"White? Black?"

"Sorry."

"And the plates? Were they familiar?"

"Plates? What is a plate?" Feiga asked.

"Sorry, that's police talk for license plates," Raquel answered.

"Yes. Pennsylvania license plates. They were Pennsylvania for sure. I remember seeing that. Yes, Pennsylvania."

Chapter Thirty-Five

Vic and Raquel reached out to John Deegan. The last they knew he was somewhere in New Jersey, or at least they thought that's where he was.

They called him on his special private, non-burner cell phone. They had Vic's cell on speaker.

"Abortion clinic. No fetus can beat us," Deegan answered.

"Jesus Christ, Deegan!" Vic hollered.

"Jesus isn't in. Would you like his voice mail?"

"Okay, Deegan. Play time's over," Raquel added.

"I have my favorite pupils on the line I see. So, a *Shabbas* without a killing. This guy is filling the profile quite nicely. Three killings and then a break in the action."

"How do you know he didn't shoot?" Vic asked.

"Elementary, my dear Gonnella. First, it would have been all over the news. Second, you would have called to tell me I was wrong."

"What are you up to? Any leads?" Raquel fished.

"I have something from a demented World War Two vet. He took too many shell explosions, scrambled him pretty good. I'm pondering whether to bet on an inside straight. You know me, I don't like to chase a card."

"We have something that may also be an outside shot," Vic responded.

Raquel jumped in, "We just interviewed a Hasidic woman who claims to have seen a van in New Square, with a strange looking guy at the wheel. We wanted you to know about it."

"New Square. Hmm, let me think for a second. That place is so tight our guy couldn't find a street with more than forty yards to take a shot. Too dense. But it's possible he was just window shopping," Deegan conjectured.

"Could be a dead end," Vic added.

"Tell me about the van," Deegan asked.

"No color or year, guy is mid-twenties, strange looking according to the witness. Van has windows in the rear only. Oh, and Pennsylvania plates."

Deegan went quiet.

"Hello? John?" Vic asked.

"I'm still here. Just playing a bit of chess in my mind."

"What's up, John. I hear you thinking," Raquel blurted.

"Looks like I'm going to Pennsylvania tomorrow," Deegan replied.

"It's a big state, Deegan," Vic noted.

"I have a town name and a GPS." Deegan ended the call.

"Deegan?… Deegan? What town?… God dammit!" Vic yelled.

"How the hell does he do that? How is he always a step ahead?" Vic asked.

"He's a damn genius, remember?" Raquel countered.

Chapter Thirty-Six

Vic and Raquel asked to see Chief Frank and Mike Sassano late Sunday night at Ramapo HQ.

The two investigators wanted to bring the Ramapo Police Department up to speed on the Pennsylvania license plate lead they obtained from Feiga Aberman.

Vic addressed Frank and Sassano. "We will have a detailed written report for you tomorrow but we wanted to bring this information to you immediately. Could be something or nothing but it needs to be checked out. We followed up on that lead you gave to us from Bergen County on the jewelry store in Monsey. Our investigation led us to a young woman, a Hasidic mother in New Square. She claims a strange vehicle, a van, was driving around the community the day of the second shooting. She can't recall the color of the van but she was certain it had Pennsylvania plates."

Sassano was looking at Vic, then quickly looked at his boss. Vic and Raquel sensed something was brewing when Chief Frank seemed to look uneasy. His face began to show patches of red.

A long, pregnant pause followed.

"We know about the van with the PA plates," Chief Frank uttered,

"How?" Raquel asked.

Chief Frank squirmed a bit in his chair.

"To be totally transparent, in early 2020 the governor approved automatic license plate readers for Monsey and New Square. We had a hate crime up here with a maniac who attacked a few religious people with a machete, and the Orthodox leaders put pressure on the governor to heighten security.

"We know about the case. Do you think we live in a bubble in Manhattan? The perp was a mentally ill man, Grafton Thomas. He slashed five people at the home of one of the rabbis at a Hanukkah party," Raquel seethed.

Frank responded, "Correct, and the governor ran down from Albany to see the Rabbi the next day and jump in front of the cameras calling it a hate crime, and an act of domestic terrorism. Fancy catch words. Christ, we have hate crimes against Jews twice a week up here. We collared Thomas who was caught by an eyewitness who memorized his license plate number. We found the machete in his car with blood and hair all over it. Five million in bail to a guy who is off the wall crazy. Next thing we know, it's a federal hate crime and news trucks and FBI are all over us like we are total assholes."

Sassano added, "Then the governor announces that almost seven hundred thousand dollars being appropriated to us for the tag reader system. Covid delayed the installation but it's finally operational. We have photographs of that van downloaded into our computer database. It took us a while but we've tracked the van in New Square and on Route 59 in Monsey on the dates of each shooting. We can show you the…"

"So why is this the first time you're telling us about this? That's not transparency in my world," Vic interrupted the detective. His slightly raised voice gave the impression he was pissed off.

"You must be joking?" Raquel added.

"First of all, we think this is the shooters vehicle but we're not entirely sure. The plates turned out to be reported stolen from a car near Allentown almost a year ago. Our people have hit a wall on the plates and the van. It's a white 2000 Dodge Ram. Do you have any idea how many of these vans are sold in Pennsylvania? Thousands! And we don't really know if the shooter is from that state, so add tens of thousands of these vans sold in the tristate area."

"Did you bother to go back six months to see of that van was in Rockland County before the shootings? This is what needs to be done, among a shitload of other things," Raquel said. She was on the edge of her seat.

Vic was furious, "Listen to me, both of you. We were invited to come up here and help find a potential serial killer. We now know that he is indeed a serial killer. Now you are withholding information from us that could be critical to help you solve this case. It sounds to me that you Chief, and you detective are looking to take the credit for a collar. God forbid the gumshoes from the big city get to the killer before you do. This is total bullshit and you know it. By holding this back from us, you are overtly risking the lives of members of your community because of what? Ego?"

'Calm down, Vic," Sassano blurted.

"Don't tell me to fucking calm down. You fucked up here and you know it. You got caught with your fingers in the cookie jar," Vic hollered.

Chief Frank lowered his eyes.

Sassano cleared his throat to speak.

"You're right. We fucked up, plain and simple."

Chief Frank spoke up. "I'm embarrassed by this whole damn thing. It's not an excuse but you both heard it when Wright said it's now a federal case. We look like Andy of Mayberry yokels up here who can't play in the big leagues."

Raquel stood from her chair. "This is not our first rodeo with the FBI. Everyone knows they're a bunch of credit crazy, media loving cock-suckers. Guys, that's not us. We want to help catch a murdering bastard, or if you want, we can go home tonight. We get paid for our time either way. No problem. What did you think? Gonnella and Ruiz were going to come up here and wave a magic wand and catch this prick in for-ty-eight hours? There is a process to collar a serial killer for fuck's sake."

Sassano and Frank were pinned in their chairs, both looking at Raquel with a sort of admiration for showing balls by going right at them.

"All I can say is that we're human. We make mistakes. We have feelings even though we're not supposed to. Yeah, we thought we could handle this ourselves. It's clear we need help, and I'm asking with all sincerity and humility for your help," Chief Frank declared.

Vic and Raquel looked at each other for five seconds. Vic winked at his partner.

"Okay, let's take a look at the photos of the van," Raquel uttered.

Chapter Thirty-Seven

Avi Nussbaum had bigger problems than the FBI at his doorstep.

Word gets around very quickly in the Hasidic community. From Williamsburg to Kyrias Joel to Money, New Square, Toronto, South Africa, Rotterdam and anywhere else Hasidic Jews are congregated and do business.

Nussbaum was tied to the Mendel Glick murder. Innocent or not, like it or not his reputation was besmirched.

Why did it take the FBI to visit him for Nussbaum to suddenly come up with the money to pay the widow for a loan he was trying to avoid? Could Nussbaum have wanted to eliminate Glick in the hopes of erasing his large debt to the deceased? Was there some other nefarious business dealing that Nussbaum and Glick had been immersed in?

Rumors were enough to assure the Hasidic community would shun Nussbaum and his new and now precipitously thriving business.

Suddenly his busy office, with the cluster of Orthodox women answering phones and taking orders was virtually silent. A few calls came in from creditors within the community looking for prompt payment on their invoices.

Nussbaum asked for his controller to step into his office.

"Jacob, what am I to do? I had nothing, absolutely nothing to do with murdering Mendel Glick. Some people won't even return my calls or texts. Even *mishpachah,* my own family. I will be ruined for sure."

"Three of the order takers quit this morning. The others are all asking questions," Jacob answered.

"What questions? I am an innocent man. I even paid my debt. What more am I supposed to do?"

"Maybe ask the FBI to issue a statement that you are cleared of any charges."

"They won't. I asked already. I called that nice one, with the Polish name. He said they are not a public relations firm and until the case is resolved I'm still under suspicion. It's *mashugana.* Absolutely crazy!"

"Maybe you have to go see the Rebbe. He can form a *Beth din* with three rabbi judges and exonerate you. If he does that it will mean something."

"As long as I am under suspicion, I'm finished," Nussbaum whined.

"So maybe we should close down the office for a while?" Jacob asked.

"That will make me look guilty of something for sure."

• • •

Chief Frank took Raquel's advice and ordered the technicians at the Ramapo PD to go through the laborious and boring task of looking through license plate surveillance tapes for any white Dodge van's in the vicinity starting the day before the shooting of Mendel Glick. Vic and Raquel aided the technicians with a broad assumption, narrowing down the video tapes from the main thoroughfares of Route 59, Route 306 in Monsey, and the entrance way to New Square off of Route 45. Looking for a license plate was relatively easy on the computerized system. That came up empty. The plate number came up with a zero result. Now, they were forced to look at any white 2000 Dodge van of which there would likely be many.

This exercise could take days to put together and no one was certain the eyewitness account of seeing a van in New Square had legs.

• • •

Deegan made his way to Pennsylvania in his rented SUV. He needed a new disguise, away from the pin-striped businessman look. He decided to make himself look like a Mennonite, a group of Anabaptist Christian pacifists that are often confused with the Amish. There were many of that sect in Pennsylvania. Mennonites dress plainly but not with the strictness of the Amish who do not even allow the use of zippers, preferring buttons alone. The Mennonites use automobiles instead of horse drawn buggies and churches rather than their own homes as the Amish do for religious gatherings.

Deegan Googled Mennonite community near Broomall Pennsylvania, and discovered the town of Ambler where he found the Ambler Mennonite Church.

Ambler was a mere seventeen miles from his Broomall destination.

Deegan purchased clothing from a store in Ambler. It had everything he needed.

Tan Timberland boots, blue Osh Gosh overalls, a couple of plaid shirts and a tan straw hat with a black and red two-inch band made him look like the average older Mennonite man who lived in the area. He kept his eyeglasses and bushy eyebrows to further enhance his disguise.

Only forty-miles from Philadelphia, Deegan felt as if he were in another country. He stopped in a German restaurant where he used his language skills to hear the dialect of German the Pennsylvania Deutsch used. Deegan enjoyed a late lunch of chicken and dumplings and a stein of Becks beer.

Deegan was ready to find what he was looking for, that is, if the demented old World War II veteran he met back in Paterson, New Jersey had had a moment of mental clarity.

Deegan had been on the road way too long for a man his age. First, he needed a good night's sleep. Deegan checked in to a Motel 6 thinking about his next move. He checked his cell phone noting and ignoring the calls and texts from Vic's phone. Deegan called Gjulianna at her cousin's home in Yonkers, telling her he was fine and enjoying the case he was on with Vic and Raquel and would be coming to see her soon. He then fell fast asleep.

Chapter Thirty-Eight

Vic and Raquel tried several more times to call John Deegan. Either he was intentionally not answering, which was entirely possible knowing the eccentric Deegan, or perhaps he was in an area that was out of cell phone range. Deegan was somewhere in Pennsylvania was all they knew. Bringing Deegan up to speed on the information about the white 2000 Dodge van may have been helpful in his search.

"I'm worried about him, baby. I have a very bad feeling about this one," Raquel said.

"He knows how to take care of himself," Vic replied.

"He's not getting any younger Vic. This shooter is slick. He's smart enough to change the plates on his van and he's covered his ass pretty good so far. The only thing he's left for us is the bullet."

"Deegan has nine lives, and when he runs out of them, he'll invent a tenth."

"But we don't have a clue about where he is in Pennsylvania. He has no back up and is totally exposed. He's out in the middle of the ocean without a life raft," Raquel uttered.

"Knowing him, he won't come out second."

• • •

Early the next morning Raquel and Vic headed over to the Ramapo PD to see if there was anything new on the white van status. Chief Frank and Detective Mike Sassano were already on the job.

"This is a labor-intensive job. So far we have nothing but a lot of tired eyes and frustrated technicians. Everyone is fully invested in finding this vehicle," Frank announced.

"If we had more technicians, we would be doing this 24-7," Sassano added.

Raquel rolled her eyes. "Are we going down that jurisdiction road again? Have you thought about sharing this with Wright?"

"We did. I told Wright all about the witness and the white Dodge. He offered no help and seemed to be of the opinion that it's an exercise in futility. He and the agency seem to think we have a shooter who blew his load at three killings. They also like the rule of large numbers," Chief Frank noted. He made an obvious smirk when he made the remark.

"What does that mean?" Vic replied.

"The more activity the shooter has, the more clues he will leave and the chance of capture is greater," Frank replied.

Raquel laughed aloud, "Tell that to the Rebbe and the families of the soon to be dead."

"Forget that bullshit. We need to get this guy before he strikes again. Look, we know from the tire tracks at the Heshey Weissman shooting that there was a van where the shots came from. Then the witness in New Square. It's the best we got other than the ballistics."

Sassano added, "And I wish we had something else more-meaty."

"I have a question about these video tapes," Raquel stated. "So can the techs program for white Dodge vans or do they have to go minute-by-minute, day-by-day on three roads until they see something?"

"If we were in New York City they could absolutely. They have a much more sophisticated and expensive system. Up here, it's not as specific. And let me tell you something. There are a ridiculous number of vans out there and we have to look at every one of them to match and cross-reference repetitive registrations. So far, the stolen plates did not come up prior to the shootings, but if we get a few hits on a similar van, we may get lucky and get tag numbers," Sassano lectured.

"Sometimes I'd rather be lucky than good," Vic added.

• • •

Deegan started his day at the Blue Line Gun and Ammo Shop in Broomall.

He walked in and went directly to the rifles that were lined up on a wall behind a glass counter where side arms were displayed in a glass case.

The store keeper came up to Deegan with a quizzical look on his face.

"Morning. I don't get many Mennonites in here looking for hand guns."

"Good morning to you," Deegan replied. "I'm not looking for a pistol. I'm interested in a hunting rifle." He pointed at the display of rifles behind the pistol display case.

"I see. I understand. I apologize for thinking you were looking for self-protection,"

Deegan added, "I don't condemn anyone who is interested in carrying a firearm. Instead, I simply advise people to live a godly life, free of violence and ask that everyone seek the salvation of Jesus."

"Good way to go. I'm born and reborn myself but I also believe in the Constitution," the storekeeper announced.

"Yes, otherwise you would own a bakery," Deegan chuckled.

"What kind of rifle are you looking for?"

"Something with long range capability, I think."

"Well, the most common would be the thirty-aught-six over here. Or a 308, perfect for hunting deer. Most people in these parts use one or both. Another popular caliber for hunting is the .270 Winchester but I don't have that ammunition right now."

"Yes, of course. In that case, I'd like to look at a .308. Do you carry a .338 Lapua by any chance?"

"Right here, second from the end. That's a .338 Ruger Precision Lapua rifle. It's got a twenty-six-inch barrel and is consistently accurate for a good shooter up to eighteen-hundred yards with precision ammunition. But if you're looking for a hunting rifle this may be a bit of overkill, and I wouldn't recommend that one."

"Why is that?" Deegan queried.

"Well, if you are hunting deer for instance, the .338 will open too big of a hole and destroy a lot of meat."

"Oh, I see. I'm curious, what kind of ammo does that one use as opposed to the .308?"

".308 can use .308 Winchester ammo of course and 7.62X51, but that's mostly for military use. The .308, that's what I would recommend. I sell the .338 Hornady Match 285 grain ELD. Not cheap, my friend."

"Like what?" Deegan asked.

"Comes to about eight bucks a round. I have .308 ammo for under a buck."

"Eight bucks? No, that wouldn't be for me. Reason I asked, I was reading somewhere about a .338 Lapua using tungsten carbide projectiles. That must be off the charts expensive."

"Insane. Like almost twenty-five dollars a round, something like that. I don't even carry them. That's for armor piercing use anyway. No hunter in his right mind would use that."

"You sold me on the .308. How much is this one?" Deegan pointed to the Rugar.

"Runs about fifteen-hundred. I can take ten percent off if you were military."

"Wow, more than I expected. Can I think on it?" Deegan asked.

"I'm always here, my friend."

Deegan smiled and shook the shop owner's hand. "I have a silly question for ya. On those tungsten bullets. I'm sure you can make them at home for a lot less that twenty-five dollars each."

"You better have an industrial type of melting unit. Tungsten has the highest melting point of any metal. My dopey brother-in-law has a tungsten carbide wedding ring. Cost him a small fortune."

"Anyone in these parts do that?" Deegan fished.

"Not to my knowledge, not for bullets anyway. There was a guy who used it for hardware parts. He's gone now?"

"Gone?" Deegan queried.

"Yea, Covid got him. Just a couple months ago. Big hunter. Good customer of mine."

"So sad. Was his name Phillips by any chance?" Deegan fished for the name.

"Gary Olsen. Good guy. Heck, he was only fifty-four."

Chapter Thirty-Nine

R ichard Gebhardt was still upset by the gun charge being pressed against him by Special Agent Wright.

He was also paranoid because of the on-again-off-again tail that was on him. Not sure if it was the FBI or local New Jersey cops or New York State Police watching him, Gebhardt wouldn't smoke a joint in his apartment or have a beer and drive home from any bar thinking he was being tailed.

The more he thought about the blonde bartender at Crossroads ratting him out, the angrier he was. He wouldn't dare go back into that bar, so he met a fellow hater, Chris Tripp, at Rhodes North Bar in Sloatsburg.

Tripp was a biker friend of Gebhardt who did a stint at Wallkill Penitentiary for throwing a Molotov Cocktail at a church rectory in Poughkeepsie, New York. Tripp had serious anger issues from being molested as a young teenager. He and Gebhardt were drinking Heineken's from the bottle at the bar at Rhodes. They both looked at their reflections in the bar's mirror, making sure their arm and neck tattoos were showing out of their cut off sweat shirts. They flexed their biceps and fore arms like they were about to get a stupidity trophy.

"I have to get even with that skank bitch, Vera. Because of her I have to pay that Jew fuck lawyer thousands to get the charges dropped and he's not even sure I'll beat it. He said the feds may give it to the state because it was not used during a felony and they can't prove I took the gun across state lines. All because…" Gebhardt drifted off from his thought.

"All because you were trying to bang her," Tripp noted.

"Pretty much."

"She fingered you as the Jew killer and you get busted on a fucking gun charge."

"And they still think I had something to do with it. Why else would they be breaking my balls following me?"

"I wish you did shoot those smelly bastards. Ya know I hear they don't wash but once a week and they fuck through a hole in the sheets," Tripp whispered.

"I heard that shit too. I don't care what they do. Just don't do it anywhere near me."

They each took a long pull on their beers, admiring their look in the mirror.

Gebhardt continued. "Chris, I can do maybe a year if they want that charge to stick. All because of that twat."

"I'll promise you something, buddy," Tripp hissed.

"If you go inside because of her, I'll bide my time. I'll just bide my damn time."

"What do you mean?"

"I'll get her alone and slit her throat like a little lamb."

"No Chris. They got more cameras inside and outside that place than the fucking White House."

"No one fucks with one of my boys without paying a visit to the reaper. I'll figure something out. Just mark my words good buddy."

Chapter Forty

Deegan decided it was time to call Raquel and Vic.

"Where the hell have you been, John. You had us worried to death," Raquel said.

"Speak for yourself," Vic quipped.

"I'm following a lead. You remember what a lead is don't you Vic? That's when you get your teeth into something and dig in until either it's a dead end or you hit pay dirt," Deegan said.

"Very funny Deegan," Vic chuckled.

"I'm deep undercover. I'm a Mennonite if either of you even know what that is."

Vic shrugged his shoulders.

Raquel replied, "They are like the Amish. Peaceful people."

"Very good, my dear. Vic, you get a D in Religions," Deegan blurted.

"So, where are you?" Vic asked.

"Somewhere between Philly and Pittsburgh."

"C'mon John. Why the freaken mystery?" Raquel asked. Her tone showed her annoyance.

"I'm a lone wolf. Don't need six-hundred cops and FBI with SWAT teams, tanks and dogs. This requires microsurgery. If I'm right, I'll send up a flare if and when I need to."

"I guess the news we have for you we should keep to ourselves. No man is an island, John. Cut the cloak and dagger shit will ya?" Raquel seethed.

Vic jumped in. "Look, I thought we were a team. We already had it out with Ramapo PD. Everyone wants to feather their own nest and I'm not playing that game. I'm gonna tell you what we're working on. We found an eyewitness who thinks she saw a guy driving around New Square in a white Dodge van the day of the second shooting. That shooting was close to New Square. We found a van on the plate recognition system. The plate was registered in Pennsylvania and came up stolen from another vehicle. It could be nothing but we are looking into any white 2000 Dodge vans. It's the needle in the haystack thing. Okay Deegan, I showed you mine, now you show me yours."

"I'm closer to Philly. I'll keep the white van in mind."

Deegan ended the call,

"That son-of-a-bitch," Vic hollered.

"I'm really pissed off at him. Total bullshit," Raquel added.

"All we can do is hope he's on the right path. I don't really care who gets the ball over the goal line, as long as we catch this guy," Vic stated.

"I can't believe it. Deegan was a killer, an international fugitive and we are counting on him to help us. If it ever comes out that we're working with him, we are totally finished," Raquel added.

• • •

Grand Rebbe Teitelbaum sent word from his Kyrias Joel synagogue to all of the Rabbis in the Satmar sect.

"In a few days, we will celebrate another Shabbas. A sacred day in our religion and our tradition. Shabbas must remain Shabbas. Our inspiration as a people is Shabbas. Shabbas is not a day to only feast our bodies but to feed our souls and to teach our children Torah. Never should we miss one chance to teach Torah. These are difficult times for us Jews. Very bad times. We must pray to G-d that whomever is behind this hatred will soon be stopped."

Privately, the Rebbe told his staff to be ever diligent with security. New Square was like a fortress with men stationed at the entrance and nearby the main synagogue. Patrols roamed in cars around the enclave. It was the same in Monsey.

The community was anxious that the Shabbas Killer would be back again on Friday to pick his next victim. No one felt safe.

• • •

That same morning, Edward Olsen, like every day except Fridays and Sundays, went at seven in the morning to his job at Lamonia and Company. It was all he had left in life since his dad had passed. That and target shooting.

The news that morning was not good. The firm had been hit hard with a Covid outbreak. The virus was running rampant through the plant so the owners decided to go into a temporary lockdown and all of the employees were furloughed.

Edward was not capable of processing such a sudden change again in his life and stood alone in the mill area, stunned by the news.

Frank Van Houton, the plant manager, saw him and knew the history of the young man. Through a N95 face mask, Van Houton's voice was muffled.

"Listen Edward, don't worry. Everything will be okay in a couple weeks. I'll give you a call when we re-open up," Van Houton offered.

No response.

The young man stood like he was frozen in place without emotion.

"We are paying everyone while we are closed, so at least you can pay your bills. Won't be long at all."

Nothing.

"Look kid. I know it must be tough on you, losing your dad and all. He and I worked together for twenty-eight years right here in the plant. He was a good man. Too bad you have no family you can stay with."

Edward just stared ahead, then his gaze slowly rose to the metal ceiling of the large shop. The overhead fans were still and the lights were off. Sunlight came through the high windows near the ceiling.

"C'mon now. I have to close the place up."

Still. Edward looked catatonic.

"C'mon now son. We have to go." Van Houton gently took hold of the young man's arm.

Edward looked down at the older man's hand and suddenly broke out of his trance. He pulled his arm away from the older man.

"They killed my dad, you know," he said, slightly above a whisper.

"What's that? No one killed your dad son. Covid is what got him," Van Houton offered.

"They killed him."

Edward starred at Van Houton for a moment, then walked quickly to the exit door of the plant.

Van Houton shook his head in disbelief. *"Poor kid. He's a mess,"* he thought.

Chapter Forty-One

Early Thursday morning, John Deegan awoke from a restful sleep, took a hot shower and changed into his other Mennonite type shirt. He checked his look in the long mirror on the bathroom door and he smiled at what a great disguise he had developed.

Before he left the Motel 6, Deegan Googled Gary Olsen, Broomall.

A bunch of People Finders ads came up with free trials that are never free and an e-mail and credit card are required for a trial membership. Deegan scrolled to the White Pages site and found what he was looking for. Gary Olsen's address. 620 Crum Creek Road.

Deegan added the address into his Google Maps app on his iPhone and he was ready for the 17.2-mile trip.

"How did we live before Google, cell phones, GPS, bottled water and Dunkin Donuts?" Deegan said aloud.

He searched for a Dunkin on Google and sure enough there was one on E. Butler Avenue in Ambler not far from the Motel 6.

Deegan stopped for a regular coffee and a plain bagel with cream cheese backed up by two chocolate glazed donuts. He needed to be fortified for the probable disappointment he was about to experience. After all, he was spending a lot of time on the word of a demented ninety-two-year old member of Merrill's Marauders back in Burma in 1943.

• • •

Edward Olsen was ready for another long drive to Monsey. Now that the Lamonia plant was closed due to the treacherous Covid virus, Edward had nothing to occupy his time and his brooding mind.

Proverbs is a book in both the Hebrew Bible and also in the Christian Old Testament. One passage teaches "Idle hands are the devil's workshop."

This passage was true for Edward Olsen's Asperger's driven personality. While working his full concentration absorbed all of his energy. But when idle, all that possessed his mind was that the Hasidic Jews took his father from him by exposing Gary to Covid.

Edward has no idea what a Jew is. He has no conceptual understanding about religion, God. faith, the devil or anything of the sort.

Gary had taught his son to drive. He didn't need a GPS. He could study a map and get to anywhere he wanted. He only paid cash because Gary didn't introduce the concept of credit cards to him. He didn't read newspapers nor watch television, so he was never exposed to news of the Shabbas Killer.

Edward could read a physics or mathematics book and apply theory to any aspect in his narrow life he wanted, that is if he was interested in the topic.

Target shooting was a passion because much of it is theory which is turned into practice. The longer and more difficult the shot, wind, speed, projectile weight, force, the more he was challenged.

Edward had no concept of being caught shooting the Hasidic people. He didn't change the license plates on the van. Gary had stolen a set of plates months and months ago. His registration had expired and he could no longer afford to carry the insurance. His business was not viable. Covid had put him in a position of desperation financially. The van, being over twenty years old, was on its last legs. Gary couldn't even afford to buy another vehicle and kept having the van repaired, just to be able to make the few deliveries that he still had

Gary did not want to return to work at Lamonia and Company, although Bert Lamonia would have welcomed him back with open arms. Gary's pride and ego would not allow him to accept defeat, even though his business had failed due to the pandemic.

Edward packed his duffle bag and rifle case into the van shortly after he returned home from being furloughed at Lamonia.

He had no idea that as soon as that 2000 white Dodge van was spotted in Rockland County he would be stopped and arrested on the spot.

• • •

Chief Frank and his department were gearing up for tomorrow, another Friday and the potentiality of another Shabbas killing.

Detective Mike Sassano, Vic, Raquel and all of the Ramapo Police Department supervisors were present at a nine o'clock meeting.

Pando would be picking up Raquel at three o'clock. She wanted to spend some time at home with Gabriella and her mom. Vic would be going home on Saturday if there was no incident.

Chief Frank started the meeting.

"Okay, first off all days off on Friday are cancelled. Second, I'm going under a broad assumption that the shooter will strike again tomorrow around the same time he shot the last three times. Around one o'clock. We will start the blitz early in the morning and keep it going until everyone is inside, after Shabbas, when the streets are empty. I want every man we have out on the streets making a big presence. I want two men walking the beat on Maple, Route 59 and Route 306. We need a larger presence in the community. I have clearance for the County helicopter to make routine flyovers above Monsey and New Square to add a sense of added security for the community. Special Agent Wright will have twelve agents, two to a car driving around the main streets in Monsey. We will be sending out a media release that we are taking additional action to protect the community today. If the shooter sees this on the news, if he sees an army ready to pounce on him is on guard, hopefully he will realize that his chance of getting away is nil. Every car we have will have a photo of the van and our men are all looking out for this vehicle. Every car will be equipped with automatic weapons and shotguns. I don't want our people carrying them openly. This is Rockland County, not Beirut. Any questions?"

One of the supervisors raised her hand. "About the media trucks that we saw riding around last Friday and the independent news people looking for sensational photos, how should we plan to handle them, Chief?"

Frank replied, "Excellent question. They have a right to be here. They don't have the right to interfere with police action. If there is a shooting, it's our job to keep them as far away from the action as possible. We don't want a situation with a sprawled corpse all over national news. It's tricky, so use your best judgment. God forbid the shooter strikes again."

Vic raided his hand. "Chief, do the officers have a shoot to kill order if the shooter is…"

Frank interrupted, "They are being told and It's the supervisors duty to reaffirm the command to use deadly force if the situation requires. We want to collar him alive if possible."

Chapter Forty-Two

Edward Olsen tried three times to start the Dodge van. On the forth try the engine turned over and the van started.

He drove the old van for a few miles before it began to billow black smoke from the engine. Edward was not yet out of Broomall, so he decided to drive to Gus' Auto Spa where his father usually brought the van for repairs.

Gus knew Edward and knew the young man was strange. He generally stood near his father, never making eye contact or speaking. Edward drove into the gas station and sat in the van, the smoke enveloping the vehicle.

"Hi Edward. Hey, I think you should get out before the smoke suffocates you," Gus hollered.

Edward looked at Gus quickly, lowered his eyes, opened the door and stepped out.

Gus leaned in and shut off the motor. The engine made a rattling noise, shaking the van and finally shut down. Edward stood quietly in front of the van looking at the smoke as it dissipated into the air.

Gus opened the engine bonnet and hooked the metal arm to keep it open. A strong smell of burning oil permeated the area.

"I told your father the head gasket was about to blow. Here, take a look," Gus said.

Edward stepped to the van and looked into the engine blankly.

"I can try to fix it but it's gonna take at least a couple days to get the parts and try to get it back on the road for you."

Edward shook his head in the affirmative.

"Do you need a car to make your deliveries?" Gus asked. Edward said yes just above a whisper.

"Okay. I knew your dad since I opened the shop. He was a great guy. That damn Covid! Terrible! Look, I don't have a van for you but you can take that old red Jeep over there. It's filled up and it'll get you where you want to go. Just fill it back up when you come in. Figure it'll be ready by Monday-Tuesday."

"Thank you, Gus," Edward blurted awkwardly, never making eye contact.

Edward quickly moved his duffle bag and rifle case into the Jeep as Gus and his mechanic pushed the white van onto the side of the station.

• • •

Deegan parked his SUV down the street from the Olsen home.

217

The houses were all older models, built in the fifties and sixties. None of them were close to each other and with the exception of a couple of the homes which had overgrown bushes and broken-down cars on the grass or in the driveway, most were fairly well maintained. Deegan went to the front door and noted the table with a small brown paper bag on it. The bag was folded neatly at the top and looked as if it contained something.

He peered into the front door side window to see if there was any motion.

Deegan noticed the worn couch and a covered arm chair that looked as if the seat had collapsed. A dusty wood table next to the sofa had a pile of papers that Deegan determined to be unopened mail. Two cans of Coca Cola, with straws sticking out of their tops also sat on the table.

Deegan pressed the door-bell which was on the side of the door frame. He couldn't hear a chime or buzz. He pressed the button again, placing his finger firmly and holding it in. Nothing. Knocking on the door, Deegan stepped back hoping for someone to come to the door or call out. No movement or noise.

Deegan walked along the perimeter of the brick house. Each window had its worn, brownish shades pulled tightly to the sill.

He walked over to the garage which was separate from the house. Deegan noticed some fresh oil stains, with a puddle of black on the cracked, weather worn macadam driveway.

The garage door was bolted with a large silver Yale padlock. The two windows on the front of the garage had been painted white on the inside.

Deegan went to the side of the garage where three large plastic garbage pails stood. He opened the tops of the pails. Crumpled brown bags with aluminum containers that held food were stuffed into the plastic pails. Deegan moved the bags exposing chicken bones and some spaghetti. The garbage seemed recent, not showing any mold or crawling insects.

"Excuse me. Can I help you?" a voice from behind Deegan asked. He was startled by the voice; his Mennonite hat nearly falling from his head.

There stood an older woman in a green cloth coat and a blue knit fisherman beanie cap. Her gray hair stuck out of the bottom of the cap like a sick porcupine.

"Oh, hello sister. I was looking for Gary Olsen."

"In the garbage?"

"Well, I was just seeing if he was home or away."

"Mr. Olsen passed away last year. From Covid, poor man."

"Oh, my Goodness. I didn't know. So young!" Deegan exclaimed.

"Yes, fifty-four I think. I've been their neighbor since they moved in. I was friendly with Ruth Olsen. Such a nice woman. Sickly though."

"Where is she?"

"Oh, she passed years ago. I suppose you're not related."

"No, I never met the Olsen's. I was interested in some metal lathing. I understood Gary was in that business."

"Yes, he was. He worked for Bert Lamonia for many years. He did some of that work here until he passed. Terrible."

"Tell me, who lives here now?"

"Their son Edward. Poor boy. All alone now. He is Autistic or something. Ruth would never really talk about it."

"Where is Edward these days?" Deegan asked. He figured he would ask questions until the busy-body neighbor had to pee.

"He still lives here. Never see him though. Goes to work early and comes home late. Some of us leave food for him every day."

"Good charitable Christian people," Deegan added. He folded his hands as if he were about to say a prayer.

"Truly. Even the young people around here are helpful with the yard work."

"He's fortunate to have you as a neighbor."

"That may be true but he has no idea. I don't think so anyway. I've known the boy his entire life and he has never said a word to me. When Ruth died I tried to comfort him, ya know, but he clung to his father like a scared puppy. Gary was a good dad. He took Edward on a lot hunting trips. I think that boy was born with a gun in his hand. Frankly, that scared me a bit. Especially after my Jimmy passed. But Edward is harmless. I just feel so sorry for him, ya know, being alone in the world and all."

"Where did you say he works now?"

"Lamonia and Company, right here in Broomall."

Chapter Forty-Three

Edward Olsen calculated that the ride from Broomall to Monsey would take him just over two hours. The Jeep didn't have an E Z Pass so he had to pay the tolls with cash.

He wasn't comfortable when toll takers said good morning or hello when he handed them money. He would stare ahead without responding or just shake his head yes.

When he got to the Garden State Parkway in New Jersey, Edward knew he was on the last leg of his trip. Just about forty-five miles would take him about thirty-eight minutes.

As he was driving on the parkway Edward saw a father and his young son in a car it the adjacent lane. The boy was smiling as his father was speaking to him. Suddenly, the pang of losing his father exploded into a desperate feeling of loneliness and abandonment. Tears welled up in his eyes and he began to tremble. The young man's stomach tightened and he began to sob. Edward visualized his dad teaching him on the metal lathe and talking to him before they turned in each night. The memories and the loss of his father hit him hard after seeing the man and his son in the car. He bit his lower lip and began banging his hands against the steering wheel until they hurt, then he wildly smashed them against his head in a fit of rage.

"Don't worry, daddy. I'm going to fix things. You said they gave you that virus. Now they will see. I'll make you proud of me," Edward said aloud.

After a while Edward settled down. He began to visualize the next shooting, going over his plans to hunt his next victim. He hadn't yet decided if he would shoot a man or a woman.

He thought the men had given his father the virus, but there were also women in the office where he delivered the specially made door hinges. Maybe he caught it from them. Also, the women were the ones who had the babies. His dad would take him on a deer hunt, explaining it was good to take a few does to manage the deer population.

Edward visualized the roads in Monsey. He knew where those people walked, with their hats bobbing up and down. He was thinking about taking a much longer shot this time, just to challenge his target skills. He knew what he was doing was wrong to other people but he didn't care at all. All Edward wanted was to remove the people that hut him by giving a virus to his father.

One time, with his dad, Edward had taken a half-mile shot, exploding a pumpkin they set up as a target. Gary took a dozen photos with Edward holding the gun in one hand and a big chunk of the pumpkin in the other.

Edward was a better shot than his father because he had a better understanding of the physics of shooting. Plus his hands were steadier.

Edward thought maybe because his dad had worked for so long on the different lathe machines so his hands moved a bit.

The younger Olsen would jump up and down and laugh with glee when his father would clap and tell him what a great shot he made.

Edward thought of a shot he might possibly make. He knew his rifle could shoot eighteen hundred yards with accuracy, with the tungsten carbide projectile. He calculated that to be a 1.022 miles attempt. The suppressor could affect the shot slightly so perhaps this time he would go for a body mass shot, he thought.

Edward remembered an open area that he could take a shot at that distance. His heart began to beat a little faster just thinking of taking that long of a shot. He wished his father could be there to see if he could make that shot.

The fact that Edward was shooting a human being and not an animal that would be eaten was of no consequence to him. These pale people, in their funny clothing and hats, with hair curls and eyeglasses had given his father a virus that killed him. These people killed his dad.

Edward's heart rate was building by the second. He drove past the last town in New Jersey, Montvale/Park Ridge Exit 172. In a minute he would be in New York State. Within seven minutes he would be on Route 59 in Nanuet.

This was the place where he envisioned his next shot would be taken. The intersection of Route 59 and the ramps to Route 287, The New York State Thruway are extraordinarily busy. At this intersection, there is the Spring Valley Market Place with two-major 'Big Block' stores. Cosco and Target, which brought in a tremendous amount of auto traffic. Traffic lights and circular roadways into the market place turn the area into a veritable circus of car confusion.

Edward drove the Jeep up Route 59 to determine a spot which was just over a mile from where he intended to take his shot. He watched the odometer until it clicked at one mile. Wide World of Cars BMW was the target area. On the other side of Route 59 sat a McDonalds and a Domino's Pizza store.

Edward made a U-turn at the BMW dealer and headed back to the spot that he chose. The shot would be slightly uphill from a knoll that was covered by bushes and small pine trees, across from the Market Place.

Edward parked the Jeep on the shoulder of the slightly used Old Turnpike road. He removed the .338 rifle from its case under a blanket that he retrieved from the duffle bag. He covered the rifle, making his way to the bush concealed area.

Wiping the nervous moisture from his hands on the blanket, Edward took a prone position and waited.

This part of Spring Valley was not an area where many Hasidic people would be walking as they do a mile away in Monsey. Edward patiently awaited his next victim.

• • •

The Evergreen store and the walkways on Route 59, where Mendel Glick was killed, were jam-packed with Orthodox patrons and pedestrians, buying what they needed for Shabbas a day earlier than usual. Being Thursday, the anticipation of the Shabbas Killer striking was not a major cause of concern. The Ramapo Police Department was patrolling the area with their normal, two-car detachment. They would be out in force tomorrow on Chief Franks orders.

However, The Shabbas Killer's, next victim would fall in the Village of Spring Valley and not Monsey, and today, not the hectic day before Shabbas.

• • •

Back in Broomall, John Deegan drove over to Lamonia and Company to see if Edward Olsen was working.

When he arrived at the plant, Deegan was met by locked doors and only one car in the employee parking lot.

Deegan knocked on the main door. No response. He knocked louder with the same result.

He decided to sit in the SUV for a bit to see if the one car in the lot had an owner who possibly was in the plant. Deegan finished off the last of his glazed chocolate donut and waited.

About a quarter-of-an-hour into his wait, Deegan saw the side door of the plant open. A man exited and was searching in his front pant pocket for his car keys. Deegan slowly opened his door and exited the SUV.

"Hello there!" Deegan declared.

"Hello, sorry the plant is closed," Frank Van Houton replied.

"Oh, I didn't expect you to be closed down on a Thursday afternoon."

"We have a Covid issue. Just closed her down this morning. Everyone was furloughed, including me."

"My goodness. Sorry to hear."

"Can I help you somehow?"

Deegan kept his social distance.

"Perhaps you can. I was looking for an old acquaintance… Gary Olsen. I learned this morning he passed not too long ago."

"Yes, he did. Another Covid victim. Good friend of mine," Van Houton uttered.

"I'm so sorry. May he rest in eternal peace. Does his son Edward work here?"

"He does. I sent him home early this morning."

"Okay. I was looking to give some work to Gary. I needed some hardware made out of tungsten carbide and I remembered that Gary worked with that metal," Deegan lied.

"He sure did. He was a master at that and lots of other metals."

Do you make tungsten products?"

"We have in the past. Not too much anymore. Mostly stainless steel, copper, platinum. Government contract work on spec mostly."

"I see. I'm curious if Edward can do some of that work on the side. Does he work with tungsten carbide?"

"I have no idea. He could I suppose but he's not right you know. He can't communicate very well, ya know."

"I didn't know that. All I knew is that Gary had a son. What is he twenty?"

"Nah, like twenty-eight. Kid is all alone. I have no idea how he's gonna make it by himself."

"My goodness. He's that bad?" Deegan queried.

"Bad as can be. Good kid mind you. Never talks, no trouble, just like…messed up. My wife says he's autistic or something. She brings food to him sometimes. The ladies leave the food on the steps for him."

"Maybe I can get my church to help," Deegan lied again.

"Good luck with that. He locks himself inside that house. Bosses wife heard him wailing one night. Like an injured animal she said."

"Such a sad vstory you're telling me."

"Yup. I'll tell you what. He won't even respond sometimes. Just stares into space. But he's no dummy. He works the metal lathe like he's been on it for twenty years. Smart as a whip with that."

Chapter Forty-Four

E dward was nervous, but only about taking the shot. He didn't want to miss a challenging eighteen-hundred-yard attempt. He wanted to somehow let his father know he was capable.

Wind, normally a key factor, was not an issue on this sunny seventy- three-degree spring like day.

From a prone position under the cover of a few shrubs and a dwarf pine tree, Edward took the Sig Kilo 2400 Range Finder and looked into the sight. He selected a car that was parked in the McDonalds across from the BMW dealership. Inside the viewfinder, red dots lined up the vehicle. On the bottom, right side of the screen flashed the distance, 1,766 y. *"Close enough,"* Edward thought. He knew the suppressor would not make a difference if he calculated the shot correctly.

Using the elevation turret on the top of his scope, Edward did the math in his head. He set the reticle to 21.5 clicks up.

The young man knew the physics of the arc of the tungsten carbide projectile that he tooled himself. He thought to himself, *"supersonic, transonic, subsonic, bam."* Those were the terms he used to confirm the bullets stability at the astounding distance. Edwards mind was extraordinary.

Now all he had to do was be patient like his dad had taught him when they hunted deer. Unlike hunting deer, a deer and most other large game can hear or smell the hunter from hundreds of yards away. Today's prey will have no idea what is about to happen.

This time he would wait for a Hasidic person to walk along Route 59 in either direction. A man, or a woman pushing a carriage would be his long-range target.

Walking toward Edwards spot on the East side of Route 59, the side where the BMW dealer is located, a short, slightly overweight Hasidic man walked towards the Spring Valley Market. Edward homed in on the man placing his body into the scopes cross hairs. Suddenly, a trucks engine backfired as it passed the knoll. Momentarily startled, Edward abandoned the shot. The shooter put his head down to re-gather himself. A few minutes later, Edward looked to see if the heavyset man was still walking. By the time Edward re-grouped, he was no longer at the acceptable range. Never would the chubby fellow know that a backfiring vehicle had saved his life.

Edward slammed his hand on the ground in anger. He had to wait a bit longer for his next victim to appear.

Roughly, ten minutes later a thin, tallish Hasidic man exited the Capital Realty Company office, about one hundred yards from McDonalds. Unknowingly, the man walked directly in-line with Edwards shot making a miss less likely so long as the shooters elevation was spot on.

He thought about walking to his home but instead opted to walk to the nearest bus stop and take the Monsey Trails that went west into Monsey. The man devotedly wanted to sit on the bus and *daven* for the fifteen-minutes the ride would take.

Edward spotted the Hasidic man, in his long black coat and black hat as he walked briskly on the sidewalk of the roadway.

The shooter honed-in on his target. He double checked his math, brought his eyes up to the scope, took a deep breath in, then let it out in a steady stream. When the air was out of his lungs, he lightly pressed on the .338's trigger.

Edwards math and his 21.5 clicks up were perfect. In 3.2 seconds, the time of flight, the victim was hit in the center of his back, his chest exploding into a mass of blood with pieces of his spine and heart spewing onto the pavement. He was dead before his legs buckled and he hit the ground. Edward saw his fourth victim drop.

Edward returned quickly to his loaner Jeep. No one saw him, no one heard the suppressed shot. No one noticed the old red Jeep with the Pennsylvania license plates on Old Turnpike Road.

After he got into the vehicle, Edward returned the rifle into its soft case and stored the blanket and the Sig Range finder into his duffle bag.

Edward got out of the Jeep for a few moments, jumping up and down in glee like he did when he shot the pumpkin and his father had been so proud and happy.

Chapter Forty-Five

The shattered body of the Hasidic man was lying face down on the Route 59 walkway near McDonalds in a massive pool of blood and tissue.

The Spring Valley police who had jurisdiction over the murder cordoned off the site with yards of yellow crime scene tape.

The Rockland County Sheriff's BCI unit was on the scene carefully taking photographs and measurements of the body and the surrounding area. They searched for the projectile. The potential sniper's nest was not yet discovered or determined.

Although Detective Mike Sassano was in another jurisdiction, he was called to the scene by the Spring Valley Police Chief for his consultation and advice. The entire area was filled with marked and unmarked police cars, a Hatzolah ambulance, and three media vans with cameras vying for a soundbite or a photograph. Cars from the Medical Examiners personnel and the van that would remove the corpse, along with vehicles from the District Attorney's office turned the area into an investigatory madhouse. Patrons from McDonalds and Domino's Pizza rushed from the restaurants to see the carnage and were moved back by the police so as not to interfere with their investigation. Traffic was diverted on Route 59 in both directions. Drivers from a mile in each direction stood outside of their vehicles waiting to see what the cause of the backup was. A sea of emergency lights from the police cars and ambulance could be seen by the frustrated drivers. The body and the gore was covered to prevent the gawking media from taking their sensational photos.

Frank Sinatra once said the press was nothing more than two-bit whores. He was correct, but he was off by about ten-cents.

Doctor Angela Rush was already at the scene examining the body when Sassano arrived.

Sassano knew all of the Spring Valley detectives and brass on the scene. One of the senior detectives, Jerry West, greeted Sassano as he approached the corpse.

"Looks like your guy again, Mike." West blurted.

"Head shot?" Sassano asked.

"Nope. Took him out with a shot to the middle of the back."

"Any one see it?"

"We're canvasing now. Looks like another high-powered deal. That's my guess anyway," West conjectured.

"This is gonna turn the County into a real circus," West added.

"No shit! Lemmie take a look if you don't mind." Sassano said.

"Be my guest. It ain't pretty."

Sassano edged nearer to the body. Dr. Rush sensed someone standing behind her. She looked up with despair written all over her face.

"Looks like the same M.O.," Angela declared. Her voice was strained. She looked a bit ragged from the stress of four killings in five weeks in her jurisdiction.

"Where do you think the shot came from?" Sassano asked.

"Absolutely no idea. That's for BCI to tell us. Wherever it came from, this bullet did a tremendous amount of damage. The body was ripped open to the point that his entire chest is wide open. I can't tell without looking further but it looks like his heart was pulverized."

"Any ballistics yet?" Sassano queried.

"Not yet, but I'll bet you a dinner it's a tungsten carbide projectile," Angela guessed.

"I won't take that bet doctor."

Shock waves spread with the news of another shooting. Yet another religious man, dead from a sniper's bullet and another funeral to put more fear into the hearts and psyche of the community.

Rabbi Kreitzman was notified by the Spring Valley Police at the advice of Mike Sassano. He got to the scene with tears running down his face.

The victim was identified as thirty-three-year old Shlomo Grunstein, a Satmar follower, real estate broker, a volunteer teacher of Torah at Kreitzman's Schul. He left behind a family of seven children without a father.

As the BCI was continuing to do their thing which would likely take four to five hours, Angela Rush gave the green light for the body to be removed to the County Morgue. The shomer had just arrived to watch the body so all bases were covered. Angela and her staff would be working late to meet the religious demand to bury Shlomo on Friday.

As the M.E. techs were preparing to tag and bag the body, three unmarked cars with all of their emergency flashers blinking almost in tandem pulled up to the site.

Special Agent Rob Wright and five other FBI agents exited the cars like they held dominion over the crime scene. In truth, they actually did.

Wright walked up to the body like John Wayne did in many of his one-hundred and forty movies. Wrights stern faced men moved around the scene like ants at a picnic.

"Hold on gentleman. This is a federal matter. Our forensic team is on the way. Fifteen minutes out," Wright announced. His voice was authoritarian. None of the Spring Valley police would utter a sound in protest.

"Agent Wright, the deceased has been declared dead. Rockland BCI is doing the forensics as you can see for yourself. I'd like to honor the tradition of next day burial," Angela Rush appealed.

"Unlikely. Not rushing this process." Wright replied. His answer was curt and left no room for debate.

Sassano broke in. "Hey, Rob. Why the sudden hardass?"

"I have no ass left Mike. I got a call from D.C. Got my ass reamed like never before. The boss said maybe I was too soft for the job. He said if I let the locals run the show, I'll be in fucking Albuquerque before month end. I'm running the show now. Plain and simple, Mike."

"So, you think you can do better that all of us together?"

"I have to. This is now a national, no an international front-page story. Clearly, it's a hate crime. And clearly, we have no clue who the fuck is shooting these citizens. I'm sending Gonnella and Ruiz packing. Seriously, and I'll deny saying it but other than looking at her, I see no value in what they're doing for this case. I'm calling in sixty agents from New York and D.C. I have Carte Blanche, full backing from the highest office. The White House is all over the Director and he's all over me. Mike, If I don't solve this case and Jews don't stop dropping like cupie dolls at a state fair, my career is done."

"Have it your way Rob. What can Ramapo do for you at this point?" Sassano ask.

"Just do what you're told on the investigation. The rest of the policing is up to you," Wright bellowed.

• • •

The entire Hasidic community was in full blown panic. Men and women fled from the stores and synagogues for the safety of their homes. Those who could manage financially were making plans to leave Monsey. It was seemingly open season on religious Jews. Many in the community were scampering for flights to Europe, Israel and Canada. Most were being thwarted due to Covid-19 restrictions. Many were making plans to go to Orthodox friendly hotels in Miami. Children were pulled from their schools by frantic parents. Countless telephone calls were being made to local police, FBI headquarters, FBI field offices, local and state government from town council people to the governor in Albany. The White House switchboard was awash with calls from the panicking religious and white supremacy wing-nuts who were happy with the shootings.

The New York Post online late edition read: *SHABBAS KILLER STRIKES AGAIN. Now a day early.*

New York Daily news late edition was less kind.

PANIC IN ROCKLAND. "No clue" on the Shabbas shooter.

Chapter Forty-Six

Sassano retuned to Ramapo PD HQ to report to his boss, Chief Frank.

Frank was in his office meeting with Vic and Raquel.

Sassano looked like he just went through the ringer. His countenance seemed down and his eyes told that he was a bit annoyed. His normally neatly combed hair seemed as if he hadn't looked in a mirror recently.

"Hey Mike, glad you're here. We just got off the horn with G.G. in Washington. She picked up the Covid virus. She was able to talk a bit from home. She was ranting on about how careless people are when they sneeze. She's blaming everyone from the office personnel to some group she belongs to. I think she said the Mensa high I.Q. thing. Anyway, she won't be of much help to us for the time being. Hey Mike, everything Okay?" Chief Frank said.

"I just left Wright and a slew of his agents. None of you are gonna like what he had to say," Sassano stated. He sat back in his chair and folded his legs still looking aggravated.

"Go ahead. Hit us with it. After this news, today nothing will shock me," Frank responded.

Sassano took a deep breath. "First of all, Wright has now totally taken over the case, and he made no bones about it. All he wants us to do is patrol, just like nice country bumpkins. The investigation is now totally federal. He got his ass kicked by the Director. Wright wants the locals, in his boss's words, to stand down. Second, Vic and Raquel, you are both out. He doesn't see your value anymore. Real asshole attitude."

Raquel laughed.

"Fuck him," Vic shouted.

Chief Frank stood from his chair behind his desk. "I'm not one to say I told you so, but I told you so. He's just like the rest of today's modern FBI. Corrupt media hungry scumbags who just want to make us all look bad for their own glory. J. Edgar Hoover is rolling in his grave. Check that, he's spinning in his grave."

Vic was smiling. "What we all forgot about the nitty gritty of crime investigation he will never know. I can't wait to tell my friend Lewandowsky what I think of the lot of those fuckers."

Raquel jumped in. "As far as I'm concerned, he can shove our deal up his ass. We are not leaving if it's okay with you, chief."

"Fine by me. Like you said Raquel, none of us can wave a magic wand and collar this guy like he's an everyday perp. This guy is a cunning murderer."

Sassano spoke up. "This shooting today may be a bit different. If my guess is right, and it's only a gut feeling because there is no ballistics yet. No hard facts. It's possible the shooter took a much longer shot than the other times. I looked at possible locations when I was down at the scene. I don't think he was on top of any building. There really isn't one in the area. I'm just thinking it could have been a shot that came from a long way off. If' I'm right, we are dealing with an expert marksman, who may be mocking us. He seems to be having fun."

"I have an off the wall question. Could the shot have been from a moving vehicle?" Raquel asked.

"Anything is possible but I doubt that. That kind of shot requires the shooter to have a clear shot with a steady hand. Look, I can be totally wrong about this. I'd like to hear what BCI has to say. Anyway, Wrights taken that over, too. He's bringing in his own forensic team. Next thing ya know he'll demand an autopsy," Sassano stated.

"I hope he does. I guess he doesn't remember when there were three-thousand orthodox Jews demonstrating at the coroner's office years ago because they were planning an autopsy on one of their own. I remember it like it yesterday. I was there. It was like a sea of black coats and hats. They had everyone and the governor on their side. He's fucking with the wrong people up here," Chief Frank added.

"Wright said if he didn't close this case soon he would be in Albuquerque. He makes this bonehead move and he's off to Nome, Alaska," Sassano laughed.

• • •

Deegan heard about the shooting of Shlomo Grunstein on his SUV's radio. He got an instant gut feeling that he was on to something in Broomhall.

Deegan was surprised and shocked that the latest killing took place on a Thursday and didn't follow the killers pattern of the afternoon before Shabbas. Deegan knew very well that many serial killers loved to follow their handiwork thru the media. It was an ego rush. He loved following his case on television and in the newspapers when he was on his own killing spree. He asked himself, *"Why would the Shabbas Killer strike outside the Shabbas parameters?"*

It could be purely coincidental that Edward Olsen was furloughed today and on a whim, went up to take another victim. But what about the white Dodge van? Deegan couldn't fathom how the shooter could drive the van up to Rockland County and not be spotted by everybody and his brother in law enforcement not spotting it. Catching this guy was equivalent to a PHD in law enforcement. It would be a career builder like none other.

Deegan ran everything through his computer-like mind. His mental game of chess took him a good thirty-minutes, sitting in his rented SUV, before he worked out the details. Assuming Edward Olsen was the killer, Deegan now had a master plan.

Deegan knew his limitations. He was no longer a young man. It was time he got on the phone and called for Vic and Raquel to back him up.

Chapter Forty-Seven

Through his English interpreter, Rebbe Aaron Teitelbaum spoke with the New York State Governor Mike Lappi

"Mr. Governor, yet another of my followers has been murdered in Rockland County. Three Satmar men and a Lubavitch woman. This is an unacceptable thing for every religious Jew in the world. I ask you, plainly, what are you doing to protect us?"

"Rebbe, first let me offer my deepest condolences to you and the entire Orthodox community. There is no bigger priority that we have in the State today. The capture of this madman is foremost on my mind. Every available person in law enforcement in the State is on full alert. I know the local departments are doing the best to try to protect every citizen from this killer," Lappi preached.

"Their best? That isn't good enough. We need more than what the local police can offer. We need you to take more action," the Rebbe hollered.

"Rebbe, you know I've been a big advocate for the Jewish people. Probably the most active for Jewish causes in recent memory. I can only do so much under the circumstances. As you know the FBI is on the case with all their power looking to end these egregious acts."

The Rebbe removed is eyeglasses, putting them on the table beside him. His normally pale complexion was dotted by scarlet blotches on his round cheeks.

"The *fakakta* FBI. You know from this word? In English, it's called crap to be polite. I hear they are so corrupt inside and out they are a laughing stock. Ha, the FBI! And tell me, in a month what has the FBI done? Nothing. Then today I'm told the latest victim, this FBI of yours delayed a burial of a religious man, whose family is already so bereaved, now they have to be insulted and their beliefs are mocked. I'm telling you, and hear my words, if this FBI man wants to do an autopsy like I've heard, you will see thousands of us protesting. It will not look good for you. We have been on this road before. And one more thing while I have your attention. Has the CIA looked into Zionist organizations that want us to accept the State of Israel or make us vanish as a people?"

Lappi responded, keeping his voice low, "I haven't heard of any CIA involvement. I'll look into that and get back with you," Lappi e rolled his eyes while putting his left hand onto his forehead.

"As Governor, you must do more. This can't continue. My people are fleeing for safety. Those who cannot escape the area, are in hiding, like we were forced to do during the *Shoah*. Hiding in basements, in attics, in sewers. We as a people have said never again. Never again will we be punished because of our faith. I am asking you now to call out the national guard. I want to see a ring around our communities that will not be penetrated by a hate filled individual or organization. Who knows? Maybe it's Arabs, Nazi's. And I want to remind you that we vote as one."

"Rebbe, your support has not gone unnoticed nor has it been unrewarded. Your want for the National Guard is understandable. I have considered it. I must tell you that it is not as easy as it sounds. I'm not saying no to you Rebbe. I will be discussing your request with my staff and with the military commanders and see if we can do something to put your community's mind at ease."

The Rebbe went on a diatribe demanding military intervention without coming up for air.

Lappi pressed the mute button on his desk phone and spoke to his Chief of Staff and two aides.

"I can't take it anymore. Not for nothing, thirteen people were killed by guns in New York City last Saturday night. Maybe we should call the Guard out and have them lock down the five boroughs," Lappi said sarcastically.

The Rebbe finally stopped his raving. Lappi pressed the mute button to speak.

"Rebbe, with all due respect, I need a bit of time to get back with you on your request. Please, I have your community's best interest at heart. There is bound to be a break in this case before long."

"In the mean-time what do I tell my people? Do I tell them to hide in their homes and only come out when this maniac is apprehended? Do I tell them to leave like their families were forced to leave Europe and before that Russia, and before that I can name other countries? Do I need to remind you of the Exodus from Egypt, Governor?"

"No Rebbe…you don't. Please give me some time to build a solution for us all," Lappi offered.

"Governor, I like you. My people like you because I say I like you. I hope I'm not going to be disappointed."

Mike Lappi got off the phone and looked at the three-people sitting in front of his desk.

"Don't you love being threatened? I can't blame the Rebbe for being so pushy. The optics on this are just terrible. I can tell you one thing, I don't want to be remembered as the Governor who was one of the shooter's victims. If we don't act fast, I can kiss reelection and anything further good-bye.

Lappi reached for his cellphone, scrolled down to Vic Gonnella and mashed the button.

"Hey, Mike," Vic said.

"Vic, I have the itchiest case of the clap you can imagine. What in the fuck is going on down there in Rockland?"

"Truthfully, we don't have much Mike. Only one or two bits of forensic evidence that leads nowhere. Besides that, the FBI just fired us," Vic announced.

"What? Who said that?"

"Listen pally. I don't want you running in there like my kid brother and making a fuss to get this job back. Frankly, Raquel and I are still on the case in spite of these suits. We'll wind up settling with the feds for our fee but the primary goal is to catch this prick now...dead or alive."

"I'm catching hell from the Rebbe, Vic. You have no idea!"

"Yea I do. I sat with him recently. Between us, he's a whack-a-do. This whole Zionist thing is Twilight Zone stuff."

"But he's as powerful as they come," Lappi retorted. "And who knows? Maybe the shooter is indeed part of that crowd. Until we catch him, he could be one of a hundred different groups that hates Jews."

"See how smart you are. That kind of judgement will put you in the White House. Me, I'll wind up in the out-house," Vic laughed. Lappi did too.

Chapter Forty-Eight

Vic and Raquel were at the Ramapo Police Headquarters flipping back and forth on the various news channels that were broadcasting the latest events from Spring Valley.

With them were Chief Frank and a grim looking Mike Sassano who was still smarting from his talk with Agent Wright.

"What a mess. The aerial shot makes the area look real small," Sassano blurted. He was referring to a news helicopters view of the crime scene.

"That gives me an idea. Let's get a map of Spring Valley up on the computer screen. I think we need to at least take some assumptions on where the shot came from," Raquel offered.

Chief Frank said, "Great idea. Maybe we are taking a back seat to the FBI guys but I'd rather be thinking than watching."

Vic's cell phone rang. It was John Deegan.

"Hi my pupil. Can you talk?" Deegan asked.

"I can listen," Vic replied.

"Raquel there?"

"Yea, I'll have to tell her later."

"Okay, gotcha. Too many ears. Just listen then. Vic, I think I may be on to something out here. Long story but if I'm correct, which of course I normally am, what did I say, ninety-something percentile? If I'm correct I may have a beat on the shooter. I have to connect the dots but it may be worth a trip for you guys to get out here,"

"Where's that? "Vic replied. He had his best poker face not to give up anything to Frank and Sassano.

"Broomall, Pennsylvania. Not far from Philly."

"Really? Are you okay?"

"I found a guy. Well he's as dead as Kelsey's nuts, but he worked with tungsten carbide. He worked for a metal lathing company over here for years and had a home shop. His son may know how to fabricate bullets."

"Did you call the doctor?" Vic hinted.

"I haven't put eyes on the machinery yet but it's likely the real deal. The dead guy fabricated tungsten parts. It's a gut feeling but the kid may be of interest. I can text you the names," Deegan offered.

"Okay. I'll check out that joint."

"Call me when you have something. I think I may need backup on this one kiddo. Not a spring chicken anymore. But I have a plan.to get inside."

"Don't do that by yourself, Dad,"

Deegan replied "Gotcha. Let me know when you have something. Can you get here before dark?"

"Sure thing Dad." The phone went dead.

Raquel's puzzled look spoke volumes. Vic's father was long dead.

"Raquel, we gotta go, my dad has a problem," Vic declared. Raquel knew it was Deegan.

"Everything all-right?" Frank asked.

"Not sure. He has a little dementia. We'll be back tomorrow," Vic lied.

The couple left the office and headed for their car.

"What the hell is going on?" Raquel asked. Her eyes were as big as saucers waiting for an answer."

"Deegan thinks he has something. He's gonna text intel." Vic replied. "We're headed for Broomhall, It's near Philadelphia.'"

"Philadelphia?"

"Think about it for a second," Vic hinted."

"Fuck! Pennsylvania license plates," Raquel answered.

"Yup. Wait a sec… here's a text from Deegan. *Gary and Edward Olsen. When you get near Broomall text for a meeting place. Don't call'*.

Vic punched in the information into the cars GPS. Suffern, New York to Broomall.

"Two hours, twenty-two minutes. Unless we have to pee," Vic said.

"I'm good. You can use a bottle," Raquel replied.

• • •

Edward Olsen was giddy. He was so pleased that he made the almost one mile shot that he was snort laughing. "See daddy...see, I knew I could do it. I knew it. You used to tell me I was a good shot," he said aloud.

He drove down Route 59 to make a U-turn to get on the highway and saw a White Castle hamburger place. Gary had taken him to the Whitehall, Pennsylvania White Castle a few times when they went on a hunting trip. Edward remembered how fun it was to eat those small burgers with his dad and count the little boxes to see how many they ate.

Edward pulled in, parked the car and went inside. He wouldn't use the drive-thru because he didn't want to speak into the machine to place an order.

The masked lady behind the plexi-glass order window looked at Edward.

"Sir, you need to wear a mask," she said in a Haitian accent.

Edward looked at her and didn't move.

"Sorry, but you can't order without your mask."

Edward put both his hands up in front of his face and offered his ten fingers. He pointed to the burgers. He wanted ten of the White Castles. His dad used to call them 'belly bombers' and laugh.

The Haitian woman could tell there was something wrong with the young man and took pity on him. She decided to serve him without his mask.

"Okay, sweetie. That will be seven-eighty please," the woman said.

Edward reached into his pocket and took out seven dollars and slowly counted eight cents.

"You are number twelve. But I will call you when the order is ready." *"Pov ti gason,"* she thought. Poor boy.

Edward took his burgers back to the Jeep. He opened the bag and the oniony aroma wafted up to his face. He recalled how much his dad loved the unique smell of his belly bombers. He took one of the small flat burgers and stuffed the whole thing into his mouth. He was happy to remember his dad when they were laughing and happy. He started the Jeep and headed toward the highway. He could see the traffic backing up on Route 59. A few police cars with lights and sirens blaring passed him on the left heading toward the dead man left on the walkway. Edward thought nothing more of it as he took the exit for Route 287.

Chapter Forty-Nine

Edward Olsen left Rockland County for Broomall just about the same time Vic and Raquel did.

While Vic drove, Raquel was on the phone with their office running Gary and Edward Olsen's background and police records.

Edward didn't come up at all. No credit, property, court hearings, licenses or criminal records. No social media, nothing. There was a social security number on file but other than that, Edward Olsen was a non-person.

Gary came up with a few interesting red flags, but nothing that was earth-shattering. He had one Driving While Intoxicated charge that was dismissed about twenty-three years ago. The DWI took place in Delaware County, Pennsylvania, which happens to be where Broomall is located. The reason for the dismissal was not reported. That would take more time and a lot of digging to uncover.

Gary's records also showed the town of Broomall had an open lien on the property at 620 Crum Creek Road for unpaid land and property taxes. His credit rating was poor at 420. He also had a pistol carry permit and three registered side-arms.

There was also a corporation listed at that same address in Broomall, Olsen and Son, LLC. It was terminated upon the death of Gary Olsen.

"I don't think we should go right to this address when we get to Broomall," Vic stated. "Deegan was specific that we should text him when we get near."

"Yup, who knows what he has planned. We just can't knock on the door to see if Edward Olsen is there or if he even lives there anymore."

"Deegan's not even exactly sure if this is our perp. I'm just happy we aren't driving to the asshole end of Pennsylvania," Vic added.

Raquel paused for a few seconds.

"Hmmm, Pennsylvania. That's probably why he disguised himself as a Mennonite. There are a good amount of those folks in that state. Who would think that a multiple murder serial killer would make believe he was a religious pacifist."

"That's Deegan for ya," Vic responded.

Vic's cell phone rang. The name came up on the car's screen. Mike Sassano.

"Hey Mike, what's going on up there. Raquel is on the speaker with us."

"Good. We may have something big guys. Our license plate video technicians finally found something on the Dodge van. They tracked a van fitting the description and year. Seems that van was up in the county a few times. It has a different Pennsylvania license plate. We tracked it to a shop in Monsey. Tov Affordable Doors. It's in an industrial park in town. I'm heading over there now to do a check in. Van is registered to a Gary Olsen in a town called Broomall. I'm going to contact Pennsylvania State Police to take a looksee

Vic and Raquel looked at each other in amazement. Raquel mouthed, "FUCK!"

"Hey Mike. You trust us?"

"Absolutely, no question about it," Sassano replied.

"First off. I bullshitted you about my father. He's been dead for years. That was my guy on the phone and I didn't want to show our hand."

"Thanks. No big deal. I've done it many times myself," Sassano replied

"Good, I'm glad I got that off my chest. Then I'm going to ask you for a big favor. Hold off calling the State police for a bit. One of our operatives is on this Olsen lead already. Matter of fact we are heading there now to meet up with him. He's deep undercover and I don't think calling in the cavalry right now is the best move," Vic asked.

"Same guy on Crum Creek Road?"

"Roger that."

"Holy shit!" Sassano uttered.

"Gary Olsen, the owner of those plates is dead. He had a son that may live there now who can possibly be our guy. We promise you that if anything comes of this, you and your department will get full credit. This way, you are the guys who break the case and they will stop calling your department Andy of Mayberry," Vic added.

"I'm with you."

Vic replied. "One more thing, Mike. I hope you haven't already, but keep Wright and his FBI guys in the dark on this."

"I wouldn't piss on him if he was on fire. Fuck that prick. Sorry Raquel."

Chapter Fifty

As Vic and Raquel raced to Broomall and Edward Olsen drove under the speed limit back home, Richard Gebhardt met his ex-con friend Chris Tripp at the Rhodes North Bar on Sloatsburg.

Rhodes was empty. They had the bar to themselves. Rhodes was between the busy lunch crowd and dinner service.

"You still being tailed?" Tripp asked.

"I'm so fucking paranoid. I look in my rear-view every ten seconds. The other day a cop car was behind me and I was sure they would pull me over and harass me. To answer your question, I don't know but I assume they are," Gebhardt answered.

"Listen up. I'm taking off for Arizona. I got a friend who owns a big body shop in Scottsdale. He's killin it. Big money out there. He's offered me a job. I just wanna get out of this fucking area. Start a new life out there. So, I was thinkin. Let me take that twat out before I drive out there. She deserves it fingering you for these Jew killings," Trip said.

"I just got a court date for the gun charge. The state took over the case from the feds. My lawyer say's I'll probably get a year. It's sucks the big one."

"She's a whore. It will look like someone slit her throat when they were trying to bang her. I'll leave some coke behind to throw them off. They won't think it was you. Especially if you have an airtight alibi, ya know. Be in a public place with a lot of people who see you. And if they are following you, even better."

"I don't know Chris. I'd like to forget the whole thing," Gebhardt said.

"Look, when you are doing time in a Jersey prison with all those coons and spicks, you'll wish you had. It's getting even, dude."

"Lemmie think about it."

"I'm packing my shit and leaving in five days. Don't wait too long," Trip advised.

• • •

Edward Olsen wasn't even enjoying the beautiful scenery on his trip back to Broomall. The trees and bushes were beginning to bloom and the colors of some of the highway flora on this beautiful, sun-lit day were stunning.

Edward was fixated on stopping at a few of the places his dad had taken him over the years. He wanted to sit by a certain stream where he and his father would sometimes fish. He wished he has brought his fishing rod and some tackle and bait to maybe catch a few trout. Gary would cook up any fish they caught and they would enjoy their dinner, and the next day's lunch while his dad would tell him what a great fisherman they both were.

He was so lonely at home that he was in no rush to get back to the house. As of late, he had started to look into the room where his father died, never entering it, but starring at his dad's death bed. He also started avoiding the kitchen again. He began looking at the kitchen floor where years ago he found his mother dead on the floor. Most nights since Gary passed, Edward would cry himself asleep with his text books lined up on the bed and the remaining tungsten carbide bullets that he made under the covers.

When he reached the trout stream, Edward sat on the ground next to the water day dreaming about his dad and he, fishing for the big ones. He could see the trout going into attack mode feeding on the caddis flies, splashing and fluttering as they ate. He started counting how many fish he saw feeding and laughed when a big one nearly jumped out of the clear stream.

Edward spoke aloud. "Daddy, we could have caught so many today. If it wasn't for those people who gave you the virus, we would have had a great meal together. Anyway, I got another one today. I'll be going back out there when the van is ready."

Chapter Fifty-One

Hanna Glick was sitting on a lounge chair in the backyard of her Maple Avenue home in Monsey. She was stifling the sound of her sobs into a terry cloth kitchen towel. The children didn't need to see another tear from their mother's eyes.

She was resting her aching back and sore feet from running to the schools to gather her children after she received word that another Satmar member was shot dead today.

Hanna, now eight months pregnant, didn't think the baby would wait another four weeks.

Her mother saw her dabbing her eyes from the kitchen window and quickly made her way to her daughter. She carried a folding chair from the kitchen with her and placed it next to the lounge.

"This is a very hard life mama," Hanna whimpered.

"I can only agree."

"And today, I thought I would lose my mind rushing to get the children. After I hear of another shooting, this time on a Thursday, I thought none of us are safe here anymore. Never once did I think of the widow and children and what they are feeling, and what's coming in the future," Hanna said.

"So…now you have a chance to think, and your heart reaches out to the family. You are a good person daughter."

"It feels like a wound has been ripped open. I remember the night Mendel was late for Shabbas. When I think…when I think about the police coming to our door. Now another poor woman has to get that visit, and her tears will flow until they make an ocean."

"The Talmud tells us, "Be careful if you make a woman cry because God counts her tears.""

"The Talmud. I feel like I've lived my life listening to Talmud and parables and six hundred and thirteen commandments to tell me what to do, what to think, how to behave, what not to do. Mama, I'm sick of this already," Hanna blurted.

"Bite your tongue. That is not how I taught you, Hanna."

Hanna sat up on the lounge. "And this baby inside me. I think he is coming very soon. Why does he want to rush out into a world like this? He's better off not being born."

"*Kein ayin hora,*" her mother shouted.

"More superstition. More nonsense to keep the evil away. I want to gather myself and the children and run. Just run away from these chains of this so-called faith."

"This is just a set-back for you. Trust me Hanna, the baby will be born. If it's a boy we will have his briss, and the children will help with the baby. It's another blessing. Your life will go on and the family will flourish."

"How can we flourish? How can we go on pretending that Hashem is watching our every move? Mendel was taken from us in the blink of an eye. Mama, let me tell you what I did last week. I broke the Rebbe's order. I went on the internet. They don't want us to learn because they want to control our thinking and our lives. I've had enough of this life," Hanna yelled.

"The internet Hanna? That is forbidden."

"This is forbidden, that is forbidden. This is allowed that is not allowed. I learned how to look up information. There is an entire world outside of the Rebbe and Monsey. I wanted to know about what being born is about. I found a quote. A German, Nietzsche. He said 'The best of all things is something entirely outside your grasp: not to be born, not to be, to be nothing. But the second-best thing for you is to die soon.' Maybe that is best for this baby. Not to live in this torturous world," Hanna preached.

"A Nazi!" Mama yelled.

"No mama, he was alive long before Hitler. I'm trying to make a point."

"He's still a Nazi! This is all blasphemy. What would Mendel think? He wanted his family to follow the Rebbe. To follow our faith.

"I am no longer following blindly. Not for anyone and certainly not for a dead husband's memory. I want to be free of this craziness. I don't want my children to have a target on them because they are religious. I hear so many women are leaving us. Especially in Brooklyn. Why? Because they don't want to be told how to live. They want to find their own way in this world," Hanna announced.

"I can't believe my own ears. I think we should send for the Rabbi. He will know how to calm you."

"I'm not interested in seeing the Rabbi. He will quote Talmud, tell me Hashem will look over us and all that other stuff just to keep us in line with this thinking,"

"Hanna, you will be breaking with hundreds of years of our tradition. How beautiful is it when your daughters help with Shabbas? They help with preparing the food, lighting the Shabbas candles. They sing with such joy. How would they be in a world without faith? I'm begging you to just try to relax and let some time pass. You will see that the shock which you, and everyone in your house experiences will soon pass and your lives will be fruitful."

"Think of that woman who was shot dead as she walked her baby. I'm told she was a brilliant woman. Musically gifted and she tossed her life aside to follow rules and commandments that were made by men for a man's world. My daughters will not be able to pray with men. They can't even dance with men. Why is it that men are held up above women? We have no free choices. It's all laid out for us in those silly books. My daughters can only have freedom if I take them away and..."

Hanna's mother exploded in anger, "Stop it, Hanna. Enough of this rebellious talk. This is who we are. Our lives are to have children and teach them the right way to live by following Torah. I won't listen to this another second."

The older woman stood from the chair, folded it and began walking toward the rear doorway which lead to the kitchen.

Suddenly, Hanna felt a sharp pain in her lower abdomen. She felt a gush of water came from between her legs soaking her underwear.

"Mama, help me. The baby."

Chapter Fifty-Two

Vic and Raquel didn't waste a minute on the long drive to Broomall. They worked on the telephone calling their office for updates on anything related to Gary or Edward Olsen. They learned, as John Deegan had, that Gary had worked for many years at Lamonia and Sons doing metal lathing and left to start his own metal fabricating firm.

Vic's office also learned that Gary Olsen died from Covid-19 and was otherwise healthy. Death records in Delaware County and the Social Security Death Index confirmed that Ruth Olsen died in Broomall. No record indicated Gary Olsen had remarried.

An hour into their trip to meet up with John Deegan, Detective Mike Sassano called Vic and Raquel.

"Hey Mike. We're still on the road."

"I have some interesting information for both of you. First off, a friend of mine at Spring Valley PD tells me that Wright told their Chief not to release any information on today's shooting to anyone without his personal approval. Because I have friends and he doesn't, my buddy tells me the Rockland preliminary ballistics came in. They found the bullet that killed today's victim and it's a match to the other projectiles." "Tungsten carbide with a similar grain weight as the others. And get this, and it's not yet official but the shooter likely took a much longer range shot than the first three," Sassano offered.

"Yea, how long are they saying?" Raquel asked.

"You're not gonna believe this. Just about a mile. A mile shot. Looks like he shot it from a spot in Nanuet. That's another town for Christs sake," Sassano bellowed.

"That would be an expert shot. Not many people can make that work out with that much accuracy," Raquel added.

Vic changed back to the shooter. "I'm no expert by any means, but the shooter has to have sophisticated knowledge of weaponry, don't you think?

"I guess so. That ain't your everyday hunter," Sassano replied.

Vic added, "Let's think about another angle. A mile shot, using armor piercing ammo. It smells of military training to me."

"Could very well be military, but I know a few competitive marksmen that can make that shot," Sassano said.

The list keeps getting longer," Raquel added.

"Let me tell you what else I discovered today. I went to that door place in Monsey today. All Hasidic. They knew Gary Olsen. He made specialty hardware for them. Ya know, for certain doors that needed better knobs and hinges. Olsen would deliver them himself, From Pennsylvania. I have copies of the invoices with Olsen and Son on them, plus the packing slips. And guess what? Right after he was there last year, the office in Monsey was shut down with Covid. Half the staff was infected. Three or four were hospitalized but survived. Here is something you two are not gonna believe. Gary Olsen called them complaining that they gave him Covid. I debriefed the lady he spoke with. She said he was very polite, he just wanted them to know he thought he got Covid from them and told her they should all get tested."

"Get the hell out of here!" Raquel replied.

"And one more thing. A month or so later they tried to call and all they got was an answering machine. They called a few times and never heard back," Sassano informed.

"That's because the poor bastard died," Vic stated.

"Vic, your choice of words!" Raquel admonished.

"Okay sorry, the poor bastard succumbed," Vic laughed.

Sassano laughed. "Gonnella, you are a real pissa."

Chapter Fifty-Three

"*Go three-quarters of a mile and exit on the right, Broomall exit, then take a right.*"

Vic's GPS broke a ten-minute silence. Both Vic and Raquel were both lost in their thoughts about the case. Raquel was hoping that Deegan's lead would not be just a coincidence. She was reviewing every one of the shootings in her head and thought about how sad the families would be having a loved one murdered in this way. She began to count the children who were left without a father or a mother. The tears began to well up in her eyes.

Vic wondered how Deegan could have gotten to the Olsen's before the license plate recognition system came up with the information on the Dodge van. His mind also went to Special Agent Wright. Vic wondered what the look on his face would be if the case was broken without the FBI. By nature, Vic was as competitive as Raquel was compassionate.

"I'll text Deegan on your phone to let him know we're here," Raquel offered.

"Okay, then I really have to take a leak." Vic replied.

"Me too. And grab something to eat. I'm starved."

Deegan replied to the text immediately. *2601 West Chester Pike, McDonalds.* He replied.

Vic blurted, "Perfect, we can use the head and have a Happy Meal."

"Yuck," Raquel replied.

"Or…you can give me head and forget the fries."

"You are such an idiot Vic."

"Why thank you, my love."

Raquel punched the McDonalds into Google. 2.2 miles on the left.

Vic walked quickly into McDonalds and headed directly for the men's room. He looked around the restaurant and didn't spot Deegan. Raquel went to the ladies' room. She didn't see Deegan either.

The couple met outside the rest rooms a few minutes later. Raquel wasn't one of those women who took twenty-minutes to pee.

"I don't see John," Raquel uttered. They both scanned the place. There were six or seven people sitting at tables and no one in line for food at that time.

"Me either. Let's get some grub and sit down. He'll find us."

Vic waited for the food and Raquel went to pour the drinks from the soda dispenser.

As Vic walked to a booth, Deegan walked up to him.

"Didn't you see me sitting over there? Did you get me a Whopper?" Deegan asked.

"What the fuck? I saw you and had no idea it was you in that fucking get up."

Raquel walked up to Vic and Deegan "John? I would never have known it was you. Holy shit. A real Mennonite."

"A genius. A Master of disguise you guys called me when you were chasing me down."

"By the way, Whoppers are at Burger King, genius," Vic added.

"All the same garbage to me. Let's get to work!" Deegan said.

Deegan started the discussion. "I did some preliminary investigation. The Olsen house is locked up tighter than a crab's ass. There is a garage detached from the house where the old man did his metal work. That's locked up too."

"Hold on. Let's back up. How did you find out about the Olsen's in the first place? Vic asked.

Deegan chuckled. "Let's just say brilliant detective work."

"Yea, right! One thing you need to know is that this Gary Olsen's van was seen in Monsey months before the shootings. He made some deliveries up there. His van finally came up on the plate ID system," Raquel added.

"Good, so all roads lead to Broomall. I'm going out on a limb and saying we are onto something here," Deegan said.

"Now the hard work of proving it. What do you have on the son?" Vic asked.

"He's got problems. Seems to be mentally challenged. Sounds like Asperger's to me. On the Autism spectrum. Highly functional. Could be brilliant. Socially inept. He's on furlough from his job in the metals factory," Deegan offered.

"When did that happen?" Vic asked.

"Just today. I interviewed that plant manager. Plant was shut down. Covid."

Raquel jumped in. "So, he was laid off today and maybe drove up to Rockland and popped a Hasidic man? Pieces fit but very coincidental."

"But plausible," Deegan added.

"We have to case the house. Take a look see inside maybe. You said you were there, John?" Raquel asked.

"Correct. No Edward, no van. That was earlier today. I got a room for you two. Let's go to the CVS and get you guys a toothbrush," Deegan spouted.

Chapter Fifty-Four

Hanna made her way into the kitchen with her mother's help.

Hanna's mom called out to her grandchildren in Yiddish, "Girls, come quickly. I need help with your mama."

Hanna leaned against the granite countertop, holding its edge until another contraction passed.

"Mama, I think I need to go," Hanna said. She was breathing heavily through her mouth, waiting for another contraction. She remembered the pain she experienced having the other children. The pain this time seemed very different. Hanna began to panic.

"Girls, run up and put together a bag. Make sure she has her head covering and a nice slip," Hanna's mother ordered.

"Do you see mama. Even now, even when we are in the pain of childbirth we have to obey the *Halakha*, the Jewish laws that control our every moment."

"Now is not the time Hanna. I'm calling for Hatzolah."

"Mendel could not even touch me when the babies were born. He couldn't even rub my back in the hospital. And he couldn't watch the babies come out of me. Why? Stupid rules. I'm sick of this life," Hanna screamed.

Another contraction, which came within eight minutes, almost brought her to her knees.

"Hanna, please. The ambulance is coming. You should be praying to Hashem for a healthy baby."

"I should do this...and I should do that. My Mendel should be here with me, that's what should be. He should be here holding my hand but even that is not allowed."

The ambulance arrived within ten minutes. The Hatzolah volunteers, both trained EMT's and paramedics, are more familiar with childbirth than any other organization. Among the Hasidic community, the average number of children born per family is six. The workers consider it a blessing to bring the mother to the hospital to help fulfill God's word in Genesis, *"Be fruitful and multiply. Fill the earth and subdue it. Rule over the fish in the sea and the birds in the sky and over every living creature that moves on the ground."*

• • •

While Hanna was being rushed to Nyack Hospital by Hatzolah, other members of the community were in Rebbe Teitelbaum's office in Kyrias Joel. They drove up in a mini-van which was owned by the synagogue.

There were four Satmar men, well known and well-respected members of the community. They were driven by Rabbi Kreitzman from their shul in Monsey. The men were all nervous and apprehensive meeting in such a small group with their famous leader. They were not stopped by the heavy security at the entrance to Kyrias Joel.

Unlike the meeting with Vic Gonnella and Detective Mike Sassano, these men were met in the vestibule of the Synagogue.

The Rebbe walked in, moving slowly with his head down in reverence to being in the holy place. He wore his father's prayer shawl which was like a holy relic in the community.

"We are meeting here so after we discuss what you came for we can all go into the temple to form a minyan. We have much to pray for," the Rebbe stated. He nodded his head at Rabbi Teitelbaum.

"Rebbe, we are here to appeal to you for you to make a judgment on a very serious matter that affects everyone in our community. These good and decent men came to me with their request and I am not able to grant them what they are asking," Rabbi Teitelbaum announced.

"Yes. I think I know why you are here. I will listen."

"Rebbe, after the fourth shooting, our community is in total panic. No one feels safe to walk. Not to the stores, not to places of business and not to the synagogue. These men are appealing to be able to drive cars or charter busses to take our followers to shul on Shabbas," Teitelbaum pled.

The Rebbe stroked his beard slowly and thought for a while. He looked at each and every man who stood before him. Everyone remained silent including the seven men that were with the Rebbe.

He spoke in a clear, loud voice which bounced off the vestibule walls.

"According to the *halakha*, operating any vehicle is prohibited on Shabbas as we all well know. The cars create a spark, it is like igniting a fire and is prohibited. There are lights involved as well, lights that go on and off when the vehicle is used, which is also not allowed to turn on during Shabbas. We also must consider the law of *techum Shabbat*, which limits the distance we can travel to the synagogue. So, we can't drive around like we are going to business or anywhere else. This is why we walk to services and to *daven*. Also, there is the combustion of fuel which isn't permitted. Our laws are clear on these matters.

The Rebbe paused and was deep in though again, looking at all of the men standing before him. All of the men stood in rapt attention, awaiting the words of their spiritual leader.

"However. Human life is more important than any rule and any tradition. Our *pikuach nefesh* is called into play here. This maniac who is shooting us is a clear danger to us. The preservation To safe of human life is paramount in our beliefs. This is what has helped us to survive as a people. I grant permission to use motor vehicles on Shabbas, but only until this danger is over. Please, Hashem, take this yoke of terror away from us."

Chapter Fifty-Five

Vic, Raquel and John Deegan rolled up to the Olsen house in Vic's car. They drove by slowly. No white van in the driveway or on the street. It was getting near dusk and the house was totally dark.

Vic passed the house and drove to the end of the street, making a U-turn in the driveway of a newly built home.

They headed back to the Olsen house.

"I think we should go in," Vic stated.

"Not gonna be easy. There is a busy body old lady neighbor who can hear a bird fart in a tree," Deegan advised. "I met her earlier. She's a real *yenta* if you know what that means?"

"We took Yiddish 101 in New Square," Raquel replied.

"I say we wait until dark. Maybe the old broad goes to sleep early. Then I'll pick the lock on the rear door," Deegan volunteered.

"Nothing doing. I'll do that. I don't want your prints on anything Deegan. Plus, I'm a great lock-picker," Vic said.

"Are you trying to tell me your lock picking skills are better than mine?" Deegan chuckled.

"John, Vic has told me many times in his day he could take the panties off a cloistered nun without her even knowing it," Raquel added.

• • •

Edward Olsen fell asleep at the trout stream dreaming of he and his dad fishing. His dad was smiling at him and he was catching the big ones, piling them on the ground next to the water. His father had brought a picnic lunch on their last trip and they were eating hard boiled eggs and some peanut butter sandwiches.

The sound of crickets and a bull frog croaking nearby woke him from his dreamy sleep. It was already dark and he had to gather his thoughts as he didn't remember where he was.

Edward rubbed his eyes and was finally able to find the Jeep. He climbed in and finished the last three cold White Castle Hamburgers.

He didn't like driving at night. Edward had a good amount a phobias and night driving was one of them. He sat in the driver's seat of the vehicle and decided he would go into the rear of the Jeep and fall asleep again. He used the blanket from his duffel bag and the bag became his pillow.

"Maybe I'll go back there in the morning and take another one. I have everything I need." He thought. He used his father's expression when they went hunting. They would "take a deer," Gary used to say in hunter terminology.

• • •

It was dark enough now for Vic, Raquel and Deegan to go into action. Vic had a small toolkit in the trunk of the car that had what he needed to pick the backdoor lock of the Olsen house. They parked up the street from the home, next to a wooded area.

One at a time, separated by thirty yards, they walked in the moon-less night to the house.

Deegan held his cellphone light up to the door lock as Vic did his work. Raquel stood guard just in case anyone came by.

"Come on Vic, I have a meeting in the morning," Deegan joked."

"Shut the hell up you, maniac," Vic replied.

"Genius maniac to you."

After a few minutes, Vic opened the lock. In seconds, the trio was in the dark kitchen. Deegan kept the cellphone light low so as not to bring attention if anyone was passing by. He panned the light around the kitchen. There were no dishes in the sink. It looked as though the kitchen hadn't been used in a while. There were some papers on the table. Raquel used the light from her cell to take a look at the papers. They looked to be some old bills and a few fishing and hunting maga-zines. An unopened Primatine Mist inhaler and a crumpled CVS bag were also on the table.

Deegan moved into the living room. The mess he saw from the front door earlier that morning was untouched. There was an older por-table television on a wooden table across from the easy chair. Deegan couldn't remember the last time he saw a T.V. set with a big bulgy back.

Vic pointed to the next room. The door was locked. He pointed to the upstairs where the bedrooms would be.

They each walked slowly up the creaking staircase, keeping their cell lights low, pointing them to the stairs. At the top of the flight there was a bedroom on the left. The door was closed but unlocked. Vic opened the door slowly. Neither he nor Raquel had drawn their handguns. Nothing but an old bedroom set and a sheet less mattress. The ceiling had some water stains from the roof and peeling paint dotting most of it.

Deegan led the way into another smaller bedroom. Raquel followed with Vic behind her.

"Looks like the kid's bedroom," Raquel whispered.

The covers were crumpled on the twin sized mattress. Empty cans of Coca-Cola and Poland Springs water were all over the place. An empty box of tissues was on the floor next to the bed. Vic noticed the text books first.

"Science text books. Heady stuff. Advanced Mathematics, Physics, Engineering. Someone has a brain," he offered.

Deegan pulled back the covers and the sheet. There was a photo in a silver frame of a man and a woman.

"I suspect these are Edwards parents. This kid sleeps with this, strange to say the least," Deegan uttered.

Nothing else in the room pointed to anything that would lead them to believe Edward was their shooter.

"Let's go see what's in that locked room downstairs," Vic said.

As they were going down the stairs, a light from the outside rippled into the house. The trio froze like they were home burglars. Vic quickly moved down to the first floor. He peeked out from the side of the drawn shade. "Nothing. It must have been a neighbor's car," he said.

"Hope it wasn't that old biddy," Deegan added.

Vic moved to the locked bedroom door. It was a hollow wood door and the lock was a cinch to pop open.

Vic led them into the room.

"Holy shit, would ya look at this place," Vic blurted.

Chapter Fifty-Six

"Mrs. Glick. Mrs. Glick. Can you hear me?" Shoshana Gottlieb gently tapped Hanna on her hand.

Hanna's eyes fluttered as she slowly came to. She looked around the hospital room, trying to remember how she had gotten there. The sound of voices, the clanking of metal and doctors being paged on the public-address system began to bring Hanna back to her senses.

"Mrs. Glick, you are going to be fine. Doctor Chani Grossbaum is here. She is the best there is. Doctor Chani will be in to see you in a couple of minutes."

"Who are you. How am I here?" Hanna asked the woman in the surgical mask who woke her.

"I'm your nurse. A neonatal nurse. My name is Shoshana. I am Chabad-Lubavitch. You are in good hands here. You should know that we follow *halakha* here. All of your doctors and nurses are women. To answer your second question, you came in here by Hatzolah *Baruch*

Hashem. They really know what they are doing. You came in here unconscious, but now you are back with us."

"My baby," Hanna felt for her abdomen and felt the baby move."

"So, we have a fetal monitor on the baby. Everything is fine, Hanna." Shoshana said.

"Is the baby coming now?"

"Doctor Grossbaum will explain. Oh look, here she is."

Chani Grossbaum is an Obstetrician Gynecologist. She is also an Orthodox Jew. Her dark brown *sheitel* was parted down the middle, the wig's hair falling to her shoulders. Hanna could see from her light blue eyes that Doctor Grossbaum was a pretty woman. Her surgical mask hid the rest of her beauty. She didn't even look old enough to be a doctor. Her diminutive size made her seem almost like a teenager.

"Hello Hanna. I'm Doctor Grossbaum but most of my patients call me Doctor Chani. Such excitement coming in by ambulance. This child can't wait to meet you. We've been monitoring your vital signs. Your blood pressure was a bit low when you arrived but is coming up nicely now. Your baby is fine. I ordered a fetal monitor because the baby is breach. Not to worry Hanna. We are preparing a room to do a Cesarean section. In no time, you will be hugging and kissing your baby and saying your Thanksgiving Prayer to Hashem for this wonderful gift."

"Will I be, awake? Like with my other children?" Hanna asked.

"No...no. The anesthesiologist, just arrived, also a *shomer Shabbat* woman. She will be administering a wonderful thing we call a full spinal block. You won't even feel a pinch."

"The baby is coming too soon. *Oy vey iz mir,*" Hanna cried.

"*Oy vey nothing.* The baby's weight is fine. The sonogram is fine. Now, just breathe nicely. You are coming in to see me in just a few minutes."

"Thank you Doctor Chani. May God bless you."

"I'll be into see you afterwards. I am very happy to meet you, Hanna."

• • •

Vic, Raquel and John Deegan were all inside the unlocked room. After the holy shit moment, their cell phone lights were all focused on an eight-foot wood workbench.

The first thing they noticed was the two-foot single stage sky blue bullet press which had a long stainless-steel arm and a black knob on its top.

Everything needed to make cartridges was neatly laid out on the bench. Brass casings for a .338 Lapua round, CCI 250 primers, a keg of Hodgdon H 1000 gunpowder, various dies, a digital scale, a grinder which was connected to a small Raspberry Pi personal computer, with a built in keyboard, led casings and various metal tools.

"Everything he needed to make homemade rounds," Raquel offered.

Deegan answered. "I'm no metallurgist but I'd bet these tools over here are tungsten carbide."

"And that's what the grinder is for I imagine. That's how he makes the projectile by grinding down the tools into a projectile, Vic added.

"Look at the sticky note next to the scale. 90.8 grains. That's a reminder for the amount of gunpowder which would go into each cartridge. He is pretty precise," Deegan said.

"So, he didn't have to melt the metal. He just grinded it out to fit into the casings," Vic noted.

"Guys, look in the corner," Raquel announced.

There were six fully assembled rounds, lined up in a row, neatly placed on what looked like a piece of cheesecloth.

"Who wants to bet with me that those projectiles match the ones that were found near the bodies in Rockland." Deegan expressed.

"That's two bets that neither of us will give odds against Deegan," Vic muttered.

"I say we don't touch a thing. This is all forensic evidence at this point," Raquel said.

"Now all we have to do is wait for Edward to return home," Vic added.

"The question is, do we wait inside here or do we hide somewhere out-side until he gets home and come in with the local cops," Deegan asked.

"I say we wait outside. First off, we didn't have a warrant and did the B and E thing. That could look bad in court. Second, I gave my word to let Sassano be the one that cracks the case. After all, he had a bead on this address from the license plate ID and held back. Lastly. No matter if Sassano comes or the local or State PD show up, Deegan, you have to high tail out of here," Vic said.

"Always the bridesmaid. My job is done here. All of the fun of the chase is gone for me now anyway. There are no coincidences here, this is the real shooter. All that's left is the cop stuff and I know how it will end," Deegan offered.

"How will it end oh genius teacher?" Vic asked. He said it with all reverence.

"I'll write it down and put in an envelope for you. Now, I will make my exit stage right. I'll get back to my hotel, get into my car and meet Gjuliana and her family. Maybe spend a couple of days in Manhattan and get back to my beautiful serene and boring life on the lake."

"John…I don't know what to say. You are amazing and once again we are your humble students," Raquel declared. She put her arms around Deegan and kisses him on the cheek.

"Deegan. I'm not gonna kiss you but an Italian hug is from my heart," Vic muttered. He grabbed Deegan, pulling him in for a long hug.

"When the next school break comes, I'll send a jet for you. Bring my dear Gabriella and the beautiful Olga. I will not take no for an answer," Deegan offered. He turned his light off, made his way to the back door of the Olsen house and was gone into the dark night.

Chapter Fifty-Seven

Vera, the blonde bartender at Crossroads bar in Mahwah, New Jersey was about ready to close up for the night.

On weekends during Covid they were mandated by the state to close at ten o'clock every evening. Even though the ban had been lifted and Crossroads could have stayed open later, this particular Thursday night the place was empty.

Earlier in the evening, Cindy stopped in for a few drinks and to see if any men were on the prowl. There weren't any, so Cindy chatted it up with Vera.

"So, what ever happened to that guy. You know, the one that looks like Christian Bale and was questioned on the shootings in Rockland," Cindy asked.

"That creep! I swear the way he told me about the shootings, I would swear it was him. One of the Mahwah cops that comes in here said they found an unlicensed gun or something and they are pressing charges. The way that guy looked at me still gives me the creeps," Vera whispered. There was a couple at the end of the bar and Vera was careful they didn't hear her.

"Did he ask you out?"

"Yea, but I get asked out a lot. These guys want one thing and it ain't free drinks," Vera laughed.

"What about that guy Carl? He's so freakin hot. He could put his boots under my bed anytime," Cindy said.

"Yea, and a big tipper. I wonder what else he has that's big. Haven't see him in a while."

"Well if he shows up mention my name," Cindy spouted.

"I will. I'll tell him you're a lesbian so I can get first dibs."

"Bitch!" Cindy laughed out loud.

They chatted about Covid and the difficulty getting the vaccinations. Vera didn't want to take the two injections because she didn't trust the government and was afraid the vaccine would make her get the virus. Cindy wanted the shots. She believed in Doctor Anthony Fauci. Vera called him a dick.

Vera set the alarm, closed the bar door and locked it. Usually there were a few drunks sniffing around her at closing but not tonight. She got into her Mazda3 sedan, put on her Country and Western radio station, turned up the volume and headed to her apartment on Franklin Turnpike.

Vera never noticed the Ford F110 that was following her.

Chris Tripp decided not to wait for his buddy Richard Gebhardt to give him the nod to get even with her for saying he was the Shabbas killer. As a matter of fact, Vera had no idea that Gebhardt even knew it was she that told Carl Shuster about her conversation with him about the shooter.

Tripp was moving in a few days to Arizona and figured getting even with Vera was a good farewell for now gift for his drinking buddy.

Vera pulled her car into her designated spot at her garden apartment complex and sat in her car for a few minutes while she finished a call to a friend.

Tripp shut the lights of his truck off, parked his truck in a visitor's spot, well away from Vera, got out of his vehicle and lurked in the shadows.

Unsuspecting what was about to happen to her, Vera took her keys and walked to her first floor, corner apartment. Tripp, took notice that her left-side, next door neighbors lights were out.

"*Excellent,*" he said to himself. "*This is gonna be fun.*"

Vera found the key hole with her key and opened her door. Her apartment was pitch black. Before she knew it, someone pushed her into the apartment, placing a big hand around her mouth. He pulled her down to the floor, kicking the door shut with his work boot.

"If you scream, I'll snap your fucking neck like a twig," Tripp whispered.

He let his hand go loosely from her mouth but didn't fully remove it.

"My money is in my purse. Take it and don't hurt me," Vera pleaded.

"Why, thank you bitch. I was planning on taking your money anyway."

Vera panicked and began kicking her legs but Tripp had his weight on her, rendering her kicks useless.

"Please don't hurt me. I have AIDS," Vera lied.

"I'm not here for your pussy darlin. I'm here to get even with you for what you did to my friend," Tripp uttered. He brought his other hand around and snapped it around Vera's neck, squeezing it hard.

Vera's eyes bulged from their sockets. It was too dark for her to make out who her assailant was. The smell of beer and tobacco on his foul breath almost made her vomit.

She grabbed at the hand which was wrapped around her throat with both her hands and scratched for her life.

"You fucking twat!" Tripp yelled as he felt his skin be torn away by Vera's nails.

He pulled his hands away, grabbing them in a reflex motion. Vera rolled and was able to get out of his clutch.

Suddenly, her door was smashed open. Unbeknownst to Tripp and luckily for Vera, Tripp and his buddy Richard Gebhardt were both being tailed by undercover New York State and Mahwah police. The sound of the door made her cover her head with both arms as she lay on the floor.

"If you fucking move, I'll put two into your head mother fucker," Carl Shuster hollered. He and two Mahwah police grabbed Tripp, flipped him over and cuffed him. He made no attempt to resist.

Chapter Fifty-Eight

"I think this might be the worst pizza I've ever had in my entire life," Vic blurted.

"It's not that bad baby. Look, we're not back in the Bronx. What can you expect?" Raquel replied.

"Taste of Italia! It tastes more like a matzo with American cheese."

"Just eat it and stop whining. We have to get back to that house in case he comes home."

"We had to eat and go to the bathroom and you had to pick this dump."

"Nothing else is open. It's almost ten. We got the last few slices before they closed or we had to get 7-11 hot dogs. Now let's go," Raquel ordered.

"Seriously Raquel, how can people live like this?" Vic said in all sincerity.

"What an aristocrat you've become. A real Italian snob."

"Pathetic," Vic seethed.

The couple drove back to the Olsen house and passed by it slowly, hoping there would be some signs of life. The van, maybe a few lights on, something that would indicate Edward Olsen had returned. It was as dark as when they left twenty-five minutes ago.

"What if he doesn't return tonight?" Raquel asked.

"We've both done surveillance like this with the NYPD. Even with our company when we first started. We just hunker down until he does get home. If not tonight, maybe tomorrow. We can take a break before dawn, have a shower at the hotel and get back here. Who knows, we may get lucky and he'll show up any minute."

"I have a feeling he's out for the night," Raquel guessed.

"He's not exactly the type to shack up and get laid."

"You really have a one-track mind. Sometimes it's nauseating."

Raquel was right, Edward didn't return home that night. They went back, showered fast at the hotel and grabbed some coffee, bottled water and egg sandwiches at a nearby deli.

• • •

Edward awoke the next morning to the sound of birds and watched the sun come up. He wondered how long his furlough from Lamonia and Company would be. He heard someone say fourteen-days but couldn't remember who said it. Maybe it was his supervisor or maybe Frank Van Houton.

He peed against a tree, got back into the Jeep and headed back to New Jersey and to Rockland County. Edward calculated in his head that he would be arriving in the Monsey area at about 8:30 that morning. Plenty of time to find a place to scope out his next shot and get back home in the early afternoon and not worry about driving in the dark.

Edward checked his gas gauge, there was plenty in the tank to make the round trip. Maybe the van would be ready at Gus' shop.

He wasn't at all hungry. Every time he burped, the familiar taste of the White Castle 'belly bombers' filled his mouth.

Traffic was a bit heavier than normal so Edward stayed in the right lane for most of the trip. In his mind, he visualized the streets of Monsey and where those people liked to walk. He remembered a building where they would walk in and out of. If he could find a place to put the jeep. Maybe he would go back to that cemetery. There were plenty of good spots in there to line up a shot.

Edward wished his father was there to help him. Gary had a hunting blind that he would sometimes bring on their trips and wait for a nice buck to get into their sights. The blind was the pop up camouflage kind that had a platform, with plenty of room for both of them. He loved those trips. Because of those people he would never do that again with his dad. They had to pay.

Edward pulled off Route 287 at the Nanuet exit. He made his way to Route 59 and made the left that brought him past the knoll where he took the mile shot. He smiled to himself at his accomplishment and drove past the spot where he dropped the last man. Driving a few more miles into Monsey, he noticed that there were no people walking. The area was deserted.

Passing the spot of his first shot, he noticed that the big store on the left was empty. "*Maybe everyone is furloughed,*" he thought.

He made the left after the big store. There were plenty of cars driving on the roads, but no people walking. He saw a man walking his dog, but he wasn't dressed in the black hat and long black coat. Then there were two men, in shorts and tee-shirts jogging. But they were black. He needed to see those pale, long coated people.

Edward looked in a few cars along Maple Avenue. He could see the men that were driving had the hats and the curls in their hair. He wondered why every one of them wore the same kind of eyeglasses.

Shooting into a car was not for him. He didn't like the idea. Edward wanted a clean shot of a man or woman walking, like a deer in the woods.

Edward passed the cemetery, made a left and turned back around. He saw some of the people with the long coats, hats and curls going into a tan building which had the writing he couldn't read. He spotted a good place to park the Jeep. It was the wooded area near where he took his second shot. He calculated the woods to that tan building was about 450 yards, maybe 500.

Edward pulled the Jeep along-side the woods, got out of the Jeep, opened the back and took out the rifle and his duffle bag. He tossed both of them into the woods and hurried back to the Jeep.

Driving a short distance, Edward made a right turn and parked the Jeep about fifty yards on the right. He parked in front of an old home with a few cars in the driveway. Still, he saw no one. "*It's still early. Maybe they come out later,*" He thought.

He walked briskly back to the wooded area and gathered the rifle and bag, going further into the trees. He walked a bit into the woods until he saw an opening where the tan building could be spotted. There was a house, with three levels on his left, just after the trees ended.

Men were walking in and out of the tan building, getting in and out of cars. A small yellow school bus pulled up alongside the building, dropping off three men.

Edward couldn't make a shot from a prone position because there were too many low, thick bushes blocking his view.

This shot would have to be done while he was standing. *"A good marksman can make his shot from any position,"* Gary used to say. He took the cap off his scope and aimed the rifle at the building. He made sure the sound suppressor was fitted correctly on the rifles nozzle. He used his range finder. 486 yards. It was a relatively straight shot and the wind was dead calm. Edward kept his scope on the steps of the tan building. Sooner or later, one of them would come out. He waited.

He heard a ruffling behind him and the snap of a twig. It startled him and he lost his breath for a moment. Edward lowered the rifle and looked around. Two squirrels were chasing each other around and up a tree.

He raised his rifle again. He knew from this distance the time of flight for the bullet would be .6 seconds. Not nearly the time of his mile shot at 3.2 seconds.

In the scope, he saw a man walking down the stairs carrying a dark blue velvet pouch.

Homing in on the man's head, Edward took a deep breath in and didn't let the breath out, as he normally would. He squeezed the trigger at the exact moment he saw the target drop his pouch. The man had bent to pick up his prayer books. Whether it was fate or divine intervention, the bullet missed its mark, shattering the tan brick wall behind the Hasidic man.

The shattering sound of the bullet smashing into the building and the puff of brick flying into the air sent everyone in the vicinity to the ground screaming.

Edward couldn't believe his eyes. He was dumfounded with disappointment. He dropped the rifle to the decayed leaf covered ground and began to pummel his own head with his fists.

Panic stricken by the screaming from the building and his own failure, Edward quickly covered up the rifle and his duffle bag under some leaves.

He walked through the wooded area, made the short walk back to the Jeep and drove out of Monsey. The sound of police sirens wailing in the vicinity made Edward panic even more. He bit his lower lip so severely is gushed blood. He banged his both hands on the steering wheel and emitted an animal like cry. "Son of a bitch," he hollered. He heard his father say that on a few occasions when things didn't go right.

Chapter Fifty-Nine

Bedlam spontaneously erupted in Monsey. Hasidic men who were near the shooting fled for the safety of the synagogue. Those who were driving when they saw the panic and heard the screaming, took off at great speed to get away from the Schul and head to their homes. Mothers, hearing of the shooting, hurried to their children to take them from their schools, clutching them closely and literally praying out loud for the Lord to save them all.

Squad cars zipped out of Ramapo Police Headquarters, all racing to the Maple Avenue location where reports of shots fired were all over the police radios.

Detective Mike Sassano had an early morning appointment with his urologist. An All-Points Bulletin cell phone text message alerted him to the second shooting in two days. Sassano bolted from the doctor's office to his unmarked car. He was looking for an excuse to avoid the dreaded annual digital examination. The timing was perfect.

When Sassano pulled up to the Synagogue, the area was swarming with police, both from his own department, Rockland County Sheriff's office and New York State Troopers, many with automatic rifles and shotguns drawn.

The veteran detective assessed the situation quickly. No one was dead on the ground, thankfully. There were no Hasidic Jews anywhere to be seen as they had all rightfully fled the area or were inside the synagogue taking cover.

Sassano saw the gaping hole in the tan brick next to the stairs. He looked down the long road and saw police fanning out with their weapons at the ready. He knew that the Rockland County BCI unit would have to analyze the hole in the building to try and recover any ballistics. They would also attempt to discover where the shot came from and look for any evidence left by a shooter. He wondered because there were two shots taken in two days if there was a chance of a copycat shooter. This shooting didn't follow any pattern.

Sassano decided to call Vic and Raquel. He walked away from the synagogue so he wouldn't be overheard by any of the platoon of police.

"Vic?"

"Hey Mike," Gonnella replied. Raquel is here. You're on the car speaker.

"Look guys, we've had another shooting in Monsey. The shooter missed his target. No one was hit."

"We are on to the shooter, Mike. We staked out his house all night. Now we know why he never went home. He went to Monsey for another hit instead," Vic informed.

"It sounds like he may be headed home," Sassano guessed.

"Exactly. Mike, how fast can you get to Broomall, Pennsylvania?" Vic asked.

"Where the hell is that?"

"Outside of Philly. One hundred and thirty something miles from you."

"What's goin on Vic?"

"We found our guy for sure. We found his shop, inside his house, long story. I'll explain later. We want you here for the arrest. We'll call Pennsylvania State when you get here."

"I guess two and half hours. Something like that," Sassano replied.

"C'mon Mike. This guy can walk in on us anytime in the next couple of hours. Use that helicopter for Christ's sake," Vic implored.

"Not as easy as that. There's a whole protocol with the County to use that thing," Sassano replied.

"Listen to me Mike, you've been a cop there for a hundred years. Use your clout. Call who you have to call or I'll call the fucking governor and he'll call. Tell them whatever you have to tell them. Call me back," Vic shouted. He ended the call.

"I have to say something. In some ways, these Rockland cops are really like yokels. We're handing them the case on a silver platter and Mike's telling me about protocol. Christ, show some balls will ya?" Vic said to Raquel.

"You've been out of NYPD too long. How would you have gotten a helicopter in the air in a snap? Never happen," Raquel replied.

"Trust me. On a hot, visible case like this I would've moved mountains. Did you forget when we were chasing Deegan from the states to Europe? We had carte blanche."

Vic's phone rang ten minutes later.

"Forty to forty-five minutes. I'm bringing the Chief with me. Our pilot contacted Broomall Fire. They have a field where we can land and we'll get to you. Text me the address," Sassano blurted.

"Okay, don't show your cards to local PD. When you get here come in quietly," Vic responded.

"Better yet, just meet us at the McDonalds parking lot, its two minutes away from the house. We don't want this guy to be scared away, if in fact he's headed home," Raquel proposed.

"Roger that. See you within the hour. I just hope you guys are right about this. My neck is sticking way out there on this one," Sassano said.

"Hey, Mike, no guts no glory. We are, without a doubt on the money on this one," Vic replied. He ended the call.

Sitting in the car, Vic drew his 9-millimeter HK P30 handgun from his shoulder holster. He checked to see if his magazine was full. He counted fifteen cartridges. He pulled back the slide, putting one in the chamber.

Raquel took her SIG Sauer P365 ten shot 9-millimeter pistol from her ankle holster and did the same.

"I hope we don't need to use these things," Vic stated.

"Let's hope not. But I'll tell you right now, no matter what, we are both going home to see Gabriella," Raquel declared.

Chapter Sixty

Hanna Glick was in her hospital bed, breastfeeding her new baby girl. She thought the baby looked like Mendel in so many ways.

The day before when Hanna realized her pain would be blocked by the spinal, Hanna had asked Doctor Chani if she could give birth naturally. Hasidic women, like most Orthodox Jews, believed that the pain of childbirth was a necessary blessing. Doctor Chani allayed all of her concerns telling her this C-section was absolutely necessary to preserve life. That comforted Hanna tremendously.

Upon seeing her daughter, Hanna recited the *Shehecheyanu*, the same prayer that she had said with her other daughters. *"Blessed are You, Lord our God, King of the universe, who has allowed us and has enabled us to reach this season,"*

In that moment, Hanna realized that passing on her beliefs and age-old traditions to her beautiful baby girl must remain intact. All of her rebellious thoughts instantly vanished. She realized that she would wait to present her baby at the synagogue, in a week, before the Torah to name the child. She would name the baby Chava, Eve, the meaning in Hebrew is living, the first woman God had created.

In Judaism, it is believed that girls are born completely spiritually. Meaning that girls do not have to make a treaty with God, because, unlike boys, they have already made the treaty.

Doctor Chani and Shoshana entered Hanna's room together.

"Look at this beautiful moment," Chani said.

"Thanks to God and to you Doctor Chani," Hanna replied.

"It was all God, Hanna. I'm just his servant. And now we have another woman to keep our faith going."

"I will admit to you both that my faith was tested, but seeing this child brought me back completely," Hanna offered. Her eyes filled with happy tears. "My Mendel would have been so proud."

"I'm certain. By the way, you will not be receiving any bills from me or from the hospital. We are all very proud of you. As a matter of fact, I've made arrangements for kimpeturin heim for you. You will stay at a convalescent home for a few days to help you recover and rest, right here in Rockland. In New Square. The community will cover the cost of your stay."

"How can I ever thank you Doctor Chiam?" Hanna asked.

"My dear Hanna, you already have."

Chapter Sixty-One

Edward Olsen was intent on getting home, getting a few more of his homemade bullets and returning the next day for his rifle and duffle bag. He planned on shooting two people the next day. Maybe even a couple of school boys to get at their parents.

Upset that he missed the last target, Edward was seething with anger as he drove back to Pennsylvania. His hands were so tight in the two and ten positions on the driver's wheel his knuckles were nearly pure white. He could still taste the blood in his mouth from when he bit his lips in anger and the sides of his head still were sore from where he pummeled them.

Edward never listened to the radio while driving as his dad had. Instead he would test himself with mathematical equations and sometimes, he would play multiplication games using the passing license plate numbers. On this trip, however, Edward was focused only on the driving, staring straight ahead at the road looking maniacal to drivers who passed him.

He stayed within the speed limit on most roads. On the Garden State Parkway, the speed limit is set at sixty-five miles an hour but Edward never went above fifty-five. Over that rate of speed, he would begin to panic and hyperventilate so his ride back to Broomall would take a bit longer than most drivers. When he calculated the time of his trip, he would factor in the average rate of speed for his arrival time.

He was getting hungry and hoped to be home in an hour and fifteen minutes. Hopefully one of his neighbors would have left him something for him to eat on the porch's table.

• • •

While Vic and Raquel were still staking out the Olsen house, Mike Sassano called. MIKE SASSANO read on the cars screen. Raquel pushed the green button to answer.

"Hey Mike, what's your twenty?" she asked.

"Just about eighteen minutes out. I have some news for you two."

"I hope it's good news," Vic added.

"One of my guys found the .338 and a duffle bag. In a small wooded area. Pretty good distance from the missed target. The shooter tried cover up the evidence with leaves and branches. Definitely the gun the shooter used. Even found a couple of the tungsten carbide cartridges in the bag."

"Nice find!" Raquel blurted.

"Yup. There should be plenty of prints on the weapon and probably enough DNA to tie back to this guy. He went from giving us no clues to dropping off a truckload," Sassano offered,

"You will see a lot more when you get here. It's like a mini bullet factory," Vic said.

"I really can't wait to meet your associate who tracked him down. Guy deserves a metal," Sassano stated.

"Let's not celebrate just yet Mike. Let's lock this guy up and let these people live in relative peace again," Raquel pronounced. She ignored the allusion to John Deegan.

"Okay, be there before you know it." Sassano finished the call.

Raquel was starting to feel the anxiety of seeing this serial killer. It was the same hand sweating, stomach churning feeling, she had when she spotted John Deegan at the Piazza Barberini in Rome, Italy and the same twirl in the stomach she experienced meeting the serial murderer in Punta Cana last year. As time passed the feelings became more intense and Raquel had to focus herself on the job at hand. Approach, subdue and cuff. It's as easy as that.

Vic called a contact he had made years ago with the Pennsylvania State Police. Danny Lucente. They met each other at a water park when they were both rookie cops in their early twenties. They both had kids the same age. Both divorced and both hooked up with Latina women. They could have talked for days. Danny went from a Trooper to a Lieutenant Colonel and Deputy Commissioner of the Pennsylvania State Police. Vic went from an NYPD beat cop to an internationally known security expert. They both had done ok.

Vic explained the situation in Broomall. He got down to brass tacks.

"Danny, all I'm asking is that your guys help with the collar and not come in as cowboys. We can't afford to chase this guy away. Lives literally depend upon us capturing this knucklehead," Vic said.

"I have just the crew for this. Smart guys, no bullshit. Follow orders to a T. You have my word. Where and when?"

"It's in your jurisdiction, thank God. Town called Broomall. If I'm right, the shooter will be back within the hour. I have a chopper coming in as we speak. Ramapo PD, Rockland County. It has to be their collar. I gave my word to one of the detectives there," Vic said.

"Your word is the same as mine. That's all we have my friend. Especially now-a-days," Lucente replied. He continued, "My guys will be in touch via your cell. Be safe pal."

• • •

Edward Olsen crossed the Pennsylvania State Line. He calculated he would arrive at home in forty-minutes.

His stomach was growling. It was Friday and one of the neighbors usually left him a fried flounder sandwich with some homemade cole slaw and some potato chips. The thought of having his lunch made his mouth water.

He looked at the gas gauge on the Jeeps dashboard and it was just a tad above empty. He calculated he had enough to get home, have his lunch and go to Gus' to get the tank filled. *A deal is a deal,*" he heard his father's voice say.

• • •

"Vic, look up. There's an old lady approaching the Olsen house," Raquel blurted. Vic was busy looking at his cell phone waiting with bated breath for it to ring. As soon as Sassano called, he and Raquel would rush over to the McDonalds.

"Oh, shit. This is all we need," Vic uttered.

"Relax, she has a brown bag of something."

The busy-body lady, the one that approached John Deegan was making a food delivery for Edward Olsen.

"Okay, now be a nice old lady and go back inside and take your nap," Raquel said.

Instead, after she dropped the bag on the table, the woman looked down the block where Vic's car was parked. No other cars were on parked on that side of the road. The old lady took a double take and paused. She pushed her neck forward like a swan, as if she could see better. She paused again, then started walking toward Vic's car."

"Fucking shit!" Vic mumbled.

"Go. Get the hell out of here. Don't wait here anymore. Go to McDonalds to pick up Mike and the Chief," Raquel blurted.

Vic did just that. He started the car and started rolling in the woman's direction. The old bitty stopped and waited for Vic and Raquel to pass, bending low, trying to peer into the cars windows. Vic turned his head to the left and Raquel gave the old woman her biggest smile and waved her hand rapidly to confuse the woman. It worked. The woman stopped and slowly waved back as if she thought she should have known Raquel.

"If she comes out when something goes down, I'm going to take out my dick and wave it at her. Maybe that will make her run back inside," Vic laughed.

Raquel looked at Vic with pity. "Maybe you'll get lucky and she'll fall on her knees out of force of habit."

Vic feigned he was vomiting.

Chapter Sixty-Two

The Rockland County Bell Jet Ranger helicopter, operated by a volunteer pilot, landed at the ball field near the Broomall Volunteer Fire Department at the exact time the pilot predicted.

One of the fire fighters, who wore a blue and gold Vietnam Veteran hat saluted Chief Frank who was in uniform and shook Mike Sassano's hand. He drove the two policemen, no questions asked, to the McDonalds restaurant to meet Vic and Raquel as planned.

In Vic's car, on the way back to the Olsen house, the discussion on the shooter began.

"Here's what we have, gentlemen. I know it's illegal but we broke into the Olsen house on a tip. What we found was a bullet factory inside of a locked room. This is without a doubt our guy. His name is Edward Olsen. From all indications, he's not right upstairs but he's a brilliant kid. We found the tungsten carbide cartridges, and everything he needed to build them. He never came home last night and then we got the call from you that he took another shot. It's an assumption but he's probably coming back here today," Vic opened.

"He has to come back at some point," Raquel added.

Sassano asked. "Where is your associate? How did he get this tip?"

"He's back in Manhattan on another big case. He did a great job. He doesn't need to be in on the collar. That's for you guys," Vic lied.

"I have to be honest with you two. If you broke into his house, the defense lawyers will have a field day with that. You know as well as I do, even though you had reasonable suspicion, it could still make things difficult. Without a warrant? I don't want to see us all embarrassed in court and in the newspapers," Chief Frank said.

"There are now only five of us who know we broke in. If we forget about it, and just arrest him on suspicion when he gets here, that could backfire too," Vic added.

"And we can't get a verbal warrant here that fast," Raquel said.

"I don't think a verbal no-knock warrant is valid," Chief Frank offered.

"Hold on," Vic blurted. He called Daniel Lucente and explained their predicament. Lucente agreed with Chief Frank.

"Fuck it then. This fucker will never see the light of day anyway. The Jews are a powerful group of people. We need Olsen off the street. Let the fucking lawyers play their games," Sassano almost yelled.

Minutes later, Vic arrived with the others at the Olsen home. Still no car in the driveway and the food package left by the elderly neighbor was still on the table on the front porch. Vic and company drove past the house and returned to the surveillance spot and waited.

Vic received a text from the Pennsylvania State Police team. They were ready for their orders. Vic called the number given on the text.

"Vic Gonnella here. I'm with three other officers, one in uniform in front of the suspects home at 620 Crum Creek Road. Single family home. Suspect may be returning shortly."

"Lieutenant Harris sir. We are in a white Ford panel van. Six Troopers, three in uniform. We're rolling toward your destination. We have two cars backing us up. They will hold a position nearby and roll upon orders."

"Thank you, Lieutenant. Please come in slowly. You will see my car on Crum Creek down from 620. Gray Mercedes, New York plates. Park behind in front of us please."

"10-4. ETA three minutes."

When Harris and his men arrived in their van, Vic ran down the potential moves they should make when Edward Olsen arrived home.

"The best for a clean collar is to move quickly and get him before he gets in the door. He knows the inside of the house better than we do. Lieutenant, I suggest you put three of your men at the rear of the house now, so we can move in quickly," Vic said.

"Roger that," Harris replied.

"If he sees us and decides to make a run for his vehicle we need to block his exit. Depending on where he parks, I think we need to block his exit with your van Lieutenant," Chief Frank advised.

"Right. I'll pull up behind him when we make the move," Harris replied.

Raquel brought up Edwards emotional condition. "People on the autism spectrum sometimes go into themselves. If that's the case, we get him on the ground as quickly as possible. On the other hand, he may freak out when he sees us. If we can keep him calm, that would be best."

"Agreed. Let's get this done and Lieutenant, you will take him into custody as it's your jurisdiction," Chief Frank stated.

The three undercover Troopers made their way to the rear of the Olsen house. They spread out, each man carrying a hand-held, two-way radio.

Everyone waited, keeping their attention on Crum Hill Road for any vehicular movement.

Twenty-three minutes later, an older model, red Jeep Laredo came down Crum Hill Road toward the Olsen house. The Jeep slowly pulled into the driveway, pulling up to the doorway of the detached garage.

Vic whispered to Raquel, "A Jeep. No wonder he was under the radar the last few days in Rockland. Everyone was looking for the white Dodge van."

Harris put the word out on his hand-held. "Hold," was his command. He saw an elderly woman walking across the lawn.

"Edward, what's going on? You didn't come home last night. Are you all right? "

Edward Olsen walked quickly to the front of the house. The white Ford van pulled up behind the Jeep. Edward saw the movement of one of the undercover Troopers coming around the corner of the house. He turned quickly and saw Sassano, Chief Frank, Vic and Raquel coming on to the property. Harris wheeled the Ford van quickly into the driveway, blocking the Jeep.

Edward bolted toward the front door, keys in hand and grabbed the brown paper bag off the table on the porch.

"Hold it right there Edward. I need to have a word with you," Vic hollered.

Edward made a strange grunting noise. He quickly got his key into the lock of the front door. In an instant, Edward was inside the house, locking the door behind him.

"Edward!" The old woman yelled. "Why are you men bothering that poor boy!"

"Shit, how the hell did that happen?" Raquel yelled.

Harris called in the backup cruisers. Suddenly, two dark gray Ford SUV's with bold white TROOPER lettering on each side, next to the official police emblem, came roaring down in front of the Olsen house.

One of the undercover men guided the woman away from the front of the house telling her they were police. He nearly carried her away back to her home.

"Go away. Go away." Edward was screaming from one of the second-floor windows, which he opened about six inches.

The troopers crouched behind their vehicles, drawing their Sig Sauer P227 semi-automatic pistols.

"Leave…now. I have a…gun. Go…away. This is…my property," Edward yelled. His voice was choppy and childlike.

Mike Sassano couldn't believe how things had unraveled so quickly. "Jesus Christ Harris, this could end very badly. Pull your men back," Sassano advised the Lieutenant.

"I'm not doing that. Look, from what we're told, this guys a killer. I'm going to protect my men. If he starts throwing shots at us what would you expect me to do?" Harris asked.

Being a cop for thirty-nine years, Sassano couldn't argue the point Harris made. These men all wanted and were entitled to go home tonight to their families.

"Hold on a second. Would you at least give me a chance to talk to him?" Vic asked.

Harris quickly answered. "The book tells me to call in our negotiation team. They are trained to handle situations like this. I have to make that call Mr. Gonnella."

"Leave me...be. Get away...now," Edward yelled.

"Listen to him will ya? He's a sick kid," Vic stated.

"With all due respect sir, he's murdered four people according to you. In cold blood," Harris added.

Suddenly, Raquel called up to Edward. She had made her way behind one of the police SUV's.

"Edward, my name is Raquel. No one wants to hurt you. Listen to me. You're a very smart guy. Just come out and talk to me."

"I can...talk. Here."

"Okay. Edward come outside. Talk with me on the porch."

"My dad is...dead. They killed him...I killed them. Now go away."

"Edward. The virus made your dad sick, not those people. What you did was wrong. Now come down here and we will take good care of you," Raquel shouted.

"I miss...daddy."

"We know you do Edward. Come down now. We can talk more about it."

"No...go!"

"Can I come in to talk with you?" Raquel asked.

Edward didn't answer.

Vic ran with his body crouched down to the SUV where Raquel was.

"Raquel, forget this. Let the team come in and take over," Vic said.

"I think I can do this."

"Remember what you said to me? We're both going home to see Gabby.

"He's gonna get killed," Raquel blurted.

"I get it. He's a stone killer. Stay put."

Edward went to his bed to get his mother and fathers photograph. He opened the back of the silver frame and removed it, placing the picture inside his front belt buckle. The old photo was facing out. He went into his closet, retrieved his father's hunting rifle and some ammo. From an old wood box, Edward took a nine-millimeter German Luger, that was his father's Norwegian grandfathers trophy, taken from a Nazi soldier he killed. Edward put the Luger in his belt next to his parent's photograph.

Lieutenant Harris called the Broomall PD for backup. He also called in negotiators to attempt to talk Edward into surrendering. A tactical unit was also on the way. Broomall PD sent a small army of uniforms. They blocked off Crum Creek Road and told any neighbors in harm's way to take cover in their basements.

Edward went down the stairs cautiously in case the police had gotten in the house.

He flung open the front door and walked out onto the porch. The rifle was slung over his right shoulder.

Screams of "Drop the gun" seemed like an echo effect. Edward just stood on the porch scanning the scene from left to right and back again.

Raquel, and Vic drew their handguns. They were still behind and protected by the police SUV. Raquel yelled out to Edward.

"Edward, I want you to drop the rifle and lie on the porch. You're going to get hurt Edward. There is no need for this."

"I miss him, they killed…him," Edward said. His voice was hardly heard. He was looking at the ground, his head tilted to the right when he said it.

"Edward, listen to me. The people you shot had children too. Those children will miss their daddies too. Now let's just calm down and get on your knees so we can take you to see the doctor," Raquel pleaded.

Edward shook his head no. He kept his eyes looking at the ground. Slowly, almost deliberately, he began to remove the rifle from his shoulder.

Shouts of, Drop the gun, drop the damn gun, drop the fucking gun, don't do it", bounced off the house and police cars.

Edward raised the rifle to his eye and looked out of the scope toward one of the police vehicles. It was the SUV where Vic and Raquel took cover.

"No! No Edward!" Raquel screamed.

As he moved his finger to the trigger, a hail of bullets hit Edward sending him stumbling backwards into the open front door of the house. He was killed instantly.

Chapter Sixty-Three

The smell of gunpowder filled the air in front of the Olsen house. The sharp odor moved down Crum Hill Road with the slight breeze, reminiscent to the Fourth of July Broomall town fireworks.

A small group of neighbor onlookers formed, leading the pack was the old woman who was pulled away from the scene.

Raquel was sitting behind the police SUV, her Beretta hanging from her hand between her knees. She had the thousand-yard blank stare, looking straight ahead.

Vic knelt on one knee next to her.

"You okay?" Raquel didn't respond.

Vic gently took the piston from her fingers. He dropped the magazine. It was empty. Vic knew she had a full magazine when they checked their firearms earlier. Raquel had emptied her gun at Edward Olsen.

Mike Sassano and Chief Frank walked over to Vic and Raquel.

"Not the ending we had wanted. Nothing could be done about it," Sassano uttered.

Raquel looked up at the veteran detective.

"I'll live the rest of my life thinking I could have done something differently," Raquel said.

The scene became eerily quiet. No ambulance or police car sirens. No officers shouting orders and instructions. The last of the Olsen family was lying in a bloody pool on the home where he lived his entire, difficult life.

• • •

On the drive back to Manhattan, Raquel was still in shock over her reaction at the Olsen house. Vic didn't want to dwell on it. He mentioned it was just part of the job to Raquel and she shot him a look of disdain.

When 1010 WINS radio came into range on the car radio, all the news was about the apprehension and killing of the Shabbas Killer. Interviews from Rabbis to policemen to the governor to the senior citizen who lived next to the Olsen's were broadcast. Virtually everyone except the old lady mentioned Vic Gonnella and Raquel Ruiz and their pivotal role in the case.

Special Agent Wright had nothing to say about the case. He declined interviews and moped around his office at the FBI White Plains office. The pouting Wright was summoned to Washington on Monday. He would need a big box to pack up his office.

Another news blurb came over 1010 WINS that Vic and Raquel paid no attention to. "In Hackensack, New Jersey at the Bergen County

Criminal Court this morning, Chris Tripp of Mahwah, was indicted for attempted murder of a local female bartender. If found guilty, Tripp will likely be sentenced to life in prison as a three-time felon. He was remanded without bail to the Bergen County jail."

Raquel was still mostly staring out of the passenger window, watching the green rolling hills and trees as Vic drove commenting on the news reports.

"Baby, can you reach in the glove compartment and see if my sunglasses are in there," Vic asked.

Raquel popped open the box and saw the sunglasses. Woven into the arms of the fancy Italian Ray Ban glasses was a white envelope. Raquel looked at it suspiciously.

"There's a letter in here for us," Raquel announced.

"A letter? From whom?"

"No idea," Raquel replied.

"Well, open it and remove all suspense, Maybe its money!" Vic laughed. Raquel didn't.

Raquel opened the envelope and scanned the note.

"Holy crap. It's from Deegan," she announced.

"What's it say?"

"By the time you read this, if I'm correct which I normally am in the ninety-something percentile, Edward Olsen is already dead. I'd like to say he is with his mom and dad but you both know I don't believe in that kind of thing. So, Raquel, if I'm right, you and Vic both more than likely fired your guns. Remember one thing, Edward is far better off dead than living in a prison, both physically and mentally. You did your job. Get over it. See you in Lugano. Love and kisses, JD."

Chapter Sixty-Four

The Sunday after the Shabbas Killer was himself shot dead, the Hasidic community needed a forum to celebrate.

The streets in Monsey, and New Square in Rockland County and Kyrias Joel on Orange County were again teeming with people enjoying a beautiful sun-drenched pre-spring day. Gone was the anxiety and fear of having a maniac with a rifle randomly picking off innocent Hasidic people as they went about their daily lives.

Although some of the community had received their two Covid-19 vaccinations, the majority still had not. In spite of the warnings to keep social distancing in effect and to avoid large group gatherings, word was passed in the community that Grand Rebbe Teitelbaum was to appear at The Atrium in Monsey in the early afternoon.

There was no larger indoor venue than the spacious Atrium in Rockland County.

Thousands of Hasidic men, in their long coats and hats, most not wearing the face masks that were advised by the Center for Disease

Control, gathered to see the Rebbe and the honored guests of the community.

Hasidic women would attend in the hundreds and be separated from the men to follow the Jewish laws.

Vic Gonnella and Raquel Ruiz, and their family, new heroes of the Orthodox world along with Detective Mike Sassano and Chief Frank of the Ramapo Police Department would be honored for breaking the case.

Governor Mike Lappi, who was invited, had initially declined the invitation due to the state's mandate of social distancing due to the pandemic. His staff, knowing that an election year was around the corner, insisted that the Jewish votes were far more important than making a statement to the public at large.

Every politician in the two counties would attend. To not be seen would be a sure way to alienate the Orthodox community. Rockland District Attorney Edward Welch, who has political aspirations to one day be Governor of the State of New York, and his Assistant District Attorney, Mary Jane Cunningham would join Vic and Raquel on the dais, along with Governor Mike Lappi. Sassano and Frank would also be on the dais as the New York media would be swarming the event. Governor Mike Lappi greeted his old friends, Vic and Raquel, with hugs and smiles and got a great photographic moment.

The Rebbe made a blessing and a short speech about recent events and how the community was strengthened buy their solidarity. He prayed for the murder victims and their families, asking the community to gather *mitzvahs*, helping them in any way possible in their time of need. Naturally, he used the venue to remind everyone of the Satmar disdain of Zionism.

In the grand ballroom of The Atrium, live Yiddish music was played and groups of men formed circles and danced with each other as a show of celebration. The Rebbe clapped his hands to the music in a show of his approval.

Raquel and Vic were spoken of as heroes of the Hasidic world. Gabriella and Olga were present and amazed at the wonderful celebration and festivities. They sat with the other women on the upper level of the Atrium looking down at the sea of hats and long coats the men wore.

Raquel did not wear a mask. She wore a conservative outfit that befitted an honored guest of the Orthodox community, making sure she covered her legs and arms out of respect. She wore a head covering, which was appropriate for the mass gathering.

At the end of the celebration, Vic and Raquel left the dais to raucous clapping and Yiddish singing.

The crowd of men opened an aisle for them to exit the building.

Near the exit to The Atrium an old Hasidic man, aided by a thick black cane, approached the beaming couple.

In a thick Yiddish accent the man spoke.

"I vant to thank you both for helping us. Vat you have done for us is beyond evaluation," the man said.

"Thank you very much sir," Raquel remarked.

"I vould like to shake your hand Mister to remember dis moment."

Vic offered his hand. The elderly man gripped it with such strength that Vic was taken aback. He pulled Vic close to him, whispering into Vic's ear.

"And…if you don't come to see us in Switzerland, I vill kick your both asses."